THE UNEXPLAINABLE FAIRY GODMOTHER

THE UNEXPLAINABLE FAIRY GODMOTHER

GODMOTHER

THE INSCRUTABLE PARIS BEAUFONT™ BOOK 1

SARAH NOFFKE

MICHAEL ANDERLE

DISRUPTIVE IMAGINATION

Copyright © 2021 LMBPN Publishing
Cover copyright © LMBPN Publishing
A Michael Anderle Production

LMBPN Publishing
PMB 196, 2540 South Maryland Pkwy
Las Vegas, NV 89109

First US Edition, March 2021
eBook ISBN: 978-1-64971-626-2
Print ISBN: 978-1-64971-627-9

THE UNEXPLAINABLE FAIRY GODMOTHER TEAM

Thanks to the JIT Readers

Dave Hicks
Veronica Stephan-Miller
Micky Cocker
Dorothy Lloyd
Deb Mader
Zacc Pelter
Jeff Goode
Angel LaVey
Larry Omans

If I've missed anyone, please let me know!

Editor
The Skyhunter Editing Team

Once again and a thousand times more, for my muse, Lydia.

— Sarah

To Family, Friends and
Those Who Love
to Read.
May We All Enjoy Grace
to Live the Life We Are
Called.

— Michael

CHAPTER ONE

If love was what made the Earth go 'round, then it was about to freeze on its axis. Few people knew the repercussions of love being created or, more importantly, of love being lost.

A fairy godmother knew. It was her job to ensure matches were made and love achieved. The problem was fairy godmothers weren't what they used to be, and it was creating a domino effect across the globe.

Marylou Goodwin stood behind a concrete pillar in the London Underground. She wore a long blue gown with a hood over her gray curls to keep the cold chill off her shoulders and head. She wore it like that for practical reasons but also to keep her cover. It was always better if fairy godmothers weren't spotted by those they were spelling.

The old fairy godmother had been patiently waiting for her "Cinderella" to arrive on the platform. Hopefully, the woman, a Miss Amelia Rose, would show soon, or the timing of matching with her Prince Charming would be off. Also, Marylou's feet were throbbing from standing for so long. She wasn't as young as she used to be, and she felt her age more with every case.

"I'm getting too old for this," she muttered under her breath, willing the blood in her feet to circulate as she toggled her weight between them.

The truth was that Marylou had been old when she became a fairy godmother. Most were, and after a few centuries of matchmaking, this tired fairy godmother was out of stamina. There were bigger issues as well, and they were about to become very apparent for the rest of the world.

"Oh, about time," Marylou said as she caught sight of Amelia Rose striding down the walkway to where her train would be stopping in five minutes.

The Cinderella was on her cellphone chatting with Bryce Tyler, the man who had been pining for her affection since they graduated from college last year. Her long blonde hair was pulled back in a braid, and she had only a small bit of makeup adorning her face.

Amelia forced a smile, which on her elegantly beautiful face still lit up her large brown eyes even though it was absent of any joy. Her words were barely audible over the clacking of her smart high heels and the rush of the other trains on neighboring platforms.

"Yeah, I'll talk to you soon," she replied to the guy on the other side of the line after a pause. The smile on her pink lips disappeared. "I miss you too."

She didn't. Marylou knew that much. Bryce Tyler's mother missed him. The friend he'd had since preschool missed him. His sister who worried he'd never get married missed him. But Amelia Rose had never missed the redheaded financial advisor, even though she appreciated his friendship.

Lasting relationships were built on friendship, but more importantly, they started with a spark. Those relationships that made the world go around, anyway.

Amelia Rose ended the call. Her lack of enthusiasm over Bryce

Tyler was heavy on her face as she passed a well-dressed man standing on the platform, his attention on his own mobile device.

Marylou twirled her finger around and pointed at the two from her hiding place behind the pillar.

A handkerchief slipped from the back of Amelia Rose's purse and gracefully floated to the concrete, where it landed close to the man—Mr. Grayson McGregor.

The old "drop the handkerchief" technique was tried and true, and Marylou had used it for centuries to get the attention of a Prince Charming for one of her Cinderellas.

To the fairy godmother's surprise, Grayson McGregor didn't notice the handkerchief. Marylou sighed. She hoped this wasn't going to be as difficult as the last case. She poked her wrinkled, bony finger in the air and stirred the embroidered handkerchief around the legs of his slacks.

That got his attention. Grayson glared down and picked up Amelia's possession. He was eyeing the initials when Amelia spun and spied him with her handkerchief.

"Excuse me." She strode back in his direction and reached for the linen square. "That's mine."

He brought his blue eyes up and smiled playfully pulling the handkerchief out of her reach. "Can you prove it? What are your initials?"

She sighed and looked for the train. She'd be late for work if it didn't get here soon. One more time and she'd get fired. "They're A.R."

He shook his head. "These are B.T."

She frowned. "Those are my boyfrie—friend's initials."

"Well, is he a friend or a boyfriend?" Grayson still held the cloth, a flirtatious expression dancing in his eyes.

Amelia narrowed her gaze at the stranger—her one true Prince Charming.

Marylou let out a frustrated breath. This wasn't going well...

again. She wisped her finger in a small gesture and made a gust of wind take the handkerchief from Grayson's fingers and send it down the platform.

Amelia regarded him incredulously when he simply watched it fly away.

"Well," she said in a demanding tone. "Are you going to get that for me?"

He glanced in the direction of the handkerchief flying down the Underground, their train speeding in their direction. "Sorry, but my train is coming, and I can't be late."

Amelia's mouth popped open. "But you lost it."

"I did not!" he argued at once.

"I'm wearing heels." She pointed at the red heels that matched her striped skirt and blouse.

"Well, I don't know why your impractical decisions have to affect me," he countered, anger flaring on his face.

She balled up her fists, her face growing as red as her shoes.

Grayson rolled his eyes. "Oh, fine. But I better not miss my train." He sped off, racing after the square of cloth flying on the wind directed by Marylou. By the time he'd recovered the handkerchief, the train had come and gone, but Amelia had stayed, growing more furious by the second. She couldn't lose Bryce's handkerchief. It meant something to him. However, now she was late.

Marylou knew that if the two shared a taxi, they would feel the spark, and the rest would be history.

Grayson threw up his chin, the handkerchief crushed in his hand. "Seriously? I missed the train! Not today."

Amelia held out her hand. "I'm sorry. I'm probably fired now."

He cut his eyes at her hand and then her face. "Well, my apologies. Maybe I can offer you a job at my company, McGregor Technologies."

She blinked at him. "McGregor Technologies? That company

turned me down for a position last year when I graduated from college."

He was supposed to offer her a job, and she would accept, and they'd work together and fall in love. From the angry expression on both their faces, romance was not budding between them—the exact opposite. There was a fine line between the two.

He shrugged. "We like our candidates to have experience."

"I have experience!" she argued. "Plus, I'm a quick learner."

"But you're not quick on your feet," he pointed out between breaths, taxed after the run to get Amelia's handkerchief.

She yanked it from his hand. "Do you always insult people whose stuff you take?"

He grinned at her. "I didn't take it. You dropped it. So you make poor clothing choices, can't run after your own things, and you lose stuff. Never mind the job offer."

Amelia's mouth formed a hard line. "What is your name?"

He lifted his chin proudly. "Grayson McGregor."

She nodded. "Grayson, consider yourself warned. Your company is utter rubbish to me."

The guy laughed, his teeth perfectly straight on the top and cutely crooked on the bottom. He was very handsome, with his short brown hair and boyish dimples. "And who will I have the pleasure of attributing my downfall to? *If* it happens."

She started down the platform, her heels clicking against the concrete. After a few steps, she whipped around and narrowed her eyes at him. "Amelia Rose. One day you'll hear my name and know I'm the one who undercut your prices, stole all your customers, and sank McGregor Technologies."

"I cannot wait, Amelia Rose. Bring it on."

The two stormed in opposite directions, each raving mad.

Marylou groaned and leaned against the pillar. The thing about a spark was it had the potential to ignite a brilliant love affair or to burn the bridges between two lovers. It was a delicate balance, one a fairy godmother was supposed to be good at keeping. It appeared, yet again, that Marylou Goodwin had failed. She knew the repercussions of Amelia and Grayson not falling in love would have far-reaching effects and would undoubtedly hurt the world at large.

CHAPTER TWO

Strong hands grabbed Paris Westbridge's shoulders, yanking her hard off the giant she was assaulting. He was easily double her size and a lot uglier by anyone's standards.

"Don't," she hissed as she struggled to get out of the grasp of the detective who was trying to pull her off the giant. Detective Nicholson was stronger than Paris, but she was nimbler. She dropped her body weight, diving under his arm and backing up several feet as the stupid giant Madow threw his fist. The attack was meant for her but slammed straight into Detective Nicholson's face, sending him back several feet.

Gasping, Paris grabbed him as he stumbled and kept him from falling to the ground. Madow, realizing he'd made things ten times worse for himself, turned at once and sprinted down Roya Lane, fleeing the crime scene like the coward he was.

Detective Nicholson held the side of his face as he turned and looked at Paris. He shook his head and squinted with his one open eye. The fairy lowered her chin, knowing there would be no fleeing for her. She had to face this and knew from experience it wouldn't be pleasant.

With an authoritative glare, Detective Nicholson pointed at the building at the end of the street. Paris had been in there many times. Hell, she lived there lately, but not by choice.

Swallowing her pride and not needing any more directives, she marched in the direction of the Fairy Law Enforcement Agency, where she was certain there was a jail cell with her name on it. At this point, she should keep a toothbrush there as if it was a boyfriend's place—if the boyfriend was a warden who served really bad food and kept her rap sheet on his desk since he referenced it so often.

Trudging toward the office, Paris sighed. This was her third strike in so many terms. She wasn't getting a slap on the wrist, and both she and Detective Nicholson knew it.

Paris Westbridge was in a world of trouble, and there would be no talking her way out of it this time.

CHAPTER THREE

At the glass door to the Fairy Law Enforcement Agency, Paris caught her reflection. She grinned, proud that she looked a lot less messed up than Madow. The fairy was pretty sure she'd given the giant a black eye and loosened one of his teeth with her fists. She chuckled, thinking it was an improvement on his ugly face.

In contrast, Paris' shoulder-length blonde hair was hardly mussed and fell straight around her face. Her blue eyes blinked back at her, and she was grateful to see no scratches or swelling from the fistfight. To her disappointment, her favorite leather jacket had a rip in the arm, and her boots were scuffed. As she and most fairies in the modern world usually did, her periwinkle-blue wings were glamoured not to show, but she was confident they were unscathed.

"You know where to go," Detective Nicholson told her when they entered.

Paris nodded and walked past the reception desk where Charlotte sat filing her nails as her sparkly blue wings fluttered behind her. Since she hardly left the magical area known as Roya Lane, she never bothered to glamour her wings.

"Oh, good to see you, Paris." The receptionist popped her gum. "Do you want some green tea? I have a new Moroccan mint flavor."

Paris was about to respond when Detective Nicholson cut her off. "This isn't a social visit, Charlotte. She's in police custody."

Paris flashed the receptionist an apologetic smile as she passed, heading for the detective's office down the long hallway.

"So, no tea, then?" Charlotte called. "I have a hibiscus flower one too. John, it would be good for you to drink some tea."

The detective shook his head as he followed Paris into the messy office. "Just coffee for me."

"Please," Paris added and threw herself into the chair on the other side of Detective Nicholson's desk. The vinyl was ripped in places, and the metal armrest was rusted.

"What's that?" He sat behind his desk, which was piled high with folders and day-old donuts.

"You forgot to say please," she explained. "Just coffee for me, *please*."

He shook his head of short white hair as he picked up a file folder and pretended to read it. Almost at once, he gave up the charade and thumped it back down on the desk, making it slide off a stack of papers. "Seriously, did you have to pick another fight with Madow?"

Daringly, she nodded. "He started it."

Detective Nicholson sighed and shook his head. His face was swelling from the assault, but he ignored it. "Someone else always starts it, Paris. That's always your excuse."

She held out her hands. "It's true, though. He was totally bullying a couple of elves. They were about to give over their money, afraid that Madow was going to snap off their pointy ears."

Running his hands through his hair, the detective groaned. "It's not your job to fight bullies who steal other people's lunch money. That's my job."

Paris wanted to point out that the detective wasn't doing his job if she was stepping in so regularly, but she didn't think that would go over so well for her. She knew he was overworked and understaffed, so instead, she stated, "I was trying to help."

He pressed his hand to his face, the throbbing from the attack registering as the adrenaline subsided. "That's just it. You're always trying to 'help.'" He said the last with air quotes. "Like last week when you stole Levoroxy from those gnomes at the market."

She narrowed her eyes, the recent memory burning her up again with anger. "Those gnomes were taking advantage of the magician who needed it. He's ill, and when they realized he needed that medicine, they jacked up the price. He was about to sell his possessions to get that drug."

Detective Nicholson shook his head. "That's the thing—it's a free market. That's the gnomes' prerogative. You can't go around enforcing things because you think they're wrong."

"Then who's going to?" she blurted and instantly regretted it. Paris knew she was only making things worse for herself, but as usual, she didn't know how to keep her mouth shut.

"It's my job to uphold the law," he argued. "It's the magical law enforcement agency's job. Yours is to mind your business and stay out of trouble, but after this, there's little hope of that happening."

Paris dropped her head, feeling the inevitable about to befall her. "Detective Nicholson, I promise that I'll—"

"Don't call me that," he interrupted, a punishing look on his face. "You're not doing yourself any favors by pretending."

Paris laughed. "By pretending that you're not my uncle and I'm not a criminal?"

His blue eyes flashed with annoyance as Charlotte brought him a steaming cup of black coffee. "Things are hard enough without you acting like you're some fairy on the street I've brought in for breaking the law yet again."

"I'm not asking for any favors, Uncle John." She offered a dry smile to the receptionist as she left the office.

"No, you never do," John Nicholson agreed. "Unfortunately, there's no way I can grant you any leniency." He picked up the file that had her name on it and was, not surprisingly, thicker than most of the others on his desk. "I've bent every rule I can for you, Paris, but I have management breathing down my neck now. If they find out that I've let you off again, there's going to be hell to pay."

"I don't want that for you." She suddenly felt the weight of her bad decisions. Paris didn't want anything to happen to her Uncle John. He'd always been there for her. When her parents had up and left town, deserting her, Uncle John took care of her. She was little then and hardly remembered them, but she remembered the man who took her in, ensured she ate and fostered her magic.

Then, when Paris was older and couldn't pay her rent, it was the man before her who helped. Uncle John had been there for her when her dumb ex-boyfriend left her with a mountain of debt. This was how she was repaying him? Paris felt awful, but that wasn't fixing anything.

He shook his head. "I don't know what else to do at this point. If my superiors find out about this incident, which I suspect they will since Madow can't keep his trap shut, they might have my badge."

"Then put me in jail," she instantly stated.

The look that snapped to his face made Paris' heart ache.

"I don't know if I can do that." His voice was gruff. "The sentence for the charges will be quite long. You could be locked up for ages."

She shrugged, pretending not to care. "I'll make the most of it. I'll pick up a hobby. Learn a new language. Take up meditation. Maybe try some yoga."

A smile nearly cracked Uncle John's lips, but he covered it up by sipping his coffee. It was too hot, judging by the grimace he made. "What if there was another option? A community service of sorts?"

Paris sat forward fast. "No. Please don't send me to Tooth Fairy College. I can't. I'll take jail. I'll do whatever it takes. Just don't throw me in with those goth fairies and their emo music. I. Won't. Survive."

He chuckled. "I think those delinquent fairies are the ones who wouldn't survive you, Pare."

Uncle John was right. One day with those juvenile fairies who wore all black and talked in monotone voices while reciting Edgar Allen Poe's poetry would push Paris to her limit. Most knew that underage fairies who broke the law were sent to Tooth Fairy College for reformation and to fulfill their sentences for wrongdoing. At the age of twenty, Paris was almost over the limit, but her uncle could get her in there if he wanted to. She desperately hoped he didn't because the last thing she wanted to do was collect gross teeth from mortal children's pillows for the next century. Anything but that.

"I can take a few years in jail," she argued. "Do what you have to do, but I don't want you suffering for my actions. Punish me, so you don't get punished."

She expected him to argue, but instead, he picked up the phone and dialed a number. Paris remained quiet, listening for the voice on the other side of the line. Unfortunately, when the person picked up, she couldn't hear what they said.

"So, I have a proposition for you," Uncle John began, talking to the person on the other end. "Rumor on the street is that your enrollment is down. What if I help you out?"

He waited and listened. After a moment, he said, "You know my niece Paris Westbridge, right?"

There was another pause. "Yeah, she's a good kid. Just..." Uncle John glanced at Paris before adding, "spirited. She needs discipline, that's all."

Paris felt like sliding down in her chair and muttering a few curse words but refrained.

"Great!" Uncle John cheered, a genuine smile spreading across his mouth. "Then we have a deal. I'll send her over—well, if she agrees." With that, he hung up and gave his niece a measured glare. "I have a proposition for you, Pare. You're not going to like it, but hear me out."

CHAPTER FOUR

The lilac-infused breeze that wafted through the open window of the fairy godmother college made the lacy drapes sweep up like a woman's dress after a gust of wind. Willow Starr glanced out at the grounds of Happily Ever After College, enjoying the spring weather. It was always springtime here. It had been since the beginning, some three hundred years ago.

Spring was the season of love. It symbolized birth, new beginnings, and a time when all things thrived. The college didn't have a mappable location. It existed in a bubble, very much like the fairy godmothers themselves.

Willow Starr had been the headmistress of Happily Ever After for a very long time. Back then, things had been easy. The rules of courtship were black and white. However, things had changed in the modern world, and nothing had changed at the fairy godmother college. Willow knew it was only a matter of time before the governing agency brought her in for discipline. Saint Valentine had to know what she was in denial about. Her boss would know enrollment at the college was at a dismal low, and the cases were piling up. Worst of all, he'd know the ones they worked on ended in complete failures.

Willow smoothed back a gray hair that had been knocked out of her loose bun by the springtime breeze. She simply didn't know how to fix things. She looked around her office without seeing, her eyes running over the hand-knitted blankets draped over the overstuffed mint green armchair and the many doilies that covered the coffee and side tables. For a long minute, she stared at the painting on the opposite wall, not seeing the shimmering pond and geese in the picture.

The office reeked of a grandmotherly feel, right down to the bowl of butterscotch on the corner of Willow's desk and the musty smell that wafted from the armoire when she opened it. That's where the headmistress kept the baby blue silk gowns that were the uniform of their graduates and students. The distinction between the two was the graduates wore a large pink bow tied under their chins. It had been a long time since Willow had given one of those out. It had been too long since they had a graduate at Happily Ever After.

The knock on the door made Willow start. She calmed herself and drew a breath before politely saying, "It's open. Come in."

A woman with short black hair and wise eyes entered, wearing a blue silk gown identical to Willow's, tied at the neck with the large pink bow.

"To what do I owe the honor of your visit, Professor Mae Ling?" Willow slid her lavender-scented stationery away. Writing to Saint Valentine could wait. She'd been putting it off, so what was another day?

The small woman coughed, her eyes full of uncertainty. "Marylou Goodwin has returned from her case, and she fears the results aren't ideal."

Willow pressed her lips together and nodded. "I suspect she wants to give me her report directly, then?"

"I think she wants to do more than that," Mae Ling carefully corrected.

The implications of her underlying message hung in the air.

"Take a seat," Willow offered, indicating a large armchair on the other side of her desk.

Straight away, the small woman swept into the room and slid elegantly into the chair. Mae Ling had been with the college since the beginning and had mastered the etiquette they instilled in their students—the three Ps: Poised, Pretty, and Polite. That was what Prince Charmings looked for in their potential Cinderellas and, therefore, the art form the fairy godmothers had mastered. However, something wasn't working anymore.

Willow's eyes slid to the tele-eventor on the corner of her desk. It resembled a tiny typewriter, but it worked on its own, fueled by magic.

"The results haven't come through yet," Willow explained, knowing it wouldn't take long before the device foretold how badly the repercussions of the failed match were. The magitech also gave her details on the cases assigned from Saint Valentine's office, but lately, the information hadn't helped her make assignments. What did it matter to Willow if a Cinderella had a ten-year plan before wanting to settle down? She didn't understand that. All these women and their career goals. It didn't make sense that they wanted an education over a man.

Women in the modern world were so strange. For many of them, romance wasn't a priority. Did these women not get that love was what made the world go around? It wasn't only about making smart matches resulting in long relationships and happy families. It was bigger than that. Relationships had far-reaching effects that affected the world at large for centuries. Mother Nature had made that abundantly clear when she put Willow in charge of Happily Ever After three hundred years ago.

"When do you want my help reviewing the new enrollment

applications?" Willow decided that it would be better to deal with Marylou's situation after good news.

The look that crossed Mae Ling's face made her hope plummet. "I've already finished them."

Willow blinked at her in confusion. "Say what? I thought—"

"There weren't any applications," Mae Ling interrupted, her tone apologetic.

"How is that possible?" Willow demanded. "Not a single applicant wants to attend the college this year?"

Mae Ling shook her head.

Willow sat back, absentmindedly looking out at the pristine grounds of the college. It was full of grassy lawns and fruit trees, but not even the songbirds made her feel better right then.

"If I may," Mae Ling began. "I don't think it's that fairies no longer want to become fairy godmothers."

Willow brought her gaze back to the professor. "I don't understand."

Mae Ling carefully pushed her thick black hair behind her ear. She was one of the few who didn't sport the grayish-blue hair associated with fairy godmothers, but she'd always been a rebel like that. Willow trusted her to help her see what she was missing. "I get the impression that fairies don't want to become like us."

That wasn't the response Willow had expected. She glanced at the mirror she kept on her desk that reminded her to smile when making phone calls. "Why not?"

"Well, for one, we look old," Mae Ling explained.

"We are old," Willow argued.

The other woman nodded. "Yes, but we make ourselves look that way well before our time."

"It's supposed to encourage our charges to trust us." Willow didn't see the relevant point here. "How will a Cinderella know we have their best interests at heart if we don't remind them of their trustworthy grandmothers?"

Mae Ling tilted her head back and forth. "Maybe in this day and age, there are other ways."

"Like what?" Willow questioned.

To that, Mae Ling didn't seem to have an answer. She shrugged.

Willow sighed. "So the modern fairy doesn't want to have gray hair and a refined appearance. I guess I can get over that. I still don't understand why we have zero applications."

"It might also have to do with the requirements," Mae Ling stated diplomatically.

"Requirements?" Willow asked. "What's wrong with them?"

"Well," Mae Ling began. "Finding a fairy over one hundred years old who has a perfect track record and years of charity work isn't as easy as it used to be."

"Why ever not?" Willow demanded.

"Because modern fairies aren't perfect," Mae Ling answered at once. "They have a different life than the ones we had. The world they're growing up in is different from ours. Frankly, I don't think that what we do and how we do it appeals to them."

"These are a lot of problems you're bringing to me." Deep down, Willow knew Mae Ling was right and was happy to hear it from her before it came from Saint Valentine.

"I know this isn't easy, but I think we have some opportunities if we adapt our recruitment efforts along with marketing techniques and change the college's image and curriculum, of course."

Willow's mouth popped open. "What's wrong with our curriculum?"

Before Mae Ling could answer, the tele-eventor *beeped* on the headmistress's desk. The possible results of the recent case were about to be foretold. Willow pretended she wasn't anxious to see what the little white paper the machine churned out would say. Instead, she glanced at Mae Ling, her expression demanding an answer to her question.

"The curriculum simply isn't working," Mae Ling explained. "Teaching manners and traditional dating practices seems ineffec-

SARAH NOFFKE & MICHAEL ANDERLE

tive in this modern age, but that's as much as I know. I can't offer you much on how we should adapt because I don't know. I'm not well-versed in the world outside Happily Ever After."

Willow nodded as the tele-eventor spun out its message. She read it, and her heart dropped in her chest. The result of Amelia Rose not matching with her Prince Charming, Grayson McGregor, was much worse than she could have anticipated.

"Send Marylou in here," Willow stated. "We need to deal with this and quickly before things get worse." What she didn't say was before Saint Valentine found out, and she lost the only job she'd ever had or wanted.

CHAPTER FIVE

The shamed expression on the old woman's face made Willow's heart ache even more. She pulled her gaze away from Marylou as Mae Ling led her into the office, offering the fairy godmother the armchair as she stood dutifully in the corner.

Willow reread the small piece of paper the tele-eventor had spewed out. It was hard to process potential results like this. It read: "Match failure will cause corporate rivalries, creating environmental instability, job loss, and dramatic economic devastation."

One of those was bad enough, but all three were huge. There was no way this was going unnoticed by Saint Valentine. Amelia Rose and Grayson McGregor belonged together, and anything less would prove detrimental.

The headmistress of Happily Ever After College expected the fairy godmother to start with an apology. What she said first wasn't something Willow was ready for.

"I'm quitting," Marylou said, her voice and expression stern.

The abruptness gave Willow pause. Her brown eyes slid to Mae

Ling in the corner before coming back to the fairy godmother. "I understand that mistakes have been made and you're frustrated."

"I'm tired," Marylou corrected. "My body is tired. My mind is overwhelmed. And I'm frustrated that I keep failing at my cases."

Willow nodded. "It's come to my attention that we could use some improvements in our methods. Maybe the ways we've done things before aren't effective."

"They aren't," the fairy godmother dared to agree.

Trying not to take the blunt observation personally, Willow smiled. "We need to find out how to help the modern woman and adapt our practices. That will take some re-educating for our fairy godmothers. It's going to involve us changing."

"I agree." Marylou untied the pink bow from under her chin and let the blue hood fall back to show her head of grayish-blue curls. "However, this old fairy isn't interested in being part of that change."

"But…" Willow's next words went unspoken, her heart breaking. Marylou was one of her best fairy godmothers. Worse was that she was one of her last. Many had retired, some had quit, and too many recently had been fired.

The results were on the news every single day as matches weren't made and chaos was the result. When two lovers didn't find each other, they inevitably found something else, and it was rarely something that contributed positively to the world.

"I'm too old for this," Marylou went on. "I used to understand how to bring two people together, but more and more, I'm confused by how two perfectly compatible individuals fall in love." She planted her hands on her hips with an offended expression on her wrinkled face. "Do you know that some modern women become offended if their Prince Charming wants to pay for their date? How do I manage that situation? It's outside the scope of my reality."

Willow nodded. She understood the gap in understanding. Unlike Marylou, she wasn't out for the count. No, she was ready to adapt if that's what it took. She might be old, but she didn't feel it. Maybe she needed a makeover... perhaps all of the fairy godmothers did. Mae Ling was right. They didn't need to look like grandmothers. That had worked back in the day for traditional women. In this day and age, something else might appeal to the Cinderellas and garner their trust.

Willow didn't know what it would look like, but she could get there if she simply remained open to the idea.

Happily Ever After was out of date and could use a remodel. She glanced around the office that hadn't changed in over a century. She didn't know where to start, but wanting to improve was a part of the process, she believed optimistically.

More confounding was how to change the actual school. They needed students, and for that, they needed to change the image and the curriculum. Saint Valentine would have some ideas, but if Willow could go to him with something and show she was already ahead, that would be good.

Willow tapped her fingers on the desk, having forgotten the other two fairy godmothers were still in her company. They were staring at her, waiting for her reply.

She glanced up suddenly, an apologetic expression on her face. "I'm sorry. I was off in thought. I realize there's no changing your mind on this, Marylou, and I appreciate your many years of service to us."

Standing, she offered the other woman her hand. Marylou took it and shook politely, as fairy godmothers were taught to do, displaying feminine daintiness.

Willow was about to say something else when the rotary phone on her desk rang, grabbing their attention. It was Saint Valentine. This was it.

She glanced at Mae Ling, and the head professor understood at once. Gingerly, she took Marylou by the shoulders and steered her from the room as the powder-blue phone continued to ring in front of Willow.

She drew a breath, pulling in some much-needed courage as she prepared to answer. Putting off Saint Valentine would do her no good.

Swallowing her fear, she imbued herself with confidence and picked up the phone. "Hello. This is Willow Starr, headmistress of Happily Ever After College."

CHAPTER SIX

"Hey there." A gruff voice that didn't match Saint Valentine's sultry tone echoed from the other side of the line. "It's Detective Nicholson."

Willow was relieved it wasn't her boss, but trepidation soon followed. A call from the lead detective for the Fairy Law Enforcement Agency rarely brought her good news. "Is this about one of my fairy godmothers?" she asked in a rush and immediately regretted it. "I mean, hello, Detective Nicholson. How are you?"

He chuckled good-naturedly on the other side of the line. "I'm about the same. Overworked, under-caffeinated, and in need of a raise."

Willow smiled and saw her teeth in the mirror. "Well, as always, I and everyone at the college appreciate your service, John."

"Same here, same here," he said with a cautious edge to his voice.

Willow waited for the detective to tell her the nature of his call.

"So, I have a proposition for you," Detective Nicholson began. "Rumor on the streets is that your enrollment is down."

It didn't make the headmistress feel better that those outside the college knew about her problems. Of course, there were far fewer fairy godmothers on the streets these days, so why *wouldn't* others have noticed? Especially someone like John, who observed so much in and around the magical communities.

"Well, we *are* working on our recruitment efforts," Willow began politely. "It's something I'm aware of—"

"What if I help you out?" Detective Nicholson interrupted eagerly.

That was unexpected. Willow didn't know what to say. She'd never needed help in the past.

"You know my niece, Paris Westbridge, right?" John asked.

Willow saw her image in the mirror blinking at her in confusion. What did that troublemaker have to do with anything? she wondered. Paris was supposedly a nice fairy but overzealous, often finding herself in the wrong place at the wrong time, in and out of trouble for something or another.

"I remember her."

"Yeah, she's a good kid. Just..." Detective Nicholson hesitated before adding, "spirited. She needs discipline, that's all."

"I'm not sure what that has to do with our enrollment," Willow commented, but on the heels of her statement, it all came together. "Oh." She drew out the word. "You mean, she..."

"That's right, Willow," the detective affirmed. "I was thinking, you need students, and I need a constructive way to sentence her."

There it was, Willow realized. "So, this is like Tooth Fairy College now?"

He chuckled, his tone nervous. "Not quite that desperate. I mean, she's a great kid, as I said. I think she'd make a good recruit if you taught her right."

Willow remained quiet, having to come to terms with this new reality. Happily Ever After had always had a few hundred applicants vying for a spot at the college. Tooth Fairy College, also known as Chump-change College, was full of delinquent juveniles that the FLEA couldn't afford to have clogging up their jails. Was that what her fairy godmother college would become?

"I'm asking for you to give her a try," Detective Nicholson continued. "If it doesn't work...well, I'll have to send her to someplace harder."

Jail, Willow thought. That's what the well-meaning detective was implying, and she understood the uncle didn't want his niece mixed up in that. Once the girl set foot there, things would change for Paris and not for the better. It would expose her to the worst criminals, and if she were rebellious before, she'd be hardened afterward.

"I guess we could do it on a trial basis." Willow heard the uncertainty in her voice and felt bad about it. John was trying to help her, and the angels above knew she needed it. Drawing a breath, she smiled. "If it works, maybe we can figure something out." Quickly she added, "I mean, I can't take those meant to go to jail or Chump-change College, but the less dangerous ones? We're known for our reform efforts, and maybe this is what we need to modernize ourselves."

What Willow didn't say was this might be her last-ditch effort to get students. If she had to take the rougher recruits, they would be better than none at all.

"Great!" Detective Nicholson cheered, a smile in his voice. "Then we have a deal. I'll send her over—well, if she agrees."

Willow thanked him and hung up. There were many things she still didn't know how to fix, but now she had a possible solution to one of her problems.

She looked around the out-of-date office and hoped she'd figure out how to update the college's image and solve its curriculum issues.

CHAPTER SEVEN

"I have a proposition for you, Pare." Uncle John set the phone's receiver back on the cradle. "You're not going to like it, but hear me out."

She eyed the old-style phone. "Does it involve pushing you into the twenty-first century with a cell phone? Because if so, I'll happily teach you how to use one."

He rolled his eyes in that way he often did when he wasn't really annoyed with her but rather was trying not to laugh and encourage her antics. "The place I called can only be reached by outsiders with a landline."

Paris' eyes widened with horror. "Oh, for the love of God, are you sending me to Minnesota? I know I have to be punished, but that seems cruel. Please, Uncle John, I'll totally pull the niece card. Whatever it takes not to be sent to the middle of nowhere and not have high-speed internet."

He shook his head. "I'm not sending you to Minnesota, but I'm fairly certain this place doesn't have high-speed internet."

"Wisconsin? Alaska? Montana?" She ran through all the remote places she could recall.

Her Uncle John laughed. "No, but I have a feeling you're not going to like the place for other reasons besides that most consider it stuck in the Dark Ages."

"Wow, you're not selling this like you think you are," she remarked dryly.

"Pare, I can make you a deal that will clear your record," he began.

"And keep you from getting in trouble too, right?" she cut in.

He nodded. "Yeah, I think so. It will probably buy me more than a few favors."

She leaned back, put her hands casually behind her head and smiled. "This is sounding better. Go on, then."

The corners of his mouth turned upward. "Well, how do you feel about going to fairy godmother college?"

Paris didn't hesitate, although she knew little about the place. "You have yourself a deal." She would do anything to keep her uncle from getting in trouble for something she'd done. He was too good for that. He worked too hard and had protected her for too long.

To her surprise, his smile faded.

"You'll have to wear a dress."

Her grin dropped too. "Deal's off."

He sighed loudly and picked up her file. "I know attending a college that caters to women falling in love isn't your style."

A laugh burst out of her mouth. "Not my style? I refuse to watch romantic comedies. Ballads give me hives. I slugged the last guy who hit on me. I think 'not my style' is an understatement."

"Well, as a fairy godmother, you don't have to fall in love," he explained. "Quite the opposite. You'll learn how to help others to find their one true love. You match them and help them to fall for each other, and the world is a better place."

"I have to wear a dress?" she questioned. Skepticism was heavy in her tone as though this was a real deal-breaker.

"I think they're called gowns, but yeah," he answered.

"How am I supposed to throw a roundhouse kick in a gown?"

He shook his head and opened the file in his hand. "That's the thing, Pare. You're not supposed to. That's what's gotten you in so much trouble. It's either fairy godmother college or jail."

She picked at the peeling vinyl upholstery of the chair. "Most of that stuff in my file is bogus."

Uncle John flipped through the pages. "It doesn't matter. It's stuck for one reason or another. Like this." He pointed at a report. "Arson in the fashion district in Los Angeles."

"I was trying to put out the fire," she argued. "Those fat gnomes who started it ran off, and I saw the whole thing, but instead of running after them, I tried to extinguish the shop."

He glanced at her. "I might believe you, but the three witnesses there didn't." Flipping to another page, he indicated another report. "Here, you were found breaking and entering an abandoned warehouse on Roya Lane."

"I heard kittens calling for help," she explained.

He lowered the file. "No kittens were found."

Paris shrugged. "Turned out it was a demon who was trying to lure me into the warehouse. He disappeared when you showed up after getting the call."

His eyes flashed with annoyance. "Then you assaulted a fae. How do you explain that one?"

"Oh, I did that," she admitted. "He was annoying me, so I clocked him."

Uncle John slapped the file down. "That's the thing. You can't hit someone because they annoy you."

She leaned forward. "He said a little makeup would make it so he could look at my face rather than my chest."

At that, her uncle almost laughed but controlled himself. "My point is that regardless of whether it's your fault or not, these crimes are on your record, and I can't keep ignoring them. I have management breathing down my neck, and they've told me one more slip-up from you, and they're going to want justice."

"This was my last slip-up, wasn't it?"

Regret heavy in his eyes, he nodded. "I'm sorry, Pare. There's nothing I can do. You can go to Happily Ever After College or jail."

She crossed her arms. "How long would I have to wear this gown and pretend to stomach romance?"

He blew out a breath. "That depends on you. The program is one to four years. Then you'll need to do your service, and I think that's another few years."

"If I do it," she began slowly, thinking about each word, "it will erase my record? We'll be even?"

Giving her a skeptical expression, he pursed his lips. "Well, until you're free and start getting yourself into trouble again."

"I don't get myself into trouble," she argued.

"No, it finds you," he said, and he looked like he believed it. "Maybe there are benefits here. The fairy godmothers are known for their polite behavior. I hope you'll learn some things that will help you…act differently."

"Better," she corrected and narrowed her eyes at him.

"Pare, you can't go around taking matters into your own hands," he stated wearily, having had this conversation with her a hundred times. "Bullies are my job."

"Yeah, but usually because of the law, you can't do anything," she protested.

"It doesn't matter," he replied. "Just because things fall out of my jurisdiction, it doesn't mean you get to step in with this vigilante business." They were silent for a moment, studying each other. Finally, Uncle John sighed. "I think learning decorum from the fairy godmothers might do you some good."

Paris sat up straight and forced a smile onto her face. "That's fine. I'll do it."

He blinked at her, surprised. "You will?"

"Well, yeah," she said. "I don't like the gown business. The romance part might kill me. Learning manners is going to ruin my spirit. But if I can't make positive changes on the streets, I might as well take a position where I can. I mean, I don't like the whole 'making others fall in love' part, but it helps the world to be a better place, right?"

"That's what it's supposed to do," he answered. "Love is important for creating peace and balance. You can be part of that."

"You won't get in trouble?" She needed to be sure.

Uncle John closed her file. "If you put in your time at Happily Ever After College, my superiors will see me doing my job, and it will also strengthen my ties with the school. Having a fairy godmother who owes me a favor or two is never a bad thing."

Paris nodded and stood. "Then you have yourself a deal. I'll do it."

CHAPTER EIGHT

I t didn't take long for Paris to pack. She didn't own much. A slew of worn t-shirts. Two pairs of boots. A ton of holey jeans. And of course, the essentials. She wouldn't be able to take much, according to Uncle John, so she left it all behind. All but the silver locket her uncle had given her years ago.

Uncle John had said it had been left behind in an evidence locker, and they were going to throw it away when they closed the case. He'd told her that it seemed like a waste to toss it when it was so pretty and seemed meant for Paris, having her initials and all.

On the reverse side of the locket were the words: You have to keep breaking your heart until it opens. Paris knew that quote to be from the ancient poet Rumi, but she never understood their significance.

Ironically, she'd never been able to open the heart-shaped locket. No spell she'd tried had opened the trinket, and there didn't appear to be a spot for a key. She had often considered taking a hammer to it to see what was inside, but she reasoned that the quote wasn't literal in that sense.

She wasn't sure about the locket being pretty as Uncle John had described, but she couldn't argue with the initials part. Since he'd given it to her, she always wore it or at least kept it close. She didn't really care what was inside anyway. She'd liked that Uncle John had given it to her.

Clutching the necklace in her hand, she strode to the end of Roya Lane, where a portal would open for her in the next five minutes to get her to the fairy godmother college. That was the only way one could get there. The college wasn't on a map, and only students and staff were allowed there.

Paris had lingered in Uncle John's office too long earlier, not being good with goodbyes. He wasn't either, and after a while, he'd waved her off and said he'd see her soon. She was going to college, not jail. Paris would be free to visit, so there was no reason to feel like this was a long-term thing, although she'd signed away the next several years of her life to erase her criminal record.

The whole situation still felt surreal, but Paris stood by her decision. She wasn't going to allow her uncle to get into trouble for her mistakes. Trouble *did* follow her around, and she knew he didn't want her in jail. She was willing to avoid it for his sake more than hers. Paris thought she could put the smackdown on some jerks if she were in prison, but it wasn't worth it. Uncle John would worry about her incessantly, and that was the last thing she wanted.

Not only did Paris not have many possessions she needed to take with her, but she also didn't have anyone besides Uncle John worth saying goodbye to. He had offered to see her off, but she'd refused, not thinking she could manage to leave if he was there. She needed to make a clean break, and he'd make her regret the whole thing.

Therefore, after a lifetime on Roya Lane, Paris was leaving without fanfare. As much as Paris defended the little guy, she never made friends with them. It would involve being nice to people, and that might make her throw up.

Looking to the side, Paris pretended there were others around her, waving at her and sad to see her go. It wasn't that she wanted a huge farewell, but it was upsetting to realize she'd lived this whole meaningless life where no one cared that she was leaving. Uncle John was probably right that this college business would be good for her, although she doubted it would soften her up much.

"See you all later." She glanced over her shoulder and didn't see anyone there.

"See ya," a tiny squeaky voice replied.

She froze, not having expected anyone to respond.

Paris looked around but didn't see the voice's source. Farther down the lane, elves strolled, and gnomes congregated on the magical street only accessible by magical races such as magicians and fairies, and the like. Roya Lane was full of things devoted to magic, like the Fairy Law Enforcement Agency or the Official Brownie Headquarters.

She blinked and noticed a small squirrel flicking his puffy tail on the cobbled street beside her. It wasn't unheard of to find a talking animal in the magical world, but it also wasn't common.

"Did you say that?" she asked the squirrel, feeling like a weirdo for talking to it.

He looked over his shoulder. "I think so. What did you hear? If it was 'see ya,' that was me. If not, it was the voices in your head."

She couldn't help but chuckle. "So far, I haven't heard any voices, but that might change soon based on where I'm going."

"Oh?" The squirrel's cheeks puffed out as if they were full of nuts. "Are you going to the fae kingdom? That place would drive anyone crazy."

Paris shook her head, having heard about the fae in Las Vegas a time or two. "Thankfully, I don't have to go there and lose my brain cells by hanging out with a bunch of fae. If so, I'd invite the voices into my head. No, I'm heading to Happily Ever After College." She glanced at the end of the alley. "As soon as they open the portal for me, that is."

When she turned back, the squirrel was angling his head. "Oh, I've heard of that college. What a fascinating place to study."

"Yeah, I guess," Paris grumbled. "I mean, I want to learn how to help the world be a better place, but learning about etiquette and all is less than appealing."

He grimaced. "Etiquette isn't my thing, but I meant it would be fascinating to study at the school. No one except fairy godmothers is allowed there. It's in a bubble, from what I've deduced from other conversations. So stepping foot there, from a scientific standpoint, would be interesting."

She narrowed her eyes at him. "You're a very strange squirrel."

"You have no idea." He nodded.

"What does that mean?"

"Nothing," he answered at once. "Anyway, my name is Faraday. You can call me Faraday."

Paris laughed. "Usually, when someone says my name is this or that, and you can call me blank, it's different from the original name."

"I don't do things how people usually do."

"Is that because you're not a people?"

A shadow passed over his face before disappearing. "What about you? What do you go by?"

She glanced at the wall of bricks. Still no portal. With a sigh, she turned back. "My name is Paris, and you can call me Pare… Paris." She couldn't think of anyone but Uncle John who called her by the affectionate nickname "Pare." She was going to miss hearing him call her that.

"Well, Pare-Paris, it's nice to meet you." Faraday bowed.

She shook her head. "No, my name is Paris. Call me Paris."

He pursed his mouth. "Usually, when someone says my name is this or that, and you can call me blank, it's different from the original name," he repeated verbatim.

"Ha-ha." She didn't mean it.

"I've deduced that you don't want to go to this fairy godmother college," he remarked.

"What gave it away?"

"Your demeanor for one, which lacks enthusiasm," he began. "Your regret about not having anyone to see you off reinforced the idea."

"Those were a lot of words I didn't expect squirrels to say," she observed.

"That you expect squirrels to say anything says a lot," he fired back. "You must have really strange friends."

"None, really," she confessed.

"Yes, hence the lack of people here to send you off."

"Again, 'hence' isn't a word a woodland creature should use."

He shrugged. "I don't spend much time in the woods if that helps."

"It doesn't," she stated dryly. She noticed a small glow starting at the end of the alley. The portal was opening. Paris gulped. "Well, I have to go. They're opening the way to the college."

"Okay." Faraday hopped after her as she walked toward the light, which grew bigger and brighter several yards away.

Paris froze and looked down at the strange squirrel. "What are you doing?"

"Nothing," he answered at once, his eyes sliding to the side.

"Cool. Well, catch you on the flipside, Faraday."

"Sounds good, Paris."

She took another step while saying a silent goodbye to Roya Lane, the place she'd spent most of her life, living in an apartment alongside Uncle John.

The squirrel's tail lay flat as he took several steps to keep up with her.

Paris halted and spun to face him. He froze, his chin tilting downward. "Are you following me?"

"It might appear that way," he answered.

"Why would that be?"

39

"Because I'm following you."

She laughed. "Why?"

"Well, first, because I've always wanted to go to a place like a fairy godmother college that operates independently, and this seems a perfect opportunity to sneak through a portal to get there," he began. "Second, my research could be aided by learning new magical practices such as those taught to fairy godmothers."

She crossed her arms over her chest. "Is there a third reason?"

"Well, naturally," he chirped. "All good arguments are constructed of three solid points."

"Again, you don't speak like a squirrel." She realized how ridiculous this notion was.

"Third, you seem like you could use…a friend." He said the last part sheepishly.

"You want to be my friend?" She felt suddenly embarrassed.

"Well, I don't really have any friends either," he remarked. "You don't want to go to this place and leave behind your world. I *do* want to go. Neither of us would prefer to go alone because that's scary, so it makes logical sense to me to go together."

"I don't know you." She narrowed her eyes at him.

He copied her expression. "And I don't know you."

Paris laughed at this. "You can't sleep in my bed."

"How presumptuous of you." He sounded offended.

"Do you prefer trees?"

"I prefer not to sleep," he corrected. "But when I do, I like bamboo sheets with a high thread count."

Paris blinked at him. "Now I know I've lost my mind. I'm talking to a high-maintenance squirrel with a large vocabulary."

"If that makes you think you're losing your mind, just you wait." He sounded very mysterious.

"What's that supposed to mean?"

"Nothing," he said in a rush while angling his head toward the portal. "So, what do you say? Your portal won't be open for much longer. Want company for this adventure you're being forced into?"

"How do you know I'm being forced?"

"I'm a master of observation."

Paris studied the strange squirrel. There was something very intriguing about him, and she didn't think he was untrustworthy. She had a fantastic instinct for people, and animals too.

In truth, she didn't want to go, but she didn't have a choice. Staying in Roya Lane wasn't going to do her any good. Uncle John was right. She would get into trouble if she stayed. Paris needed a change. She was overdue for it, and this weird creature had shown up at the eleventh hour and asked to accompany her to an unfamiliar place where she'd be inundated with new ideas and people and made to wear a dress. If ever she needed a friend, it was then.

Looking down at the squirrel, Paris smiled. "Okay, if you want to go with me, you can. But if you do anything nefarious, I'll turn you into a hat."

To her amusement, he grinned, showing a row of sharp teeth. "That's a deal. I think this is the start of a great partnership."

She sighed and wondered what she'd gotten herself into. "Or this is how I lose my mind."

"Who says it can't be both?" the squirrel asked as they strode forward.

The two stepped through the portal and entered the world of Happily Ever After College.

CHAPTER NINE

The grounds of Happily Ever After College were a stark contrast to Roya Lane. Whereas the cold February winds had been sweeping through the magical street in London, at the college, it felt like the perfect spring day.

"We're not in our prior location by any means," Faraday observed while sniffing the air happily.

"I think the phrase goes, 'We're not in Kansas anymore,'" Paris absently corrected. She squinted at the large mansion that stood in the distance, waiting for her eyes to adjust to the sunlight.

Faraday looked around. "This doesn't resemble the rolling plains of Kansas and the weather for this time of year is completely wrong, so I would never have concluded that we stepped through the portal to Kansas."

"Anymore," Paris added. "I meant to say, 'We're not in Kansas anymore, Toto.'"

The squirrel flicked his tail. "Faraday. I prefer to go by Faraday. I'm not sure where you were earlier, but I wasn't in Kansas."

Paris sighed and wondered if she made a mistake bringing the strange creature along. He'd used a convincing argument when he said that she didn't want to go to fairy godmother college alone. And he did seem smart, but as far as being trustworthy, that was yet to be determined. "It's from *The Wizard of Oz*. The phrase means we're in a totally different location than a moment prior."

"Wizard of Oz." Faraday carefully rolled the words around in his mouth as though he was testing them. "I've never heard of him, but you're correct that there has been a significant change to our location based on our prior coordinates."

"Seriously?" Paris muttered. "*The Wizard of Oz* is a movie."

"Haven't heard of that either."

"You've never seen one of most iconic movies of all times, but you referred to where we were as our prior coordinates? I'm certain I'll ask you this many times, but what's wrong with you?"

The squirrel shrugged. "I don't have time for the cinemas, and that doesn't make anything wrong with me—albeit one could argue that my time management skills could be to blame."

"Yeah, I guess you have to do that whole squirreling away food in the winter thing." Paris pointed at a tree. "Looks like you'll do all right here."

"I don't forage," he stated plainly, eyeing the tree as if it had offended him somehow.

"What do you eat in the cold winters then?" Paris was genuinely curious.

"Cheese sandwiches mostly," he answered seriously. "Sometimes soup."

She nodded as if this made perfect, reasonable sense. "A squirrel who eats soups and sandwiches. This is on par for this new strange life I'm living."

"On the weekend, I like to add dessert to the mix," Faraday offered.

"Peanut brittle?" Paris guessed with a laugh.

He gasped. "I don't eat nuts. I'm highly allergic to them."

Again, she nodded as if she should've expected this. "A squirrel who's allergic to nuts. Nothing weird about that."

"I also have seasonal allergies," he added, sniffing as though the spring breeze laced with floral scents was about to make him sneeze.

"Well, it appears that much like me, you know how to derail a conversation and a special event such as this." Paris looked out at the green grassy lawn that stretched between them and the large Victorian mansion. It was strangely quaint and very regal with its many turrets and balconies lined with hanging plants overflowing with flowers.

Leading to the large estate was a charming winding cobbled path with twisted oak trees lining it. In the distance, willow trees waved in the gentle breeze. The house reminded Paris of a grandmother's house with the wraparound porch and smoke billowing from one of the many chimneys. It was a three-story baby blue edifice with white trim and had to have at least a hundred rooms or more.

Paris couldn't see the back of the estate very well, but there appeared to be a greenhouse and another separate large structure. She also thought she caught sight of a lake in the distance and red stables.

Bordering the building on one side was a huge English garden with many statues and topiaries. Paris immediately longed to meander through it, smelling the giant roses she could see from even that distance. Growing up on busy Roya Lane and not having left it practically ever, Paris hadn't many opportunities to play in gardens. She'd always had to remain on Roya Lane due to Uncle John's work as a detective, and he was too busy for vacation.

On the other side of the large mansion was a thick dark forest. Shadows clung to the twisted oak trees that were dripping with moss. A chill ran down Paris' back as a sudden icy wind raced across the grounds, making the tree branches creak and groan.

She pulled her gaze away from the ominous forest and focused on the house once more, thinking that it didn't much look like an academy that trained fairy godmothers. If anything, it reminded Paris of a grandmother's house—not that she'd ever been to one, not having a grandmother herself. Really, since age five, Paris only had Uncle John, and he was pretty much the opposite of a grandmother.

Suddenly, something occurred to Paris, and she turned, doing a complete circle. There was no one on the extensive grounds of Happily Ever After College, making it feel like a ghost town in a way. Maybe she'd stepped through the wrong portal. Perhaps this had been a trick. Maybe she was stuck in time. The place did seem old and new at the same time.

Paris wasn't sure what she had expected when arriving at Happily Ever After College. Maybe a welcoming committee? There hadn't been anyone to see her off, so she didn't know why she expected anyone to be there when she arrived.

Sighing heavily, Paris started for the front door, deciding that she'd have to investigate on her own.

As soon as she took off, Faraday scampered along beside her. She paused and pointed at a nearby tree.

"Why don't you make a nest there?" she offered.

The squirrel halted too. He peered up at the tree, then at Paris, and back again. "I'm not the nest type. Or the tree type, for that matter."

"How come I didn't guess that?" she muttered dryly.

"You really should have." He snickered. "Anyway, I hoped to stay with you."

"Look," she began heavily, "you asked to tag along to this place. You didn't say anything about attaching yourself to my hip."

"No, you're right, I did not," he stated matter-of-factly. "I don't think either of us would like such an arrangement."

Paris grunted in frustration, then sighed again. "Are you always so literal?"

"Only when I'm not."

Paris nodded and chewed on her lip. "If you don't sleep in trees, where were you planning to stay?" She pointed at the dark woods on the other side of the mansion. "How about you find a hole or something in there?"

He shivered, obviously sensing the same foreboding quality emanating from the woods as she did. "I don't think so. How about I sleep in your sock drawer? It's not bamboo sheets, but I'm sure it will do. I don't take up much space, and I'm as quiet as an oscillating current that's—"

"Quiet as a mouse," she interrupted. "That's how the phrase goes."

"The mice I've been around aren't that quiet," he contradicted. "Especially if they can't get to the cheese at the end of the maze."

Paris' frowned. "I'll pretend you said something that makes logical sense coming from a squirrel."

"So what do you say?" Faraday gave her an expectant look. "Can I stay with you? I promise not to be a problem. I'll help when I can. I can be a great problem-solver. And my mission was to study the college and its unique ways after all."

Paris considered the strange squirrel again. There was something about him that was incredibly intriguing. Also, he made her laugh. Maybe that wasn't his goal, but a squirrel who was allergic to nuts and had seasonal allergies was entertaining. Paris thought her morale could use the boost. If Faraday ended up being a problem, well, she'd make a stew out of him.

"Fine," she finally relented. "But I tend to draw enough attention to myself without having a strange talking squirrel at my side. So stay out of sight and behave yourself. No dumping puddings on students' heads or anything else mischievous."

He saluted her with his tiny little arm in a very dignified manner. "You got it. I'll be the perfect picture of poise, and no one but you will know that I exist."

Paris huffed, shook her head, and doubted her sanity. She

sorely hoped that the squirrel was real and not a figment of her imagination that she created to cope with all the changes.

She made her way down the winding path to the large mansion and braced herself for the adventure ahead.

CHAPTER TEN

As the unlikely pair stepped onto the wraparound porch of the large Victorian mansion, a mysterious figure watched from the shadows of the Bewilder Forest.

The animal's green eyes reflecting the ambient light were the only sign from a distance that he lurked in the darkness. No one would expect this creature to be on the grounds of Happily Ever College since strong magical spells heavily protected it. Only those invited to enter through special portals were allowed entry to the place that existed in a bubble of sorts. But those rules didn't apply to Plato—no rules ever did.

The magical lynx watched as Paris and Faraday argued about whether she should ring the doorbell or knock on the mansion's large, stately entrance. Plato had been waiting a long time for this moment—and yet, there was still so much more that needed to happen. Paris had finally made it to Happily Ever After College as the powerful and all-knowing cat always knew she would. Now, the real work began. This was only the beginning.

The timing of everything was important, as it usually was with events as serious and complex as this. Nothing could happen to fix things until Paris Beaufont was ready. She currently thought she was Paris Westbridge, so there was much to unravel, but it would take time. Things couldn't be rushed.

Plato reasoned that he'd waited this long for the fairy to mature. It wouldn't be much longer now. Time passing was relative for the lynx. A hundred years went by in an instant. The last two decades...well, they'd felt like the longest years of his very long life.

Hopefully, all that would change soon. However, the only person who could fix things was the fairy currently standing on the grand Victorian mansion's porch and arguing with a squirrel.

Paris Beaufont was about to enter a brand new world, and it would change everything for her. If things went to plan, she'd change everything for the world in turn—which was exactly what Plato needed to happen.

CHAPTER ELEVEN

Paris had always liked doors. She collected pictures of interesting ones painted in different colors, with unique knockers and handles. Blue doors set into orange stucco or red ones on an all-white building. The thing she liked most about them was that they always led to somewhere so they were a marker of sorts—the entry to a new place, a change.

Dark stained glass windows of birds and mice entangled in a thick pink sash inlaid the double front doors to the huge Victorian mansion. Paris never read fairytales like Cinderella. She wasn't about to start either, but she knew where the references to the woodland creatures came from and it made her momentarily doubt her decision yet again. If anyone wasn't cut out to be a fairy godmother and create love for two people, it was Paris.

Honestly, the fairy had never believed in love. It was only a chemical reaction that wore off when the guy quit trying, and the girl started nagging. Love was a thing that Mother Nature used so the human race would procreate. Paris realized that she was more than cynical on the matter, but how could she not be?

All her life, she hadn't seen real love. The movies painted it as though the happy ending was the guy getting the girl, but they didn't tell the part where he got fat, and she started reading trashy novels to fill the emptiness. Love songs were usually snapshots created when someone felt fuzzy feelings, but those wore off like the overly full feeling after eating a tray of nachos or the excitement after buying a new leather jacket.

Paris glanced down at her worn leather jacket with the rip from her fight with the giant named Madow. She was overdue for a new coat, but that would probably have to wait since she was out of funds, jobless, and at a college where she was supposedly required to wear a gown. Revulsion flip-flopped in Paris' stomach as she tried to come to terms with her new reality—repeatedly.

"Are you planning to ring the doorbell anytime today?" Faraday asked beside her.

She narrowed her eyes at the squirrel, pretending he was her complete source of annoyance. In truth, Paris realized that she was stalling. Her frustration wasn't really at the mysterious squirrel but rather at her entire predicament. Faraday was the only thing that had gone right all day. He wanted to be Paris' friend, and she didn't know anyone volunteering for that position in her life.

"I was thinking of using the knocker." She ran her gaze over the bronze knob of a rabbit and below it, a large ring set on a small placard. It reminded Paris of the white rabbit from Alice and Wonderland, and she suddenly felt as if she'd fallen down the rabbit hole and had no idea where she'd end up. She'd much rather be trapped in those stories than Cinderella's, but it didn't appear she had a choice.

"I'd like to hear the chime the doorbell makes," Faraday countered. "I have to think it's enchanting and loud for a place of this size."

"I'll remind you that you're along for the ride and therefore, you get no vote."

The squirrel showed his teeth while making a biting motion. "That doesn't seem very democratic."

"Probably because this isn't a democracy," Paris argued. "This is my life, and I get to live it the way I want."

"Which is why you're attending Happily Ever After College against your will," Faraday chirped.

"I'm going to use the knocker," Paris remarked dryly.

"Can we do both?" The squirrel scampered back and forth, pausing and rocking back on his hind legs in front of a large planter beside the front door.

Paris grunted. "No, that's overkill. I want them—whoever they are—to know that I'm here, but not to be irritated by my arrival from the start."

He nodded. "First impressions are everything. So where are the fresh-baked goods?"

"The what?" Paris asked.

"Well, I think it's customary to offer treats to your host upon arrival," Faraday offered.

"They're at the store. I don't bake."

"Well, maybe you can pick some of these flowers and offer them." He indicated the begonias spilling over the sides of the planter.

"Yeah, because they won't notice that I've pulled up their flowers and given them as a gift."

"I'm simply offering you suggestions since you showed up empty-handed." Faraday crossed his arms over his chest.

"I brought you, which once fattened up, will be perfect served with a nice chutney," Paris teased.

He grimaced at her. "You make a multitude of threats."

Paris batted her eyelashes at him. "It's part of my charm."

"I simply think the doorbell makes the most sense—"

The *clinking* of the door handle cut off the squirrel's words. Paris' eyes jerked up, startled. On the other side of the stained glass was a figure.

With little time to react, Paris did the first thing she could think of and booted the squirrel to the side, making him dive into the planter. A squeal escaped his mouth as Faraday disappeared into the flowers while Paris straightened and looked into the eyes of a studious butler who regarded her with great skepticism.

CHAPTER TWELVE

The man, who Paris assumed was a butler only because he appeared to be the epitome of one with his starched black pinstriped suit and white gloves and pursed lips, craned his head before looking at Paris.

"Were you talking to someone?" he asked in a very refined British accent, still looking around.

Paris coughed uncomfortably, careful to keep her eyes off the planter where Faraday was thankfully as quiet as a mouse...or a squirrel she would murder if he made any noises.

"I was talking to myself." She forced a smile.

"Oh." The man still searched the empty grounds, but not finding anything, snapped to attention.

He wore a three-piece suit of the finest quality and was older, although an exact age was hard to pinpoint with fairies since they aged much slower than other races. Like most, he'd glamoured his wings out of the way. That was a practical thing most fairies did since they could cause clearance issues.

Really, most fairies didn't have much use for their wings in the modern world since they were mostly for show and not very practical for transport. It simply cost too much energy to use them for flying, and it was ineffective at best. Still, it was always easy to spot her kind and Paris knew the man to be a fairy. He'd neatly combed his grayish hair to the side, and he had a distinguished look in his green eyes.

"You must be Paris Westbridge. The headmistress has been expecting you."

Paris nodded. "Well, I'm here and ready."

Jeeves, or whatever the man's name was, looked Paris over, taking in her jeans and leather jacket and tousled blonde hair. "Do you have anything you need me to bring in for you?"

"Unless you want to carry me in, then no." She chuckled.

A sudden look of disapproval sprang to the butler's face, and Paris sensed he wasn't the joking type.

"I'm Wilfred Biltmore." He bowed to Paris. "I'm the butler for the Fairy Godmother Estate or as we call it, FGE." He waved his hand to indicate the mansion where he stood. After taking a step backward, he held out his gloved hand in a presenting fashion. "Please come in, and I'll show you to the sitting room where you can wait for the headmistress."

The butler's overly formal nature immediately made Paris want to crack some jokes and follow them up with, "Cheerio, old chap. Right-o. Bob's your uncle."

Instead, she casually glanced over her shoulder at the planter where Faraday was still hiding, hoping that he was okay there. She figured the talking squirrel had made it this far and probably knew how to take care of himself.

Turning her attention back to the waiting butler, she nodded and allowed herself to be led into the Victorian house known as FGE, where she immediately felt that she'd stepped into a brand new and very strange world.

CHAPTER THIRTEEN

The smell of fresh-baked chocolate chip cookies was intoxicating when Paris stepped over the threshold into the mansion. If that wasn't enough to assault her senses, she suddenly felt transported back in time.

As when she stepped through the portal onto the college's grounds, she felt like she was visiting grandma. Paris half-expected an older woman with an apron and a loving smile to toddle out of one of the many doorways that lined the long hallway.

That was the part that made the mansion all of a sudden not feel as cozy, although if she blinked, she felt that she might fool herself into believing she was in a tiny little cottage instead of a huge house.

Straight off the entrance was a long hallway that led to what appeared to be a large sunroom at the back of the house—a green lawn winked through the glass windows. Doors lined the hallway and to the left of the spacious entry was a grand staircase that led to the various floors.

To the left of the staircase was an elegant round sitting room that Paris suspected was in one of the house's many turrets. Fancy furniture that Paris couldn't picture sitting on filled it. Paisley designs and oil paintings covered the walls. Sitting in the corner was a piano and in front of the crackling fire was a cozy cat curled up on a tufted sofa. The fat orange cat cracked an eye and peered at Paris appraisingly, annoyance evident on its face for being disturbed during nap time.

"I trust that you'll be okay waiting here while I collect the head-mistress," Butler Stuffy Face said in his posh voice.

Paris should have said, "Yes, of course." Instead, she opened her mouth, and against her better judgment sang, "Capital! Pip, pip, Wilfred."

The butler arched a curious eyebrow at Paris, probably trying to figure out if she was serious or not. "Very well," he finally said stuffily. "Now, I suspect I'll see you around since you'll be here full-time."

Paris glanced out the large bank of windows and stared at the grounds of Happily Ever After College, having a surreal moment that she was now inside the mansion that towered over her moments prior. She gulped, nodded, and glanced down, suddenly worried that she'd tracked mud into the pristine room with her combat boots. Thankfully they appeared clean. However, the thick carpet was white like much of the furniture, as if they were inviting a huge mess.

"If you need anything at all, you simply must call for me," Wilfred stated. "No matter where you are in the house, say my name and I'll appear."

Now it was Paris' turn to arch a curious eyebrow at the butler. "This must be a very large place. How will you hear me?"

He nodded with his hands clasped behind his back. "There are three stories to FGE not including the basement and cellars, and over one hundred and twenty-six rooms, although the number fluctuates plus or minus ten depending."

Paris tilted her head to the side, her expression saying, "Go on."

When Wilfred didn't continue his seemingly unfinished sentence, she prompted, "Depending on what?"

He shrugged. "Many factors. The number of residents and activities as well as other things that I'm sure you'll learn about over time."

She glanced at the far wall and studied it. "So are the walls like those accordion ones that can fold in and create different spaces? I had one of those in my place where I could pretend I had a separate living room in my studio apartment."

Wilfred's eyes tightened. "The manor is not at all like your apartment, I'm guessing. It rearranges itself using the magic that governs Happily Ever After College."

"Right." Paris drew out the word. "I guess the furnace doesn't hiss and the water heater doesn't take eons to heat up."

"I think you'll find that we're very comfortable here at Happily Ever After College," he said in his refined tone. "The headmistress will be in charge of your tour. I'll go and alert her of your arrival."

Paris simply nodded, wondering how uptight this headmistress was if Wilfred was any indication.

Grabbing both of the double doors to the sitting room, the butler pulled them shut after backing out of the room, leaving her alone with the sleeping cat.

Turning back to the windows, Paris searched the front patio for signs of Faraday. Not seeing any indication of him, she redirected her attention to studying the sitting room, which was rich with decorations and furniture.

She'd never been in a place this fancy. Uncle John was a simple man who kept things pretty minimalistic. Paris always liked that about him. They never had much money, but she never went without—well, as long as he knew she needed something. In recent years, knowing she needed to start taking care of herself and not be a burden to her uncle, Paris had tried to do without and live on her own, but usually that meant she went hungry.

Paris' mind suddenly started to roam as she studied a set of black and white photographs on the wall. All featured women in long gowns. So many thoughts competed for her attention right then.

Out of the blue, she wondered about something that never plagued her—her parents. Standing in that strange sitting room with an orange cat and a bunch of possessions that had to belong to a grandmother, she wondered if her attending Fairy Godmother College would have made her parents proud. It was a tough place to get into, and Uncle John had pulled strings to get her there, although she'd picked up on the fact that the college was hurting for enrollment.

However, she was suddenly curious what her parents would think of this career choice. It had to be better than her working two-bit jobs or getting into trouble on Roya Lane. In truth, Paris didn't know because she didn't know much about her parents. Uncle John had said they were good people. They were quiet and simple. Accountants.

Apparently, they had gone to an accounting conference, and that's where they both disappeared when Paris was young. No one knew what happened to them and the investigation had been closed after no leads turned up.

Paris didn't know what could happen to simple people at an accountant conference. Maybe they died of boredom, she joked to herself with a morbid laugh.

She was able to make such bad jokes because she didn't have many memories of them. Nothing to make their absence hurt. Only blurry memories of two figures she only sensed love from. Uncle John had echoed that sentiment, stating that they'd never abandon Paris so something must have happened to them.

Their disappearance was why Uncle John became a detective, but even with all his efforts and expertise, he'd never been able to find the couple. Paris didn't like feeling sorry for herself about not having two people she didn't remember all that well. She had

Uncle John, and he was by far the best man in the world and the best one to have raised her. He'd taught her to be tough and loved her unconditionally, which was vital because Paris was one of those types who tried people's patience and tolerance. Yet, that man had not so much as ever raised his voice at her.

She instantly missed her uncle, the realization that she wouldn't be able to pop into his office between shifts settling in. However, Paris consoled herself with the notion that attending Happily Ever After College saved her uncle from getting into trouble. In the back of her mind and deep within her heart, she hoped that maybe it saved her. If she was honest with herself, Paris knew that she couldn't keep going down the same path she'd been on the last few years. Things needed to change, and that had started the moment she walked through the door to Fairy Godmother Estate.

Still lost in thought, looking out the window without seeing, Paris nearly jumped when the double doors to the sitting room burst open.

She wheeled around not to find the refined figure she expected of the headmistress. Instead, Paris found herself face to face with a small Asian woman with short black hair, dressed in plain gray clothes.

"Hi!" Paris squeaked, but the woman didn't respond.

Instead, she pointed at the cat. "Out of here, Casanova. No spying for you today."

The orange cat unhurriedly stretched to a standing position on the sofa.

"Now!" the small woman snapped, suddenly displaying great authority.

That put some fire under the feline's butt, and he bounded off the sofa and scurried through the open doors. When he was gone, the woman closed them at once and whipped around to face Paris, her eyes serious although kind.

"We don't have long," she began while glancing over her

shoulder and peering through the glass panes on the door. "Listen to what I have to say before the headmistress gets here. It's imperative that you do exactly what I tell you."

CHAPTER FOURTEEN

"You're not the headmistress?" Paris asked, then felt dumb for it. She consoled herself with the fact that there was no way for her to know. She'd never met a fairy godmother, let alone the headmistress for the college that churned them out. How was she supposed to know what they looked like? Uncle John had said they wore gowns like those in the black and white photographs on the wall.

Paris had to admit the unprepossessing woman standing before her didn't look like a headmistress or a fairy godmother. She seemed unnerved as she vied for Paris' attention.

The woman shook her head. "My name is Mae Ling, and I'm here to tell you something before your adventure starts."

"That I put my underwear on backward? Because that's how this whole thing is starting to feel," Paris joked and tugged on her pants, although they didn't at all feel uncomfortable. It was the whole meeting a talking squirrel, a pretentious butler, and an antsy woman that made her feel like she'd woken up on the wrong side of the planet.

"Your underwear is fine," Mae Ling stated. "Although you're probably old enough to graduate from Spider-Man undies."

Paris' eyes widened as she looked down and back up, then down again. "How do you know I'm wearing Spider-Man underwear?"

Mae Ling waved her off dismissively. "I know things. It's what I do. That's why I'm here."

Paris pointed at herself self-consciously. "You know something about me?"

The wise woman, who was both young and old in a mysterious way, stated, "Yes, I know that no matter what, you need to be exactly who you are here at Happily Ever After College."

Paris couldn't help but laugh, although she did feel rude about it and covered her mouth. "I'm sorry, but that seems unwise since who I am is an uneducated, unmannered heathen who is only here so I can stay out of jail." She waved her arms at the shelf of knick-knacks made of porcelain and hand-painted with beautiful delicacy. "You all, the fairy godmothers, are refined and poised and educated and everything that I'm not."

"Don't let appearances deceive you, Paris. We don't know everything, and there's much we can learn."

"Not from me," Paris retorted.

"My point," Mae Ling's voice shifted to a subtler tone, "is that it's crucial that you be you while here at Happily Ever After College. If you don't agree with something, say so or don't do it. Rebel. Whatever it is that you feel. No matter what."

Paris scratched her head, not believing that things could be more confusing, and yet they were increasingly so. "I don't understand—"

Mae Ling whipped her head over her shoulder, her eyes going wide at the sounds of heels echoing down the long hallway outside the sitting room. "No matter what," she insisted in a rush. "You must be you. Don't conform to our ways if they don't feel right to you."

"But I'm here because I'm a troublemaker," Paris argued, wondering if she could trust this harmless-looking woman. Maybe Mae Ling was trying to sabotage Paris. "I'm here to learn your ways, not to rebel against them."

The fairy godmother sighed. "I realize that what I'm telling you sounds strange—"

"It sounds like a fast way to get me booted out of here, to be honest," Paris interrupted, deciding to be bold and truthful. She didn't have time for games.

"That won't happen," Mae Ling countered. "I'll see to it. Still, it's critical that you do as I say, which shouldn't be hard. Just be you."

"I don't think I can do that," Paris said in a rush, sensing Mae Ling's nervousness about someone approaching in the hallway. "This is my last chance to make things right, or I'm going to jail. My uncle will be in trouble. I can't risk that."

Mae Ling shook her head, a deadly serious look on her face. "What we have to lose if you don't do as I've instructed is much bigger than your uncle and you. It will have far-reaching effects for the world at large."

"But—"

"If you see something you don't like, say so," Mae Ling cut in, again jerking her head to glance over her shoulder at the hallway. The sounds of footsteps were right outside the door, but Paris didn't see anyone yet through the glass-paneled panes. "If you don't want to do something, don't, Paris. This is very, very important."

It was all starting to sound much more ominous than Paris ever imagined. She thought she was going to a stupid matchmaker school. How could what she did affect the world at large? "Why?" she argued, giving the fairy godmother a pleading expression, needing answers.

"You will see—" Mae Ling stated definitively as a figure materialized on the other side of the door and entered at once, interrupting their conversation and Paris' opportunity to get information.

CHAPTER FIFTEEN

A woman who resembled much more of what Paris pictured a fairy godmother looking like entered the sitting room. She wore a long blue silk gown with a thick pink ribbon around the collar and a hood in the back. Her hair was grayish-blue and tied up in a neat bun. Like Mae Ling, this made her look old and young at the same time.

"Hello, Paris Westbridge," the woman said in a welcoming tone with a sincere smile on her face. "I'm Willow Starr, the head-mistress for Happily Ever After College." She gestured at the black-haired woman. "I see that you've already met our head professor, Mae Ling."

Paris was suddenly speechless, something that was rare for her. Mae Ling wasn't only a fairy godmother or a professor, but the head professor for the college. That seemed like someone she could trust. Someone that she should. Yet, her instructions to "Be yourself" were so strange.

That had always gotten Paris into fistfights when she saw something she disagreed with. Employers passed over her for jobs more times than she could count because of her rebellious appearance and tendency to speak her mind.

Uncle John had often encouraged her simply to think things instead of blasting her opinion. Like when she called out the guy who cut off an elderly lady so he could get out of the elevator first. Or like the crowd of gnomes who simply strolled by, watching as an elderly elf struggled to carry his heavy packages. Paris still had the burn mark from the fireball one of the gnomes threw at her. It was worth it to call out the inconsiderate behavior.

As if it ran in her blood, Paris felt compelled to fight and speak out about injustices in the world. She thought she'd put that tendency to bed when she stepped through the portal to Happily Ever After College. However, it appeared that she hadn't, or she shouldn't.

Maybe sensing Paris' nervousness or the tension between her and Mae Ling, Willow glanced between the pair. "Well, I guess that you've been orienting Paris, Professor?"

The small woman shook her head. "Not too much. Only introductions."

"Very good," Willow stated cheerfully. She had a broad smile and bright red lipstick that contrasted with her blue eyes. "Introductions are a great place to start."

She sat on the tufted couch and gestured at the armchair opposite it. "Please have a seat, and I'll tell you about the college."

Paris eyed the chair covered in white fabric as if she'd been asked to sit on a pile of rocks.

Sensing her apprehension, Willow's smile dropped. "Or you can sit wherever you like." She indicated the other chairs in the room, which were all white too.

Swallowing her hesitation, Paris took a seat, her black jacket contrasting boldly against the seat.

"Very good," Willow chirped. "Now, I'm not sure what all you know about Happily Ever After College, but it's been educating fairy godmothers for centuries. The Saint Valentine govern it at

Matter of the Heart and assignments are made by Fairy Godmother Agency." She waved her hand. "That's the boring stuff that I'm sure you don't care about. What you need to know is that we teach our students how to foster love connections between two people."

"Can't people fall for each other without your help?" Paris asked before she could stop the words.

Willow smiled politely, not at all off-put by the brazen question. "Of course, but fairy godmothers simply nudge connections that might not happen if not for our help."

"Why?" Paris questioned again. "Why not let two people do their own thing?"

Willow nodded thoughtfully. "Love is important in this world. I dare say that it's what makes the world go round. The more love we have, the better our planet. So it's our job to help two people to fall in love, creating positive feelings that resonate globally."

Paris tilted her head back and forth, not finding anything to argue with regarding the sentiment. "Okay, so we stick two people together and hope they fall for each other. That sounds easy enough."

Willow glanced at Mae Ling, who had remained standing by the door, before returning her gaze to Paris. "It's a little more complicated than that. Our primary focus is to guide our Cinderellas to help them land the perfect Prince Charming."

"Do you mean help debutantes land rich husbands?" Paris asked.

Willow pushed back on the sofa, her patience starting to wear thin with these types of questions. However, Paris could have sworn that a small smile flickered to Mae Ling's face briefly before her neutral expression replaced it. "I understand that you're not the overly romantic type." She snapped her fingers, and a thick file materialized in her hand. Willow opened the pink folder, combing through the pages. "I've had a chance to review your file."

Paris slumped. "I didn't do most of that stuff."

Willow pressed the folder closed and looked directly at Paris. "How about this? How about you use this to make a fresh start? I won't think of you as your past misdeeds, and you simply keep an open mind to what we do here at Happily Ever After College."

A fresh start… That's what Paris had thought this was all about. Instead, Mae Ling was asking her to be her usual rebellious self, which would no doubt create problems, as she always did.

Gulping down the tension in her throat, Paris nodded. "Yes, I'll keep an open mind."

The file disappeared from Willow's hand. "Lovely. Now, I must warn you that although I'm willing to give you a fair chance, there will be others here who may not understand your involvement with the college."

"Because my uncle pulled strings to get me in here," Paris guessed.

Willow offered her a polite smile. "In the past, it's been quite difficult to get into Happily Ever After College. With enrollment what it is and your predicament, I allowed you here. Detective Nicholson has helped me out a time or two. However, I'll warn you that this isn't a free ride and you'll have to earn your place here."

"I'll be tested?" Paris asked.

Another pursed smile. "There will be an evaluation, and yes, you'll have to pass to stay. That's all I require, but others might be a little less accepting. Give them time, and hopefully, they'll come around."

When Paris didn't say anything in response, Willow stood, her elegant gown brushing the floor. "Well, if there are no further questions, I think a tour is in order, but first we should get you settled in." She glanced around. "Did Wilfred already take up your things?"

Paris shrugged. "I didn't bring anything. Well, I have my toothbrush in my jacket pocket." She pulled out the blue toothbrush. "Uncle John said that you provide all that I require."

Willow nodded, studying the toothbrush curiously. "Yes, but usually students have keepsakes or personal things they bring along."

Paris thought of the heart-shaped locket in her other pocket. "I don't really have that type of stuff."

"Very well." Willow snapped her fingers. "Wilfred, if you'd join us please."

To Paris' surprise, the butler simply materialized in the middle of the room like an AI paged on a spaceship. So that's what he meant when he said that all Paris needed to do was call him and he'd help her.

"Yes, Headmistress?" Wilfred said in his regal tone.

"Would you please take Paris to her room?" Willow asked.

"Of course." He nodded, opened the double doors, and stood by.

"In your room," Willow glanced at Paris. "You'll find a blue gown like this." She indicated the one she was wearing. "Please wear it, although you'll notice there's no pink sash on yours. Students must earn those when they graduate."

It was difficult for Paris to hide the grimace at the thought of putting on the powder blue gown.

"When you've settled in," Willow continued, "please meet Mae Ling and me in the conservatory at the back of the house. Wilfred will show you where that is."

Paris simply nodded, wondering what the hell a conservatory was and if she'd get hives when she put on the gown.

CHAPTER SIXTEEN

"What's a conservatory?" Paris asked as she followed Wilfred up the stairs to the second floor. The fairy godmother manor seemed to go on for ages and Paris thought it would take her a while to get a lay of the land.

"A conservatory is a building or room having glass or tarpaulin roofing and walls used as a greenhouse or a sunroom," the butler said in a robotic voice. "If within a residence, it's typically attached to the house on only one side. Conservatories originated in the sixteenth century when wealthy landowners sought to cultivate citrus fruits such as lemons and oranges that began to appear on their dinner tables brought by traders from warmer regions of the Mediterranean."

Paris gave Wilfred a sideways look. "Why does it sound like you're reading from Wikipedia?"

"Because I am," he answered as they arrived at the second-floor landing and held out a white-gloved hand to show her the way.

"Because you have it memorized?" she questioned. "All of the internet?"

He tapped the side of his head. "I have it downloaded."

"I'm going to need an explanation." Paris strode down the long hallway of rich wood walls and floors, similar to the one on the first floor, lined with doors.

"I'm not a fairy," he answered. "Well, not entirely."

That made Paris tense. She always recognized her own. "You aren't? I thought only fairies were here."

He nodded while walking slightly in front of her. "I'm a magitech fairy, created to serve the college."

"You're an artificial intelligence." She gasped, having wondered that earlier.

"Correct. Although I'm much more. Anyway, yes, I'm the AI for FGE, serving all the students, professors, and staff. You can call on me from anywhere in the manor, and I'll show up. I have the entire Internet at my disposal so I can find most information for you."

"Much better than having an Alexa," she joked. Paris paused, raising a cautious eyebrow at the butler. "Wait, you're not annoying like Alexa and show up when I say something close to your name like, will you blah blah whatever?"

He shook his head. "You have to say my name and a request, like Wilfred, will you join me, or Wilfred, can you help me, or Wilfred, I need—"

Paris nodded. "Okay, I got it. I like it. Very handy, although it's weird to think that I was talking to a human earlier who isn't one."

"As far as I'm aware, I'm as human as you or anyone else," Wilfred corrected. "I feel, think, and have judgment."

"Of course the fairy godmothers have a sentient AI butler," Paris teased. "I'd expect nothing less."

"I'm not sure what you would have expected," he said smugly and suddenly stopped at a door. "I simply am what I am despite your expectations."

"We're going to work on your sense of humor, Wil." Paris pointed at the door where they'd paused. "Is this my room?"

"Yes, madam. I hope you find it comfortable." He opened it and pushed it back to reveal a small but elegantly appointed room.

Paris' feet brought her forward as her mouth fell open. The bed was something out of a fairy tale—a sweet pink canopy style with fluffy bedding. There was everything that she could need: a dresser, bedside table, lamp, and a giant teddy bear.

She restrained the smile seeking to unfold on her face. "This is…it's nice…thank you."

He nodded and backed up. "Make yourself at home and remember, I'm always here if you need anything."

With that the butler pulled the door closed, making Paris realize that she might have it all here at Happily Ever After College. The question was, did she want it all?

CHAPTER SEVENTEEN

T he bedroom was small, with little room to maneuver because of all the furniture, but it was also perfect. It had everything that Paris could need, well, besides the giant teddy bear. She was pretty sure that would disappear under the bed at some point.

Bright sunlight shimmered through the only window in the room, which was half open, the pink curtains blowing in the breeze. Paris also didn't know how she felt about all this pink business, although she did like the canopy bed. It felt like something out of a movie—the type that some rich girl slept in at night.

In this fantasy, the girl would have parents who tucked her in at night and named all of her stuffed animals. She'd wake up to the smell of bacon and waffles in the morning and come downstairs to find her mother smiling at her and calling her "Beautiful." Her father would be reading the newspaper and offer to give her piggyback rides around the house after breakfast. However, that was a fantasy and Paris knew it.

She looked out the open window, enjoying the fresh breeze that wafted through. The grounds of Happily Ever After stretched on for as far as she could see from her second-story view. Paris enjoyed looking at the winding path she'd taken a while ago to reach the front door, flanked by twisted oak trees. Beyond that were trees and rolling green hills and blue sky. Pristine wasn't the right word for it. The place was surreal and idyllic in every way.

A scratching noise on one side pulled her attention from the lawn and wind dancing through the trees. She stiffened, then turned to face the dresser against the wall. The sound grew louder.

Paris looked around for a weapon of sorts. What if a monster who knew she didn't belong at the college was hiding in her dresser? Or maybe it was the ghost of the last girl who had flunked out of Happily Ever After.

She shook her head and muttered, "You have an overactive imagination."

Paris held up her fist as she neared the dresser, deciding it was the best weapon and the one she was best at using. She didn't think she could punch a ghost, but it was better to be prepared.

The scratching intensified, shaking the second from the bottom drawer.

Soundlessly, Paris grabbed the handle and held her breath —tensing.

In one swift movement, she yanked the drawer open, preparing for something to spring out of it.

The small squirrel didn't fly at Paris when she opened the drawer. Instead, as if somewhat annoyed that he'd been interrupted, Faraday sat up, turning in the drawer and offering her a pursed expression that seemed to say, "Do you mind?"

Paris slumped with relief. "What are you doing in there?"

"I'm making my bed, thank you very much," he replied in his squeaky voice.

Her eyes widened as she threw her finger to her mouth. "Would you shush it? You're going to get me in trouble. How did you know this was my room?"

Paris glanced over her shoulder at the open window, guessing that's how the sneaky squirrel had trespassed. "Again, how did you know this was my room? You could have snuck into someone else's, and I told you not to get me in trouble."

Still sitting upright in the drawer of bright white socks—all brand new—Faraday pointed at the bed. "I made an educated guess since the letter there is addressed to you."

Paris whipped around, looking at the pink bed and seeing what he meant. Lying against the many rows of fluffy pillows was an envelope. On the front was her name: Paris Westbridge.

She recognized the writing at once. It was from Uncle John.

Feeling a sudden wave of nostalgia, Paris picked up the letter, looking back over her shoulder at the squirrel. "You didn't read it, did you?"

A look of offense crossed his face. "What type of person do you take me for?"

"I don't take you for a person at all, squirrel," she replied dryly, picking up the letter.

"Touché," he chirped, diving down into the sock drawer, making the scratching noises again.

"Need I remind you that you broke into my room and are rearranging my sock drawer before I stepped foot in the place?" Paris opened the envelope and pulled out a short letter.

"I'm getting my bed together," he countered. "As I told you that I'd have to do."

"Good, do that," she muttered while scanning the letter from Uncle John.

It read:

Dear Pare,

I trust that you've made it to Happily Ever After College and are settling in. I would have loved to see you off, but I respect that you're independent. I'm always here for you if you ever need anything. Also, I'm proud of you for taking on this challenge. I know that you didn't want to, but I can't help but feel this will be a good chapter for you. Still, I miss you already and can't wait to hear about your adventures. Please try to stay out of trouble and do the best you can. I know that romance isn't something you subscribe to, but you have the biggest heart of anyone I know so I think you're in the right place.

Take care and much love.
Uncle John

Paris lowered the note and sat on the bed, which was the perfect balance of soft and firm. She couldn't help but feel that she would disappoint her Uncle John if she took Mae Ling's advice. This was her second chance to make things right. Still, according to Mae Ling, it didn't seem like it was only about Paris anymore.

"Maybe I can do both," Paris muttered. "Behave and also be me."

The squirrel poked his head up out of the drawer. "I think those two are mutually exclusive."

Paris grunted. "You're mutually exclusive, rodent."

"That doesn't make any sense," he argued while scratching around in the drawer. "In the logic and probability theory, one is required to have two propositions to maintain mutual exclusivity."

"Did you fall out of a tree as a baby?" Paris asked. "Is that why you're so weird?"

"Can you define your use of the word weird in this context?"

Paris stood from the bed. "By weird, I mean that you sound like you swallowed a dictionary when you should be making chirping sounds."

"Logic would reason that if I had trauma as a baby, I'd have fewer brain cells and therefore behave less intelligently," he countered.

Paris shook her head, pulling out the drawer on top of the one where Faraday was burrowing, making him have to duck suddenly.

"Hey," he complained in a muffled voice from under the open drawer. "You nearly hit me there."

"Well, it sounds like you've got some brain cells to lose, so what's the harm?" she teased while running her gaze over the drawer's contents. It was full of undergarments that were all neatly folded and brand new. She pushed the drawer closed and checked the others, finding them all stocked with clothes that were soft and well-made.

Leaving the sock drawer open for Faraday, she crossed the room to the bedside table to find it filled with toiletries and other things she might regularly need. Paris brought her gaze up to discover the blue silk gown hanging on the back of the door. A grimace sprang to her face at once.

If she wanted to stay out of trouble, as Uncle John had encouraged her, she should wear the gown as Willow had advised. However, if she followed Mae Ling's advice, there was no way in hell that she'd be caught wearing that thing, which was the antithesis of what Paris liked to wear.

The competing struggle was real, and she suspected it would only get harder. Before she pulled her door open, Paris glanced back over her shoulder to where the squirrel continued to sort through her sock drawer. "Stay out of sight. Don't make a noise. And don't get me in trouble."

"Affirmative on all three accounts," Faraday answered. "Will you bring me a cheese sandwich at some point? I'm starving and have a lot of work to do here, making my bed just right."

Paris shook her head. "Don't tear up my socks, squirrel. Yes, I'm sure no one will notice if I nick a cheese sandwich from the kitchen and sneak it upstairs."

"Tell them that you require a late-night snack," he advised.

Laughing, Paris pulled the door shut. She would grab the strange squirrel a sandwich for dinner from the kitchen, right after she figured out where it was. First, she had to find this conservatory now that she knew what that was.

CHAPTER EIGHTEEN

I t didn't take Paris long to realize that she was lost. All the hallways on the second floor looked the same, lined with doors that she guessed led to other residents' rooms.

She reasoned that she could simply call Wilfred and he'd show her down to the conservatory, but Paris wanted to prove she could find it on her own. Pride was something she was good at harboring.

Soon after becoming lost, Paris realized that multiple staircases led up to the third floor and down to the first. She assumed that she'd missed the one they'd taken up to her room and was now totally turned around.

After finding a window at the end of a hallway, Paris glanced out and realized she was at the back of the large house. These grounds didn't look anything like the ones that her room faced. Instead, she saw a shimmering blue pool, an outdoor patio, the forest on one side, and gardens on the other. In the distance were a tranquil lake, horse stables, and more buildings.

Taking the next set of stairs, Paris was greeted by many rich and delicious aromas as she descended to the first floor. At the end of the hallway, she glimpsed a glassed-in room that could only be what she guessed was the conservatory.

Paris made her way toward it, but crying echoing from a room coming up on the left stole her attention immediately. The telltale sounds of taunting followed the noise.

"It isn't that hard, Penny," a girl said. "Jump if you want them. Or you could use magic, but chances are, you're not going to get that right."

Paris paused at the doorframe, trying to decide if she should poke her head into the room and investigate. The conservatory, where Willow and Mae Ling required her, was a little way down the hallway.

The crying interrupted Paris' focus. "I can't see without my glasses to jump or to use magic," someone whined.

"Always an excuse with you," the other girl fired back coldly.

Paris realized that she couldn't in good conscience simply stroll past what was clearly a bullying situation. She entered the room, which she quickly recognized as a large dining hall.

Stretching the length of the space was a long table made of mahogany wood and lined with two dozen chairs. There was a fireplace on one wall and a bank of windows that faced the statue garden on the other. Along the closest was a buffet with covered dishes that were steamy and gave off many of the rich aromas that Paris had smelled upon coming downstairs.

With her back toward Paris was a woman with stringy grayish-blue hair, wearing a blue gown like the one she'd left hanging on her door. The fairy godmother in training had her hand over her head and was using magic to levitate a pair of purple glasses high above another woman's head.

This one didn't see Paris even though she faced the newcomer because she was squinting upward and making poor attempts to jump for the hovering glasses. She had short curly hair that was the same color as the other girl's.

"Oh, poor Penny Pullman." The bullying fairy clicked her tongue several times and shook her head. "What's going to save you now? Maybe you can get a scholarship to help you get your glasses back? Or you can go cry to the headmistress again like you did this morning."

"Please, Becky," Penny begged. "Please let me have my glasses back."

Becky the Bully ticked her finger up, and the glasses rose. "This is why we shouldn't allow those like you to get a free ride. You can't even use magic to defend yourself. What good are you going to be as a fairy godmother?"

Paris' face instantly flushed with anger. Her fists clenched by her side. Her eyes narrowed with frustration. She didn't know anything about Penny or Becky, but she knew enough to read the situation, which she'd seen a hundred times.

Not thinking, as she typically didn't do in those situations, Paris immediately reacted. She used her magic to lift a banana cream pie that sat on the sideboard behind Becky high into the air and made it hover over the fairy's head.

"Give her back her glasses," Paris instructed in an authoritative voice, making her presence known.

Becky whipped around and saw Paris in the entry. The glasses remained floating in the air, the pie as well, but unseen directly above the bully's head. Penny continued to cry, although she seemed surprised to have someone else there to witness her humiliation.

The woman with stringy hair narrowed her eyes at Paris. "Who are you?"

"Justice," Paris fired back immediately.

The fairy ran her disapproving eyes over Paris's black street clothing. "Well, it looks like we have new help here at the college. Good, the Brownies could use help cleaning the toilets."

Ignoring the awful attempt at criticizing, Paris shook her head. "Give her back her glasses."

"Mind your own business, loser." Becky's face pinched with hostility.

Penny sniffled, continuing to make poor attempts to jump for her glasses, her eyesight so bad that she couldn't see the pie also hovering directly above the other woman.

"The abuse of others is my business," Paris retorted, thinking that she'd give the bully one last chance. "Give her back her glasses, and I'll walk away."

Becky laughed loudly. "How about I don't give poor Penny back her glasses, and you go back to cleaning hair out of our drains and scrubbing my shower?"

Paris sighed. She'd tried to be reasonable. In the end, the jerk fairy gave her no choice. "Fine, I hope you like bananas."

Suddenly confused, Becky squinted at her. "What? I can't stand bananas. What does that have to do with anything?"

"Don't worry. You don't have to eat them." Paris stepped into the dining room. "It seems time that you get your just desserts." With that, Paris released the banana cream pie and let it turn over in the air, where it fell straight down onto Becky's head, covering her hair, shoulders, and face with whipped cream, filling, and crumbs.

CHAPTER NINETEEN

Becky shrieked. The glasses hovering in the air dropped, but before they could crash to the floor, Paris saved them with magic and put them safely on the table next to Penny.

Bananas and whipped cream dripped down Becky's face, but it didn't cover how livid she was as she continued to scream. "How dare you?"

"I dared," Paris boldly replied as she crossed her arms over her chest and thrust out one hip.

"Who do you think you are?" Becky railed while wiping the banana cream off her face. Behind her, Penny was still sniffling as she put on her glasses.

"I'm your worst nightmare," Paris retorted defiantly.

She would have followed that up with a round of insults, but running footsteps from behind cut her off. Willow rushed into the room, panic written on her face. Mae Ling followed her but didn't appear as concerned or rushed.

Willow searched the three women, focused solely on Becky, and blinked in confusion. "What's going on here?"

The fairy covered in banana cream pie shot an accusatory finger at Paris. "She did this!"

Willow rounded on Paris, disappointment suddenly covering her face. "Is that true?"

"I don't like bullies," Paris stated simply, her arms still crossed.

"Will someone please tell me what's going on here?" Willow glanced between the two.

"This one was taunting her, holding her glasses out of reach," Paris explained and pointed at Penny.

Willow sighed, instantly understanding the situation. "Becky, what have we told you about teasing Penny?"

"We were playing around," Becky lied.

The headmistress glanced at Penny, who was cleaning her glasses and wiping tears from her face. "I'm certain that your idea of playing and Penny's are very different."

"I don't know who this new maid is that you've hired," Becky began, scowling at Paris, "but it's none of her business what we fairy godmothers do."

"In training," Mae Ling corrected. "You're all fairy godmothers in training."

"Paris isn't on the staff," Willow explained. "She's a student here."

That enraged Becky more. "Since when?"

"Since now," Paris answered.

"Then why isn't she wearing the gown?" Becky challenged.

"It didn't fit," Paris stated simply.

"It's one size fits all," Willow offered.

Paris glanced discreetly at Mae Ling, trying to read her expression. It seemed to be encouraging her on this path. Returning her gaze to the headmistress, she clarified, "It didn't fit in the more symbolic way."

Willow sighed. "We'll discuss the dress code later. In the future, it's not your job to discipline bullying behavior."

"It's sort of why I'm on this earth," Paris argued.

The headmistress exhaled a steadying breath and tried to quell her impatience. "Paris, I know that you're used to doing things a certain way, but here at Happily Ever After College, we don't simply act on our impulses." She indicated the sideboard. "Chef Ashton will be very disappointed to learn he has to remake this dessert."

Paris slumped, realizing her mistake. Uncle John often said that her impulsive behavior caused more work for others. Ironically, when Paris tried to defend the little guy, she usually made trouble for someone else who was innocent in the whole injustice situation. "I'm sorry. I didn't want to do that. It's just that Becky didn't really leave me any choice. I told her to return Penny's glasses, and she refused. So I did the first thing I could think of."

"It doesn't seem that you were thinking at all," Willow replied.

"She definitely wasn't," Becky fired hotly.

"As for you," Willow rounded on the fairy, "you know that Penny is sensitive and doesn't like to play your games."

"It wasn't a game," Paris argued, wondering how long Becky had coasted by with this type of behavior.

"Look, newbie, you don't know anything about this place so stay out of it," Becky threatened.

Paris propped her hands on her hips. "I know a bully when I see one."

The headmistress stepped between the two, seeking to break the tension. "Becky, go and clean yourself up. I don't want this type of thing to happen again."

The dessert-covered fairy charged past them and threw Paris a murderous glare as she left the dining room.

Willow cleared her throat and glanced at Penny, who was still sniffling. "Would you please stop crying? The whole ordeal is over with, and as far as I can see, you appear unscathed by it all."

Penny nodded, knotted her hands together, and meekly left the room, her gaze down and shoulders slumped.

When she'd gone, Willow let out a breath and focused on Paris.

She braced herself for punishment. Maybe she'd be kicked out of the college right away. That would be so disappointing to Uncle John, but Paris stood by her decision and held her chin high, willing to accept the consequences of her action.

To Paris' surprise, the headmistresses' eyes lit up when she smiled. "Well, I think we can move past all that and commence with the tour of Happily Ever After College if you'd like."

Paris blinked at the fairy, confusion heavy in her mind. "I'm not in trouble?"

"Well, I can't say that it's the best way to start things out here," Willow answered. "However, you have a passion and moral aptitude that I find intriguing. It might be very useful for you as a fairy godmother." She cocked her head. "It also might keep you from excelling here. Honestly, you aren't at all our typical student from a behavioral sense so only time will tell."

Paris glanced at Mae Ling, who had a slight smile in her eyes and again seemed to be secretly glad about all this. Paris focused her attention directly on Willow and nodded. "If I'm not in trouble, I'm ready for that tour."

CHAPTER TWENTY

The conservatory was a lovely room and Paris was instantly in love with the space as Willow led her through it. As Wilfred had explained, it was a glassed-in room at the very back of FGE. It was warmer than the cool hallway they'd come through, which was dark with its wood-paneled walls and floors.

There were a few students curled up on couches, reading or writing. They all glanced up as the three fairies strode through the area to the yard and grounds on the other side of the conservatory. All of them gave Paris strange looks but tried to be polite about their sudden curiosity.

"The conservatory is a nice place for students to lounge in between classes," Willow explained. "Many choose to study here rather than the designated space for that on the second floor."

"I can see why." Paris looked around and enjoyed the warm sunlight that fell through the glass ceiling. "I bet it's nice to be here when there's bad weather, and you can't go outside."

Willow smiled. "There's never bad weather here at Happily Ever After College."

"Never?" Paris wondered if it was like Southern California,

which she'd heard had lots of sunny weather year-round.

"Never," Willow repeated. "It's always springtime here on the Enchanted Grounds." She opened a door and led them out onto the college's grassy lawn. "That's what we call the area around the college—the Enchanted Grounds. It's always exactly seventy degrees here regardless of the time of day."

Paris couldn't help but smile. Having grown up on Roya Lane, the hidden magical street in London, she'd had her fair share of gloomy days filled with nonstop rain. To think there was a place where it was always spring, well, it seemed like a dream come true.

Willow led them past a shimmering blue pool where women not wearing the usual blue gowns were lounging or swimming in the perfect spring weather. The whole thing felt very resort-like and not at all how Paris had pictured an academy.

"The students and faculty often get their exercise in the pool," Willow explained, indicating the waters as they passed, again getting curious looks from the swimmers. "We also encourage other forms of exercise." She waved at the woods to the right of the manor. "Hiking in Bewilder Forest is nice, although mostly it's where we go to forage for special herbs not found anywhere else for spells. You should note that the forest is off-limits at night—for your good."

The headmistress nodded in the direction of the statue garden on the opposite side of the manor. "If you require a nightly stroll, the Serenity Garden is the perfect spot for that, although it's off-limits on Tuesdays."

"Because?" Paris found it difficult to keep up because she was so intrigued by all the sights. Next to the beautiful pool was a huge patio area that looked perfect for taking in an afternoon meal or relaxing and reading a book. The entire Enchanted Grounds were so...well, just that, enchanting. They were perfectly manicured everywhere she looked.

"Because," Willow answered simply as if that was a perfectly adequate answer to her question. She pointed at a round dome building on the far side of the pool area. "We have the observatory there where you'll have astrology classes."

"Wait, what?" Paris thought that had to be a joke.

Ignoring the interruptions, Willow indicated another set of buildings. "We also have the greenhouses and stables, as well as places that you'll have classes."

Paris scratched her head, confused why she'd need classes on horses or plants to be a fairy godmother. She had so much to learn. Glancing back at Mae Ling for support, she found the woman's expression stoic as she quietly followed.

"Most of your classes will be inside FGE," Willow continued, pointing back toward the mansion. "On the first floor, you'll find the main classrooms, art studio, sewing room, music hall, ball-room, theater, demo kitchen, faculty offices, as well as the living areas, main kitchen, and of course you've already seen the dining hall."

Paris nodded, although most of what Willow said wasn't computing. Why would they need half that stuff? The idea of sewing nearly made Paris cringe. She wasn't the domestic type. She was the "find her frayed clothes a point of pride" type.

"The second floor," Willow went on, turning to face the large manor now that they were far enough away from it to take it all in, "is where the student dorms are, as you've learned by now. That's also where you'll find the showers and baths, as well as study rooms, common areas, and balconies."

The headmistress indicated the third level. "The third floor is for faculty and staff and off-limits to students."

Talk about making Paris want to trespass on the third floor. All anyone had to say was that something was off-limits and it became the forbidden fruit. She silently started making a list of places to explore in her head: Bewilder Forest at night, Serenity Garden on Tuesdays, and the third floor of FGE.

Willow spun back and looked proudly at the small body of water at the rear of the Enchanted Grounds. "You'll see that in addition to the pool, Mirror Lake is a wonderful place to swim. It's also great for boating and other water sports." She indicated the red stables nestled next to the shore. "Riding the horses along the lake is always a nice leisurely activity."

Paris grimaced. She'd never been interested in riding a horse. She preferred to stay grounded and use her two legs. Not to mention that she didn't trust horses. Paris was pretty sure the animals were aliens. She chuckled to herself, noticing the idyllic boat house opposite the stables on the far side of the tranquil lake. She understood now why it was called Mirror Lake.

"Well," Willow clapped once. "I think that about covers it." She turned to Mae Ling. "Is there anything you'd like to add?"

Mae Ling offered a polite smile. "Not at the moment. I'm sure this has been a lot for Paris to take in."

"Indeed," Willow agreed. "Well, I have a few appointments before dinner, in roughly an hour in the dining hall." She grinned at Paris. "Why don't you take this time to explore the Enchanted Grounds, make yourself comfortable, and please feel free to get to know the staff and students. I think you'll find most are very welcoming, although as I said, not all will take to the circumstances of your arrival, but they will in time, I believe."

Paris nodded, excited about the opportunity to be turned loose in the place.

"Professor," Willow began, looking at Mae Ling. "Will you please ensure that Paris gets her schedule for classes tomorrow?"

The small woman simply nodded.

"Very well," Willow answered, turning back for FGE. "I'll see you both at dinner, which I'm sure will be as lovely as usual due to Chef Ashton's efforts. And Paris…"

She looked at the headmistress, waiting for her next words.

"I hope that you work out here," Willow stated. "But that's going to require that you're open-minded. Otherwise, I think our ways will be lost on you, and there's nothing I can do to help you then."

CHAPTER TWENTY-ONE

Paris expected Mae Ling to follow the headmistress up to the building and was surprised when the professor stayed by her side as they watched Willow retreat.

"Can I ask you a question?" Paris asked Mae Ling after a moment.

"I encourage it," she replied, her hands behind her back. "It's the only way you're going to get to the truth or answers or anywhere, here or anywhere else in life."

Paris blinked, not having expected the philosophy lesson right then. "Okay." She drew out the word, trying to figure out the most diplomatic way to ask her question. "It seems that you want me to be myself for an important reason, like, do you expect me to be some sort of change agent here?"

Mae Ling gave her a brilliant smile as if she was proud of this guess.

"Okay." Paris again broke the word into multiple syllables, carefully constructing her words. "Well, it seems to me that you're also a rebel here, not wearing the uniform and telling me to be myself when Headmistress Starr seems to be asking me to conform."

"That's an accurate observation."

"Then why don't you be this change agent?" Paris dared to ask.

"I do things my way and always have," Mae Ling answered with confidence. "But when I do, no one notices. When you do, I suspect everyone will notice, and maybe they'll see how different things can be."

"Different how?" Paris wondered what was so wrong with this place as she watched fairies frolic through the Enchanted Grounds, swim in the pool, or kayak on Mirror Lake.

Mae Ling's objective gaze followed Paris as if she was trying to see through her fresh viewpoint. "Here at Happily Ever After College, we're overdue for an evolution, but that usually can't happen until something changes, and that usually doesn't happen until the winds blow something new in."

Paris tried to consider everything that Mae Ling had told her. It made sense that the modest fairy godmother went unnoticed. For some strange reason, she blended in, although she was dressed differently from everyone other than Paris.

Several times, Paris had forgotten that Mae Ling was there during the tour. She was different, but she wasn't loud about it. That had been Paris' problem her entire life. There was nothing subtle about her.

A perfect breeze, not too cool or warm, passed over the grounds, running over Paris' hands and face. She turned to face Mae Ling directly and to her shock, found that the woman had simply disappeared as though she was never there in the first place.

CHAPTER TWENTY-TWO

F inding herself alone on the Enchanted Grounds of Happily
Ever After College, Paris took off for Mirror Lake, wanting
to explore. Growing up on Roya Lane, she hadn't many opportunities to be around bodies of water. She'd spent much of her time on
that narrow lane, mouthing off to gnomes and exploring the
various magical shops when not expected to attend online school.

Uncle John hadn't only done the best he could in her parents'
absence. He'd done better than most. However, his busy detective
life and protective nature had kept her on Roya Lane, far away
from magical forests or placid lakes or trees...

She lovingly looked up at the large oak and willow trees
littering the grassy lawn of the Enchanted Grounds. The smell of
nature was so...clean. Such a stark contrast from the smog and
smoke she was used to on Roya Lane.

In the distance, gliding over the water's surface and making
small ripples were two swans, heading toward the middle of the
lake. Paris remembered learning that swans mated for life and
always thought it an endearing fact about the large, lovely birds.
She couldn't imagine finding one person that she couldn't do with-

out. She worried that her skepticism would make it difficult for her to match Cinderellas and Prince Charmings.

The whole thing felt like meddling, but that was the way of most of the magical organizations, from what she could tell. The House of Fourteen told the magical world how to live. The Dragon Elite policed the mortal world. The Rogue Riders regulated criminals. The Fairy Law Enforcement Agency kept Roya Lane under control. The Official Brownie Headquarters, well, that seemed like the one place that minded its business for the most part. Anyway, it made sense that the Fairy Godmother Agency would intervene, meddling in the love affairs of others.

Lost in thought, Paris didn't notice the racing hooves behind her. It wasn't until she heard someone frantically yelling behind her that she whipped around. To her horror, she turned to find a large wild black stallion barreling in her direction—moments from running her down, ending her time at Happily Ever After College...and on Earth.

CHAPTER TWENTY-THREE

"Watch out!" a guy yelled while running after the horse but a good distance away.

Paris' heart jumped into her throat. The beast thundering toward her had its head down as if it planned to hit her like a battering ram, sending her outside the barrier to Happily Ever After.

Trying her best to maintain focus, she assessed her options. There weren't many. Really only one.

Paris threw her hand over her head, twirled her finger, and mouthed a spell. Instantly she disappeared from where she'd been on the lawn, about to get mauled by a crazed stallion. Paris reappeared in the twisted oak tree directly above her, clinging to one of the branches as the black horse sprinted underneath her, tearing up the grassy lawn as it passed.

The black stallion bucked and neighed as though sorely enraged that it wasn't going to be able to evict Paris from the college. The angry beast continued toward the Bewilder Forest, where Paris hoped it ate a chill pill herb or root that mellowed it out.

Suddenly shaking from adrenaline, Paris realized she was clutching the tree for dear life.

The guy who had warned her about the approaching murderous horse slowed when he came to the tree. He looked up until he saw Paris perched in the branches like a stuck kitten.

"Are you okay?" The guy sounded breathless.

Paris drew in a steadying breath. "I didn't get run over, so yeah." She glanced at the many branches around her, thinking that this might make a nice place for a treehouse. Maybe if living in the manor didn't work out…

"Sorry about that," the guy said, his hands on his knees as he pulled in breaths. "Rude Awakening has been resisting training."

"Can I suggest that you name the horse something different then?" Paris offered. "A name is everything, and I doubt that a stallion given that one will ever cooperate."

The guy laughed, straightening. "Yeah, you might be right. Anyway, did you climb that tree to get away? I couldn't really tell since I was looking at Rude Awakening's behind most of the time."

"I think I would have preferred to be looking at the horse's backend rather than his murderous gaze," Paris joked. "I more or less climbed up here."

"Quick thinking. That was one way to avoid getting stampeded," the guy commended. "Do you want help getting down?"

"No, thanks." Paris tried to make her way down as gracefully as she could manage. She would have magicked her way out of the tree but wanted to conserve her reserves in case she needed to escape something else here. Also, Paris quite liked the idea of climbing out of a tree since this was a first.

"If you don't mind me asking," the guy began while watching her, his tone careful as if he was nervous she would tumble down from the tree limbs and land on him, "what are you doing here at the college?"

"I-I-I'm," Paris stuttered between breaths, trying to figure out her footing. "I'm a new student here at Happily Ever After."

The guy, who had dark brown hair that wasn't short or long, but had a mind of its own and dark blue eyes, scratched his head. He was young, but not too young. Probably about Paris' age and wearing jeans and a flannel shirt, so she guessed he wasn't an assistant butler to Wilfred. And probably wasn't Chef Ashton. "Oh, it's been a long time since I've heard of a new student at the college."

"How long?" Paris dared to take a long step down to a lower branch, testing her weight on it.

"Oh, a few years." He tipped his head to the side and watched her with a worried expression. "Apparently, fairies would rather be Instagram influencers than fairy godmothers."

Paris nearly slipped, the heel of her boot thankfully catching herself as her hand grabbed a branch above her head. She didn't have too much farther to the ground now. As she'd expected, climbing a tree was fun. "How do you know about Instagram?"

The guy chuckled, covering his nervousness. "I might live in a fairytale of sorts, but I'm still on social media." He coughed nervously. "You sure you don't want a hand?"

Deciding that she was close enough to the ground to make the jump, Paris shook her head. She swung her arms to the side and jumped off the limb, landing in a low crouched position on the grass, but on her feet and unscathed, which was all that mattered to her. She checked herself over and sighed. "Oh, good thing I didn't rip my leather jacket."

The guy scrunched up his nose and pointed at her side. "Sorry to inform you that it appears you have."

Paris' gaze shot down, but she relaxed at once. "No, that tear was there already. I ripped it on a giant's teeth recently."

The guy arched a curious eyebrow at her. "You're not our usual student."

She laughed. "I'm not anyone usual anywhere...ever."

He rubbed his lips together, a smile hiding behind his eyes, and held out a hand. "I'm Hemingway Noble."

Unable to stop herself, Paris grinned. "Talk about a name."

Hemingway chuckled and nodded. "Yeah, it's better than Rude Awakening's for sure, but sets a precedent for me usually. And you would be?"

She eyed his hand still hovering before her. Finally taking it, she said, "I'm Paris Westbridge."

Shaking her hand gently, Hemingway gave her a curious sideways expression. "Paris, huh? That's a nice name."

"What do you do here?" She suddenly felt nervous and pulled her hand from his, which was calloused but not too rough.

"I'm the jack of all trades for the college. If something needs to be done and no one wants to do it, it's my job. I'm the gardener, stable boy, groundskeeper, handyman—you name it and I do it."

She pointed over her shoulder to where Rude Awakening had thankfully disappeared into the forest. "And you tame the wild animals."

He nodded. "Sometimes successfully. That one is stubborn."

"Again, maybe a different name," she offered. "How about Overly Cooperative or Doesn't Stampede? Just suggestions."

Hemingway rubbed his chin thoughtfully. "I like this new naming structure. It explains why the bunnies keep eating all the radishes."

"What are they named?"

"Gobbles and Gulps." He laughed.

Paris nodded. "Yeah, but that also might be because they're hungry bunnies who don't know the radishes are off-limits."

Hemingway gave her a sideways, appraising look. "I like the way you reason, Ms. Westbridge. It's not like most here."

"Why?" Paris knew she was different because Willow and Mae Ling had told her that, but she wanted to drill down into how.

He shrugged. "I don't think reasoning is much in the mindset of fairy godmothers in training. If it is, it's what embroidery pattern would look best on a pillow."

102

Paris' eyes widened with horror. "Oh, please tell me that I don't have to take embroidery?"

Hemingway nodded while giving her a commiserating expression. "I think it's part of the first-year curriculum."

"I'm going to have to be sick on the day of that class." Paris wasn't at all joking. She didn't understand the curriculum at Happily Ever After College. She knew that Willow had asked her to keep an open mind. However, that was in direct contradiction to Mae Ling stating that she needed to voice her opinion if she didn't agree with something. She couldn't understand why a fairy playing matchmaker would need to know how to embroider or anything about astrology or gardening.

However, Paris thought that she needed to follow both fairy godmothers' advice in this instance to get the best results. She reasoned—since her reasoning skill was something she prided herself on—that she should always be herself while also keeping an open mind.

She was about to ask Hemingway more about the college when a bell sounded from FGE.

His face lit up with a smile. "Oh, my favorite part of the day. It's dinner time." He pointed up at the large building and offered, "Shall I show you the way to the dining hall?"

Paris pretended that she didn't know where it was from the earlier incident and nodded, allowing herself to be led back toward FGE.

CHAPTER TWENTY-FOUR

U nlike the first time that Paris was in the dining hall, now it was packed with students and professors wearing the pale blue silk gown and excitedly chatting as they took their seats. The rooms smelled heavenly of freshly baked breads and roasted meats and other savory aromas, all in covered dishes at the far end of the room on the sideboard. To Paris's relief, also sitting on the buffet table was a new banana cream pie as well as many other scrumptious desserts.

As soon as she and Hemingway entered the room, the chatter subsided, and everyone turned to look at her.

Beside her, Hemingway nodded. "Oh, man, did I track fertilizer in again?" He picked up one boot and looked it over. "I'm such a goof, always the clown attracting all the attention."

Many shook their heads and returned their attention to filling their plates or their conversations.

"I think they were staring at me," Paris offered from the corner of her mouth.

"Aren't we full of ourselves?" he teased with a wink. "Why

would they have any reason to stare at you when I'm over here tracking in horse manure?"

Paris glanced down at his clean boots and shook her head. "Right. As you said before though, I'm not the typical student here."

Hemingway led her to the end of the buffet line and handed her a warm plate. "I can't argue with that. I've yet to see anyone here in a tree."

"It was my first time," she admitted, overwhelmed as the line dispersed from the buffet, revealing all the delicious-looking meal options.

"Word of warning," Hemingway said as she loaded up on mashed potatoes, smothering them in gravy.

Paris paused and glanced at him tentatively.

"Don't fill up on dinner," he stated.

"Oh, because of all the dessert options?" She shrugged. "I'm not really a sugar type of person."

He shook his head and put a slab of roast beef on his plate. "That's probably going to change. Chef Ash provides the main courses more out of custom, but do you notice a difference between the savory and sweet options?"

Paris stepped out of line and looked at the desserts on the far side of the buffet. "There's, like, three times as many desserts as main courses."

He nodded. "Fairy godmothers are required to eat a three-to-four ratio of sweets every single day. I'm pretty certain that filling up and not having enough room for dessert is a punishable offense."

Paris put back the ladle of braised Brussel sprouts she was about to load onto her plate. "I can't believe I'm being told not to eat my vegetables."

"It's strange for sure," he agreed.

"Why are we supposed to eat mostly sugar?"

Hemingway shrugged. "You're the fairy godmother in training, not me. I mow the lawn and chase horses. I think it has to do with magical reserves and being as sweet as possible."

"Are you a magitech AI too?" Paris narrowed her eyes to try and see his wings if he'd glamoured them.

He shook his head. "No, I'm a bona fide fairy. As real as they come. I need meat and potatoes to sustain myself. But I also use my energy to clean the gutters and wash the windows and not to create true love, so what do I know?"

Paris eyed the macaroni and cheese that looked so yummy swimming in a thick sauce and wished that she could load up on that instead of banana cream pie. She'd never liked sugar because it made her stomach violently angry. It looked like she would have to take Mae Ling's advice in this instance and not do as she was told and instead be herself.

When Paris turned away from the buffet, she suddenly tensed, not knowing where to sit at the long table. Thankfully, she didn't have to stand with indecision for long.

Hemingway glanced over his shoulder, nodding toward the end of the table. "There are some open seats down here. If you don't mind sitting next to a dirty farmhand, you're welcome to occupy the space next to me."

Paris contended that she was probably dirtier than Hemingway, having been hugging a tree earlier. She was pretty sure she still had leaves in her hair.

As soon as she took her seat, Headmistress Willow Starr stood at the far end of the table and tapped the side of her glass with her spoon, making a chiming sound. "May I please have your attention? I'd like to introduce our newest student to Happily Ever After College. You all may have noticed Paris Westbridge around today."

Willow held out a hand in Paris' direction. Having just taken a large bite of a steamy roll, Paris smiled nervously, waving at the many pairs of eyes on her suddenly.

"Seems like a good time for a speech," Hemingway muttered in her ear as she strained to chew the dense starchy roll.

She narrowed her eyes at him before turning her attention to the headmistress, nodding like a squirrel with nuts in their cheeks.

"I hope you all will make Paris feel comfortable here," Willow continued. "I think that she'll make a great contribution to the college since she has a diverse background."

Paris nearly choked on the roll that refused to be chewed and swallowed. A diverse background was one way of putting life on the streets and a bare-bones education.

"I don't know the family Westbridge," a professor between Mae Ling and Willow said. She wore the blue gown with the pink ribbon around the collar. Her grayish-blue hair was frizzy and half-straight and half-curly as though she couldn't decide what fashion she preferred.

"There haven't been any fairy godmothers from a Westbridge family," Becky stated smugly. "I'm sure of it."

"Paris comes to us through untraditional means," Willow stated carefully.

"Is she a scholarship kid like Penny?" Becky rolled her eyes at the girl across from her.

Penny looked better than before, mostly because she wasn't crying and had her glasses, but her gaze immediately dropped to the table in shame.

"How a student enters the college shouldn't matter," Willow stated. "The point is that once given the opportunity, they do the best they can, and I trust that Paris will make the most of things."

Many around the table muttered, not at all sounding accepting of Paris.

"She can climb a tree, so that's pretty cool." Hemingway sliced through the tension.

"You climbed a tree?" Willow asked curiously.

"Well, more like climbed down from a tree," Paris admitted.

"What a strange thing to do," a student said down the table.

"Why would anyone want to do that?" another asked.

"Is that why you're not wearing a gown?" a girl with soft red hair asked. "Did it get ripped when climbing?"

"Ummm…" Paris looked at Mae Ling for reinforcement. "The gown may not be for me. I can't throw a roundhouse kick in a dress."

That produced mixed reactions around the table. Hemingway and the guy across from them both laughed.

Willow shook her head. "I think you'll find there isn't a need for fairy godmothers to use violence. We promote love after all."

Paris took a quick sip of her water, trying to cover her embarrassment. "Right. Of course. I have much to learn."

Whereas before Mae Ling hadn't offered her any encouraging looks, now she shot her one of disappointment. Apparently, this wasn't the reaction she was hoping Paris would have. The girl didn't know what else she expected. On her first day, at the first meal, in front of the entire college, she couldn't outwardly disrespect the rules of Happily Ever After. There was time for that.

Thankfully many returned to their meals or got up to get dessert, not having eaten most of their dinner.

"So you're the reason I had to remake the banana cream pie," the guy across from Paris said.

Now that she was looking at him, she noticed he was wearing a white chef's outfit. Behind his ear was a short pencil and his head was bald and his eyes full of kindness.

"Oh, I'm so sorry," she said in a rush. "You must be Chef Ashton. I didn't mean to cause you any trouble."

He grinned and tore into his roll. "No, no. It was no biggie. I dare say, the reason for its destruction was worth the effort to remake it." The chef glanced down the table to where Becky was talking loudly about something.

"Wait, what happened here?" Hemingway cut in, leaning forward.

"I heard that Paris dumped the first banana cream pie on

Becky's head because she'd stolen Penny's glasses, yet again," Chef Ash stated.

Hemingway's mouth popped open, and his eyes widened with delight as he regarded Paris. "You didn't…"

"I did," Paris confirmed. "In, like, my first hour at the college."

"Taught that rich snob a lesson and escaped a wild stallion all in your first hour?" He shook his head, looking impressed. "I'm going to keep my eye on you."

"I promise I won't cause trouble for you all," Paris offered. "I'm really sorry, Chef Ash."

"Like I said, not a problem in the least." He waved her off. "I haven't laughed that hard in a long time when I heard what happened."

Hemingway nodded. "I'm keeping an eye on you out of pure amazement and entertainment." He looked at the chef across the table. "When was the last time we had any excitement around here?"

The chef shrugged. "It's always the same thing, day in and day out. Studies, meals, lounging, and blissful boringness."

Hemingway grimaced. "Bliss is so boring. Yeah, what we need is a bit of adventure." He turned to look at Paris directly. "I can't tell you the last time one of my horses broke loose like that."

"I have a way of attracting drama," she admitted. "If there's trouble, it will find me."

He nodded proudly at her. "So far, it looks like you're getting rid of the trouble."

Paris pushed her plate away, accidentally having eaten all of it because it was so delicious. She had no room for any dessert. "Well, we'll have to wait and see. I'm not necessarily here because I get rid of trouble on a regular basis."

Hemingway tilted his head and gave her a look that said, "Go on then."

She shook her head and looked at Chef Ash. "That meal was… well, probably one of the best things I've ever eaten."

"Why, thank you." He smiled wide. "It's nice to hear a compliment about my creations now and again."

"I tell you that your food is good," Hemingway complained, pretending to be offended.

"You tell me that my food needs more cheese," Chef Ash replied good-naturedly.

"Well, everything needs more cheese," he argued.

Not caring that she wasn't going to touch a dessert, Paris ran her finger over her plate, soaking up more of the cheesy mashed potatoes that had filled her up. "I couldn't agree more."

The guys, as well as the other students around them who had witnessed this impolite behavior all paused, regarding Paris as if she was a Martian.

However, Hemingway and Chef Ash broke the tension, laughing loudly.

"I'm going to keep an eye on you too, Paris." Chef Ash smiled again. "I suspect you're going to shake things up."

Paris glanced down the table at Mae Ling, who wasn't pretending to be watching the whole thing. She nodded and gulped. "I think that's why I'm here. But I don't really understand any more than that."

CHAPTER TWENTY-FIVE

Paris felt like she'd run a marathon when she crawled into her pink canopy bed that night. She didn't know what running a marathon was like since she'd never done one. Paris didn't run unless she was chasing down a thieving elf or a gnome who had mouthed off one too many times.

However, she knew that what she was experiencing was a new level of exhaustion. It proved that mental and emotional strain could do a number on one's body.

"Do you snore?" Faraday asked from the sock drawer.

A laugh burst out of Paris' mouth. "How would I know? I'm always asleep."

"Excellent point," Faraday replied. "I hope you don't, but I'll let you know if you do. I'll wake you up."

"It's cute that you rode my coattails into this place, now you're freeloading off me, and you tell me not to snore," Paris said dryly.

"I don't know if you understand what the word 'cute' means," he stated. "It's defined as attractive, charming, pretty, or delightful, and I'm under the impression that you don't find my behavior any of those things."

Paris laughed again. "It's called sarcasm, Faraday. You've heard of it, right?"

"Yes, that means irony, mockery, or cynicism," he stated matter-of-factly.

She rolled her eyes. "Oh good, I brought a furry dictionary along for this adventure."

"I also am good at other things," he stated smugly.

"I'm sure that I'll learn."

"Like, I prefer a nice aged cheddar or smoked cheese to this Swiss you got on my sandwich." The squirrel poked his head out of the sock drawer while nibbling on some of the rye and Swiss sandwich that Paris had retrieved from the kitchen, explaining to Chef Ash that she required a midnight snack. He had seemed skeptical and also impressed about this since she'd polished off her plate of carbs and declined dessert, much to the disappointment of Headmistress Starr. Still, Chef Ash had obliged, saying that he wished the other students had such a healthy appetite. Apparently, they hardly ate much of his food if it wasn't desserts and only picked at those, wanting to maintain their "girly" figures.

Paris never had a problem with that. As a fairy, her magic relied on her food intake. She was always so active running after bullies and criminals that she maintained a pretty athletic build. However, she guessed that since none of the students ever climbed trees or anything similar that they didn't get the same exercise.

"Oh my," she groaned and rolled over in her bed, trying to get comfortable. "A walking dictionary who has preferences on cheese and thread count."

"The socks are quite nice," he said with surprise.

"Will you not get crumbs in my socks?"

He looked down suddenly with surprise. "Oh, you're still planning on wearing these?"

She sighed. "I was..."

"I hope you like holes in your socks."

"I don't."

"I'll find you more tomorrow," he offered. "I'm guessing you're an Under Armor sporty sock type of person."

"Why?"

"Because you need something that breathes."

"You're so weird."

"You have no idea."

"Again, I'm sure I'll learn. What will you do tomorrow?"

"I'll do what I do," he replied as if that was a sufficient answer.

"I don't know anything about you except that you're a high maintenance squirrel with a strangely large vocabulary."

"The truth is in the details," he remarked in a sage tone.

When she didn't respond to this enigmatic statement, he added, "I'll explore and start my research for understanding how this interesting and mysterious place operates."

"And you'll cackle at that orange cat named Casanova as squirrels tend to do, right?" she joked.

"I think we both know that I won't."

"Since you don't do anything that a normal squirrel does," Paris guessed.

"I do the main things such as sleep, eat and breathe."

She sighed. "Which every living creature does."

"Technically—"

"Okay, many living creatures then," Paris corrected. "You're all about the semantics, aren't you?"

"I'm nothing if not precise."

"Well, while being precise and doing your research, stay out of trouble," she warned.

"I feel that advice is better suited for you," he admitted.

Paris nodded. "I fear that I'm destined for trouble here."

"I hypothesize that you are, based on the current evidence."

Paris wanted to argue, but she knew it was useless. She fell silent, thinking of her current predicament and how confusing it all was.

"If it makes you feel better," Faraday began in a consoling tone.

"I think that cat, Casanova, senses me here. He's the only threat I'm aware of that will rat me out."

Paris laughed. "Rat you—the squirrel—out, by a cat. Nice one."

He sniffed. "I don't get the joke."

"You have to have a juvenile sense of humor like me."

"I'm sure it will wear off on me," he stated. "Don't worry, you'll find your place here, or you'll make one, or you'll move on to something else. It's important to remember that we are never at a dead end in life. Only new turns that we inevitably have to take when the straightaways disappear."

"That was strangely very helpful." She was surprised by how comforting the squirrel's words were. He was right. If this didn't work out, then Paris would...well, she'd go to jail. But she'd make the most of that and pick up a new hobby while serving her time. She'd always wanted to learn how to throw a bullseye with a dart or maybe read a book or two. The latter might take up most of her sentence since Paris wasn't a very good reader.

For some unknown reason, the seemingly easy skill had always been difficult for her making it so she immediately became uninterested in whatever she tried to read. At the age of twenty, she'd never read a single book and didn't understand what the fuss was all about. She didn't know why some people spent all their time curled up, devouring stories. However, that didn't mean she didn't envy them and want to know what it felt like. Those who read got to go on tons of adventures. The ones that Paris had were all her own and usually resulted in bruised knuckles and scuffs on her boots.

She sighed into her fluffy pillow and pulled the soft covers over her shoulder as she closed her eyes. "Good night, Faraday."

"Good night, Paris," the squirrel squeaked.

"I hope tomorrow is better than today." She recalled all the strangeness from the day: Nearly getting stampeded by a horse, dumping pie on a bully's head, and the scrutiny at the dinner table.

"If I was a betting man, which I am not—"

"Because you're not a man," she interrupted.

"Precisely," he agreed. "But if I were, I'd say the odds are low that it will be less stressful than today as you start your new classes and assimilate into a magical school full of fairies who have their own established mindset, which is much different than yours."

"You could have lied and said that it would be better," she muttered into her pillow.

"I'll never give you lip service, Paris. It simply will do you no favors."

"Fine," she groaned. "Get me new socks. How about that?"

"Straight away," he promised. "And Paris..."

"Yes?"

"Tomorrow will be what you make of it. Be alert. Be engaged. Most importantly, be true to yourself so you don't have any regrets. At the end of the day, no matter your reason for coming here, you need to feel good about what you do and what this place does to you. Remember, we don't become anything without allowing it."

Paris suddenly felt wide awake, thinking that the squirrel's advice seemed similar to Mae Ling's. Whereas before she doubted this approach, now it seemed like the only path for her. She didn't have to become the type of fairy godmother they wanted her to be. She had to learn their ways and be open-minded, but in the end, who Paris Westbridge became was up to her.

"Thanks, Faraday," she finally said and closed her eyes once more.

"You're welcome." He settled down in the drawer. "Good night."

CHAPTER TWENTY-SIX

The lynx hadn't moved from his spot in the Bewilder Forest all day, watching as Paris nearly got run over by an out-of-control horse, then made her way up to the mansion. It was time for him to stop watching her, as hard as that was for Plato to admit. He'd watched Paris from the shadows all her life, but now that role had passed to someone else.

Also, other things demanded the black and white cat's attention —things that needed to be set in motion for when Paris was hopefully ready. Not to mention that Plato was seriously behind on returning messages on social media and looking after his stock portfolio.

Before he said adieu for now, he needed to lift one of the many spells placed on the fairy a long time ago. They were all there to guard her in one way or another. Some spells had made it so Paris wasn't overly curious about who she was or her background. Others simply protected her. Those weren't supposed to last forever—and technically they couldn't. The moment that Paris learned the truth, the wards would break. That had been one reason it was crucial that she not know who she was.

The spell Plato was presently lifting had been one of the hardest to put on the young fairy. Children should love to read. They should always be allowed to fall in love with the magic of books. But everyone feared that if Paris read too much, she might run across a certain history and that would lead her on a path to the truth.

So the young fairy had been spelled not to read well and be disinterested in every book after only a short while. That spell, after all these years, was being lifted. When it was, it took a weight off Plato's soul.

Now Paris would read with ease, and that would open up so many avenues for her. Hopefully, she'd learn things rapidly, whereas before her online education had to be restricted. He hoped she'd dive into book after book, falling in love with stories. Hopefully, she'd become everything that Plato knew she could.

The time for Paris Beaufont to blossom and bloom was approaching, and it would change everything.

CHAPTER TWENTY-SEVEN

To Paris' surprise, she awoke before her alarm which was a tiny little fairy figurine that played the harp to rouse her and threw pixie dust on her head. That had been the second surprise when she was lying in bed, trying to figure out why she suddenly felt so different. Sure, she'd woken up in a new bed at a college for highbrow fairies who were all about romance. That was enough to make her feel different. There was something else...like she'd grown a few inches overnight. That seemed unlikely since Paris stopped growing at age thirteen without reaching the average adult height.

Uncle John had always said that she was better off being small. "Everyone always likes small people because they're cute and unintimidating."

"Gnomes are short, and they can be mean as hell," she retorted to this reasoning.

Being short hadn't made putting poorly behaved giants in their place harder. On the contrary, Paris could slide easily through their arms and dodge their attacks due to her size.

However, after the fairy alarm went off, she stood and didn't find her pajamas any shorter so it was unlikely that she grew overnight. Yet, she felt different somehow. Like she had changed in a major way, but she reasoned this was related to the new adventure before her.

After getting ready, Paris found that she still had loads of time left before breakfast.

"I think the other students spend more time getting ready and brushing their hair, and that's why they wake you up so early," Faraday had offered when Paris glanced at the clock. "By more time brushing their hair, I mean any at all."

Paris looked in the mirror on her dresser, ran her hands through her blonde hair, and shrugged. "Why mess with a nice bedhead?"

She slid her leather jacket on, leaving the blue gown hanging on the door where she'd found it.

"You're not going to wear the uniform?" Faraday observed.

"I'm allergic to dresses," she answered while lacing up her boots.

"It's highly unlikely to be allergic to a style of clothing," he replied. "Now, the type of fabric is possible. I, for one, can't wear polyester."

"Because you're a squirrel," she muttered matter-of-factly.

"Because it gives me hives," he countered.

She threw her hands up with mock surprise on her face. "That's the same thing that happens to me when I wear a dress!"

"Are you going to take the extra time you've created before breakfast to explore the Enchanted Grounds?" He climbed out of the drawer where he'd slept and onto the dresser, looking out the open window.

She shook her head. "I figure there's plenty of time for that. No, instead I'm going to try and fix my mistakes."

"Oh, you're going to apologize to Becky for dropping the banana cream pie on her head?" he guessed.

She shot him a look of surprise. "I didn't tell you about that. How do you know?"

He shrugged. "I'm remarkable at observation."

Giving him a curious expression, she said, "No. That wasn't a mistake. I think I let Becky the Bully off pretty easy. Next time she gets two pies to the face."

"You're going to apologize to Headmistress Starr for not eating your dessert last night?"

Again, Paris arched an eyebrow at the squirrel. "How do you know that I filled up on dinner and was given a punishing look for not having dessert?"

"People talk," he chirped and scurried for the open window.

She shook her head at the squirrel. "No. I'm not giving myself an upset stomach because a fairy godmother tells me that desserts will make me sweeter. Maybe being sweet isn't my thing."

He agreed with a nod. "No, I'd say there are a lot of characteristics that label you, but sweetness isn't one of them. However, that doesn't mean you don't have a lot of heart, and I think that's probably better."

Paris pulled the door open, again struck by the strange squirrel. It was so similar to what Uncle John always said about Paris: "You may not be overly sweet but you sure as hell have a lot of heart, Pare. I wouldn't have you any other way."

Shaking her head at Faraday, Paris waved at him. "See you later and stay out of sight."

"Oh, I will." He slid out the window. "Have a good day, Paris. I'm sure it's going to feel like your whole world has opened up all of a sudden."

CHAPTER TWENTY-EIGHT

S till feeling oddly struck by the talking squirrel's words, Paris made her way down to the first floor of FGE. She heard singing from the kitchen before she rounded the corner into the room. At the threshold, she saw Chef Ash buzzing about, stirring several pots and Wilfred on the opposite side of the kitchen cleaning and singing a song she didn't recognize. She guessed it was opera, not that she'd ever seen or heard one.

The kitchen, which was filled with so many wonderful competing aromas, was unsurprisingly huge with industrial-sized stoves and ovens. Large mixers lined countertops at the back, and giant bags of flour, sugar, and other ingredients were below. There was a walk-in freezer on one side along with a bank of refrigerators. Hanging overhead were pots and pans of every size.

Paris watched for a moment, amused by how the chef and butler worked, their backs to her. They seemed happy as they cooked and cleaned. Magic was also clearly at play, helping to make the meal for breakfast. Bowls were suspended in the air, pouring batter into muffin tins and a floating spatula turned the bacon and sausages in a frying pan over the stove.

SARAH NOFFKE & MICHAEL ANDERLE

Knocking loud enough to be heard over all the noise, Paris stole the attention of the two.

Chef Ash turned, appearing confused, the short pencil behind his ear again. Wilfred spun, holding a sponge and also seeming perplexed by the interruption.

"Are you lost?" the butler asked in his refined voice.

Paris had followed Chef Ash to the kitchen after dinner the night before, so she wasn't lost and had intended to be there right then.

"No, I had some extra time before breakfast and thought I'd stop by to see if Chef Ash needed some help," she replied.

This deepened the confusion on the two men's faces.

"Paris, you understand that students aren't expected to help with chores, right?" Chef Ash asked.

She nodded. "Yes, but I made more work for you both yesterday since Wilfred had to clean up the banana cream pie and you had to remake it. I figured that since I caused you extra work yesterday that the least I could do was offer to help out with a chore or two."

Chef Ash glanced at Wilfred with an expression that seemed to say, "Oh, this poor dear. Bless her heart."

"It was your first day," he said consolingly, looking back at Paris. "As I said last night, the reason for having to remake the banana cream pie was worth it. Becky Montgomery gets away with too much in my opinion."

Wilfred nodded while drying his hands on a damp rag. "Yes, Ms. Montgomery isn't punished for her bad behavior." He shook his head. "I'm afraid that discipline is simply not the strong suit of the headmistress."

Chef Ash twirled his finger, and the pot he was stirring began stirring itself. He turned to Paris and leaned his elbows on the workstation between them. "So you see there? You did us all a favor."

Paris slumped. "I don't think Headmistress Starr wants me

taking on the role of disciplinarian. She'd probably be right that it's me overstepping my boundaries. I simply can't help it. If I see something unjust, I have to intervene. Maybe it's because my uncle is a detective."

Wilfred nodded. "It would make sense that the trait ran in your family."

Chef Ash pulled the pencil from behind his ear and jotted some notes in a notebook but kept flicking his eyes to Paris, giving her part of his attention. "I'm not sure what's wrong with what you've said. I think more should want to step in when injustices happen."

Paris watched as he drew a box with levels, curious what he was doing.

"Although your offer to help is generous," Wilfred began. "It's unnecessary. There may only be three of us on the staff of Happily Ever After College, but we manage quite well, I dare say."

"That we do." Chef Ash laughed and snapped his fingers three times in the air over his head. A moment later, a jar of spices levitated and tilted over the boiling pot three times, sprinkling its contents into the pan.

"I had the opportunity to see your class schedule this morning while serving Headmistress Starr her tea," Wilfred stated. "Unfortunately, it's quite rigorous, and therefore, I'd advise you to take this bit of respite while you can."

Paris suddenly felt overwhelmed. "Oh, that sounds daunting."

Wilfred nodded. "I fear that it will be, at least at first."

She glanced back at Chef Ash, who was drawing another diagram of sorts. "What are you doing?"

He looked up. "Oh, I'm working out the recipes for today's breakfast."

Paris' face must have registered her confusion. She totally was since she clearly saw the chef drawing a picture rather than writing a list.

"Chef Ashton has a fascination with carpentry," Wilfred

explained, reading her expression. "He approaches all of his culinary endeavors from the mindset of a carpenter."

The chef nodded enthusiastically. "I like to think of it as building flavors."

"Oh, that's fascinating." Paris smiled wide at the idea.

He grinned back. "Then with baking, well, there is a fair bit of construction with that. So often I draw out the designs, and that helps when I'm formatting the plans and spells I'll use."

"What a neat concept." Paris watched as the two returned to work. She realized then that she was serving as a distraction during their busy time before breakfast. Feeling remorse again for causing them trouble, she retreated to the door. "Well, I'll go and enjoy the time off, as you said."

"See you around," Chef Ash cheered.

In the hallway, Paris found herself smiling. She liked those two. They were easy to talk to, even if Wilfred was a little uptight…and a magitech AI. Still, she felt at ease with them and thought she'd find herself in the kitchen a lot more than in the study rooms on the second floor with all the students.

CHAPTER TWENTY-NINE

With time to spare, Paris went to the study area on the second floor of FGE. It was deserted since apparently the other students were combing their grayish-blue hair or putting on makeup or whatever girly girls did. Paris didn't know. It wasn't that she had anything against makeup or one doing their hair. It merely wasn't for her. She had her style, which pretty much consisted of looking like she rolled out of a biker gang, sans having the motorcycle or tattoos or a boyfriend named Duke...or a boyfriend.

The study area was surprisingly peaceful and inviting, with many Chesterfield couches lining the space and Tiffany lamps on neighboring tables. Under the long rows of windows that looked out on the Enchanted Grounds were low cases filled with books.

Pulling out a random book, Paris flipped it open, unsure why she had picked it or what it was. The volume was a book of spells for studying.

"Seems like a helpful book for this space," Paris muttered to herself and sat on the sofa. She often spoke to herself because, well, there wasn't anyone around to talk to most of the time. It was fine with her. She was a great conversationalist and always laughed at her jokes.

Expecting that she'd tire of the book within a matter of seconds, Paris was surprised to find herself suddenly engrossed. The material was fascinating, offering tips and tricks and spells for ways to maximize studying. There was specific music that could be played to dramatically increase information retention, exercises one could perform to master a particular skill quickly, and a spell that allowed a reader to absorb material through osmosis. Of course, all of these were either difficult to obtain or very costly on magical reserves, but their benefits seemed worth it.

Paris was surprised to have read almost the entire book by the time a large and ornate grandfather clock chimed on the far wall, pulling her attention back to the present moment. In less than an hour, she'd almost read her first book—ever. Whereas nothing had ever kept her attention for long, for whatever reason, this one had been fascinating, making her quickly devour it. Strangely, it wasn't a thrilling fiction tale or something else riveting. No, it was a book on studying techniques and hopefully had filled her with knowledge she could use.

Clapping the book shut, Paris peeled herself off the cozy sofa. She didn't know what had changed that she suddenly didn't simply like reading but was very good at it. However, she looked forward to exploring many more books, especially now that her new tricks and spells would make her more efficient. For now, it was breakfast time.

CHAPTER THIRTY

P aris realized that she could avoid getting all the strange looks and unwanted attention if she caved and put on the blue gown. She didn't want to. She liked her clothes, and she'd given up her life, her home, and decided to attend a school that didn't interest her. At the very least, she was going to dress the way she wanted. However, she wasn't going to allow herself to complain when all the other students and faculty members stared at her when she entered the dining hall. She'd brought it all on herself by being stubborn.

Still full from last night's dinner, Paris wasn't overly excited about breakfast until she looked at the spread. Chef Ash had outdone himself once again. There were trays piled high with creamy scrambled eggs, mounds of bacon and sausage, stacks of pancakes and waffles, huge bowls of fruit, heaping piles of crispy hash browns, and so many other delicious foods that she didn't know where to start.

"Try the maple bacon," an unfamiliar voice said at Paris' shoulder.

She looked up to find a student about her age standing beside her. The woman had straight bluish-gray hair, freckles, and bright green eyes.

"I don't know how Chef Ash does it, but it's the best I've ever had," the woman continued. "I try and fail not to fill up on it every morning, but I think it counts as a dessert because it has all the maple syrup on it."

"Thanks for the recommendation," Paris said. "I didn't know where to start, so overwhelmed by options."

She nodded understandingly. "I've been at Happily Ever After College for a year, and the spread never gets old. I don't think it will although some of the other girls seem less impressed." Angling her head, the woman who Paris guessed had red hair when not wearing the blue gown due to her complexion, freckles, and eyes indicated the table where Becky Montgomery and a bunch of refined-looking students sat talking excitedly.

"How could this ever get old?" Paris piled several thick strips of bacon onto her warm plate.

"I know, right?" the woman agreed. "I swear, when I go home, I'll probably just stand in front of my refrigerator, completely lost for how to feed myself."

The idea that at some point she'd go home from the college suddenly struck Paris. This was only for her education. Then what? She'd work cases, she guessed, but from Roya Lane. She didn't know how everything worked yet, although Headmistress Starr had said that Saint Valentine's organization, Matters of the Heart, oversaw the agency that assigned cases. She had a lot to learn.

"My name is Christine." The woman moved behind Paris in line, piling tons of bacon onto her plate. "Many here call me Chris, which I don't like at all. Some call me Christina because they forget. It's cute in the way that it makes me want to butcher their name."

Paris laughed, instantly liking Christine. "My name is Paris. People call me...well, usually no one calls me."

"Oh, what a nice name." Christine slid a piece of perfectly browned waffle onto her plate. "Are you French?"

Paris shrugged. "I'm not sure. I don't think so. My last name is Westbridge."

"Well, I wish I had a name like that, which is much cooler and not confused with similar ones." Christine pointed at a set of seats. "Want to sit with me over there?"

Grateful for the invite and unnerved by it, Paris nodded, having filled her plate with bacon, potatoes, a slice of quiche and a buttery biscuit, and zero sugary pastries. She knew she was supposed to eat sweets, but the idea of putting a bunch of sugar in her stomach made it rumble with unease. Plus, as Christine said, the bacon was loaded with maple syrup.

Once Paris took a seat, and before she'd picked up her fork, an envelope with an embossed wax seal materialized beside her plate. She looked up at Christine, hoping she'd fill her in on what that was.

"Oh, your schedule has arrived," Christine said excitedly.

Paris grabbed the ice water beside her plate, suddenly nervous, and drank. She remembered what Wilfred had said about her having a rigorous schedule and tensed, unsure what she'd find inside the envelope.

Maybe sensing her nervousness or trying to give her privacy, Christine dug into her food.

Breaking the seal on the envelope, Paris pulled out a thick card with flowery writing. It read:

Class Schedule – Day One

First: Cotillion

Second: Ballroom Dancing

Third: Astrology

Fourth: Gardening

Fifth: Cooking and Baking

Sixth: Exam

Paris read the card three times through and flipped it over, thinking there had to be more. Or maybe a note that said, "Just kidding. Here's your real schedule."

Glancing up at Christine, who was doing a poor job of pretending not to be paying attention, Paris held up the card. "I think there's been a mistake. None of these classes seem relevant."

Christine scanned the card. "Those are all first-year classes."

"I thought we were supposed to help people find love," Paris argued. "Not dawdle in strange hobbies meant for seventy-year-old women. Like, ballroom dancing? How does it make sense that I learn that?"

Christine smiled understandingly. "In year one, you're not to learn the art of matchmaking yet. Not until you know what a good match should be like. Our Cinderellas have to learn how to be a great catch before we can find their Prince Charming."

Paris pushed her plate away, suddenly not interested in eating. "Does that mean we have to become a seemingly great catch first?"

"Exactly." Christine took a bite of bacon and closed her eyes briefly as if having a heavenly moment. "We have to master these things so we can teach them. It's a little weird, but I guess it makes sense."

"Are you telling me that I have to teach Helen the Housekeeper how to garden before I can land her a husband to keep house for?" Paris wondered where the hidden cameras were and when the host of this prank show was going to jump out and yell, "Haha, we got you!"

Christine giggled. "Yeah, I was surprised too. It's not only matching true loves together. A Cinderella has to be of what they call 'top stock' before she's ready to meet her Prince Charming."

Paris laughed abruptly, gaining the attention of many at the tables for a moment. When they looked away, she shook her head. "I'm sorry, I'm trying to keep an open mind, but this all seems ridiculous. And the idea of me learning ballroom dancing and baking is atrocious. I don't even like to sway to my favorite songs."

Christine nodded and leaned closer. "I'm bad at it too, but you only have to know the basics so you can instruct your Cinderellas."

"Because why would Prince Charming want to marry Wifey Whitney unless she could tango?" Paris joked.

Christine covered her laughter. "I get that these methods seem weird, but it's how things are done here. We mold the perfect Cinderella so she can land the perfect Prince Charming. Then they fall in love, and the world is a better place."

"I like the last part of that whole equation, but nothing else," Paris muttered and drank more water.

"Well, maybe after you attend your first day of classes, things will make more sense to you," Christine offered thoughtfully.

Paris nodded although she didn't think that was possible. None of this seemed like it could ever make sense to her. She admittedly didn't know much about love and romance. Were only those refined in arts and culture destined for love? She thought it was everyone's birthright, but again, she apparently had a lot to learn.

When she glanced up from her plate of uneaten food, Paris found Mae Ling watching her from the far side of the table. The fairy godmother gave her a challenging look.

Returning her attention to her pile of food, Paris considered that maybe she had tons to learn. Or perhaps she simply had a lot to rebel against.

CHAPTER THIRTY-ONE

Cotillion class was in a classroom that looked like a dining room with a table set for what looked like tea service. The room also had furnishings that Paris would have expected to find in a regular classroom, not that she'd ever been in a real one. There were rows of desks and a dry erase board at the front.

Hanging back, Paris took the remaining desk after the other students had chosen theirs. She wasn't seated for more than a minute when a figure appeared suddenly beside her, seemingly out of nowhere. It was the professor who had questioned her the night before at dinner. The one with the frizzy hair and a disapproving look on her pinched face.

"I see that you're still not wearing the uniform," the woman said smugly, her chin held high.

"It doesn't work for me." Paris responded with conviction, trying not to be intimidated by being stared down.

Many of the students exchanged hushed words in front of Paris and glanced over their shoulders at her.

"I think you'll find that your job here at Happily Ever After College is to do what we've proven works," the professor stated.

"Wearing the fairy godmother gown makes us appear more trustworthy and presentable to our charges. If you were to show up to advise a Cinderella looking as you do, do you think they'd take you seriously?"

"They would probably think she was lying," Becky said with a rude laugh.

"Or not want help from a fairy godmother who can't dress properly," another woman said with a supercilious grin.

The professor nodded in agreement. "That's my thought as well. We are to instill trust in our charges."

"Or maybe they'd think that I'm the real deal and there to help them rather than keep up some fake appearance," Paris said before she could stop herself, earning gasps from the students in front of her for being so bold.

She slumped but immediately felt bad for it. What she said was how she felt, so why should she feel disgraceful for it?

The woman standing over her narrowed her brown eyes. "I'm Professor Shannon Butcher, and this class is Cotillion, where I'll teach you about proper etiquette and how to present yourself appropriately so if appearances are a problem for you, maybe you're at the wrong college."

"I heard that Tooth Fairy College was accepting rejects," Becky called from the front of the class.

Paris tried to hide the shiver of disgust that ran down her back. She'd rather go to jail than Tooth Fairy College. Talk about gross, having to retrieve teeth from children's pillows.

Professor Butcher pulled a red satin-covered hardback book from her robe and placed it on the desk in front of Paris. "Our textbook. I expect for you to read the first couple of chapters by tomorrow to catch up with the class."

Paris slumped again. Just when she was starting to enjoy reading, now she would have to bore herself with table manners and proper social behavior.

"There will be a test at the end of the week," Professor Butcher continued. "Although you're new to the college, I don't think that grants you any leniency."

"No, why should being brand-new to the college and not knowing how any of this works give me any breaks?" Paris retorted sarcastically, earning many more gasps from the classroom. She did it again, that thing where she meant to say stuff in her head, but instead opened her mouth and let it fall from her lips.

Professor Butcher apparently wasn't a fan of sarcasm as she stared down at Paris with contempt. The first class wasn't going well...

"If you don't pass my class," the fairy godmother began, "you're not qualified to progress to other classes that teach skills crucial for our Cinderellas to know to behave correctly and find love, which means you'll fail Happily Ever After College. If that happens, what will happen to you, Paris?"

The flare of anger on Shannon Butcher's face was palpable.

Paris straightened in her seat. "I guess I'll take up my second career option of working at a bowling alley. It was this or that, and the coin toss sent me here."

The professor's eyes turned to tiny slits. "Funny, because I heard that if this didn't work out that you'd find yourself in jail."

Internally Paris groaned, but she worked to keep her facial expression neutral. So the truth had leaked out. Maybe Willow had shared it with the faculty. Paris didn't think she had said this was to become public knowledge. That didn't seem like the sensitive headmistress who had said that Paris was to have a fresh start here, which meant that Professor Angry Pants was using this knowledge as ammunition.

The students were now talking above a whisper, all their voices full of shock and conspiracy.

Paris knew that she couldn't contend with this indictment so she needed to take a different approach with this professor, who obviously didn't like her from the beginning. She probably was one of those that Willow had said would be hard to win over, Paris guessed.

It made sense that professors and students who were overly prideful about Happily Ever After College would find the fact that Paris was there very offensive. They were about to get a rude awakening because she felt the same way about many of the practices at the college and Mae Ling had told her when she thought something or disagreed that she should voice the concern.

"As I'm new to this, please help me to understand how this works," Paris began, leaning forward, pretending to appear confused. "In this class, you teach us etiquette and manners, correct?"

"That's right," Professor Butcher answered in a high-pitched tone.

"You do that so we can relay those behaviors to our charges, right?"

"You might be teachable after all," the fairy godmother responded.

Paris smiled. "So then are you telling me that only women who can behave 'right' should find love?"

The furious expression that had receded flared again on the professor's face. "Only those who can behave 'right' can keep love. What self-respecting man would want a woman who doesn't know how to serve an afternoon tea or do an opera fold on a napkin?"

Paris laughed loudly, making many of the students in front of her widen their eyes in shock. "What self-respecting woman would waste her time learning such drivel when there are so many other more awesome things to know?"

Professor Butcher pressed her hands together and pushed them against her mouth, appearing as if she was trying to decide what to do with Paris at this point. "I realize that your uncle pulled a few strings to get you into Happily Ever After College."

An eruption of whispers from the students interrupted the fairy godmother, but she didn't seem put off by it. Paris thought she was happy to have leaked this information. Now the secrets were all out and would probably spread across the college quickly.

"But now that you're here," Professor Butcher continued, "you're going to have to earn your place at Happily Ever After College. There will be no coasting by in my class. I don't care who you're related to or that if you flunk out, you're going to jail."

This woman was trying to get a rise out of Paris, and she knew it, but she wasn't giving her the satisfaction. Glancing at the red book lying in front of her, Paris had an idea. She'd beat Shannon Butcher at her game.

"You're right," Paris began with a sideways smile.

"Of course I am," the fairy replied snobbishly. "Everyone must earn the grades, and something tells me that you simply don't have what it takes."

"You might be right," Paris stated flatly. "So why don't we make this fast and easy for both of us? You don't want me here, obviously, and I don't want to be here. Let's simply be honest."

"I'm listening," Professor Butcher said.

Judging by the sudden silence in the classroom, all the students were listening as well.

"Tell you what," Paris began and placed her hand on the book, recalling one of the spells she'd read about earlier. "Give me a pop test. If I flunk it, I'll go to whatever other beginner class is before this. Table manners for toddlers or trolls or whatever."

There were some giggles from the class. Some hisses of disapproval. Some gasps of shock.

Paris swallowed and continued before Professor Frizzy Hair could interrupt her. "If I pass this quiz, I've tested out of your course and can move on to embroidery or whatever other useless things you expect me to learn next."

Professor Butcher didn't respond right away, her beady brown eyes studying Paris for a long moment. "You don't know the material. There's no way that someone like you will pass a pop quiz on your first day without reading the material."

Paris pressed her hand firmly onto the book in front of her, hoping that the untested spell worked. Everything was riding on it.

"I've picked up a few things in my time," Paris replied.

"On the streets?" Becky questioned with a laugh.

"Yep," Paris chimed. "Ever done shots with giants? They're sticklers for etiquette. If you don't shoot your whiskey the right way and slam your glass with the right intensity, they'll put your head through the bar wall."

Professor Butcher grimaced with disapproval. "I don't think we're referring to the same type of etiquette."

"I think we are," Paris argued. "All cultures have their rules and customs. Just because I wear a leather jacket doesn't mean I can't dine with the king of the fae while also drinking with the gnomes. If you don't believe me, test me. If you're right, I'm out of here and not your problem anymore."

"Fine, one condition," Professor Butcher stated.

Paris raised an eyebrow. "Let's hear it."

"If you don't pass the quiz with anything less than a perfect score, you fail my class, a requirement for passing Happily Ever After College." She leaned forward, bearing down on Paris. "And that means you've flunked out of here."

Not blinking, Paris considered her options. She didn't have to do it. If she simply apologized, she could go back to learning the material and avoid this fast-track option. It was a huge gamble. However, if she did that, she'd have to sit through hours of cotillion classes with this snotty instructor, and that would probably kill her spirits. Then what would she have left?

Shaking off her indecisions, Paris nodded. "You've got yourself a deal. If I fail, I'm out of Happily Ever After College. If I pass, I'm done with this class."

Professor Butcher gave her a wicked grin. "I hope you haven't unpacked yet."

CHAPTER THIRTY-TWO

"I'll make this straightforward and fast," Professor Butcher began smugly, pressing her hand to her chest. "This will be an oral exam. Three questions. All pertain to table etiquette. However, I'll warn you that it will cover material that we haven't gotten to yet in this class, but if you are to test out of this course, you'll need to prove that you have superior knowledge."

Unflustered, Paris pressed her hand firmer onto the book, preparing the spell in her mind. "I'm ready then."

"First," the fairy godmother said, sounding victorious as if Paris had already failed. "When setting a formal dinner table, what is the proper placement of all the plates in front of a guest?"

This, Paris knew right away, was supposed to sound like a trick question. It sounded too easy, as though she was supposed to say sarcastically, "right in front of the guests." Not falling for the trick, she momentarily closed her eyes, and using the spell that used osmosis to read an entire book, she absorbed the entire contents in front of her. It was a lot all at once, both because it instantly made Paris feel overwhelmed with information and exhausted from performing the spell.

However, not only did she know the answer to the question, she also learned a lot of other very useless information, like how to greet guests at a ball and arrange a bouquet.

"The answer is that the dinner plate should be placed in front of a guest," Paris replied and paused, waiting for it.

When the obnoxious professor's eyes lit up with triumph, Paris continued. "Furthermore, the dinner plate should be placed a thumb knuckles' length from the edge of the table."

The smile that was about to unfurl on Shannon Butcher's face disappeared at once, replaced by annoyed surprise.

"The salad plate should be placed in the middle of the dinnerware since that course is eaten first," Paris concluded, daring to smile at the professor. She didn't smile back.

After a long calculating pause, the other woman narrowed her eyes at Paris. "I started you with an easy first question."

"How kind of you," Paris responded blandly, earning a few snickers from the class, although when Professor Butcher whipped her head up, everyone fell quiet.

"Second question," the fairy godmother said in a scolding voice. "Explain the proper way to set glassware for a formal dinner, and you must include all necessary glasses and their exact placement."

Paris sighed as if she was bored. She simply pulled on the information that she'd learned in the one hundred-page book inside of a few seconds. "First, you must place the water glass above the dinner knife, which is to the right side of the plate with the blade facing inward."

"I didn't ask for information on the flatware," the professor seethed.

Paris shrugged. "Oh, darn. I was hoping to score extra credit. Anyway, after the water glass, then the wine glass is placed up and to the left of it. Finally, a coffee or teacup should be put on a saucer to the right of the spoon, which is on the far right of the plate."

When Paris finished speaking, everything fell deathly silent in the classroom. She didn't say a word, simply waited for the fuming professor to reply.

"Lucky guess," the fairy godmother said. "The third and final question won't be as easy as the first two. I'm sure that you've seen a table set at some point."

"At dinner last night," Becky offered.

Professor Meanie Head nodded. "Yes, I realize that now. More important than setting a formal dinner table is table etiquette, which I didn't notice you'd mastered at meals."

Paris groaned. "Oh, did you catch me with my elbows on the table? Silly me." She'd now learned in her quick study of the textbook that elbows on a table were a big no-no. She was going to conclude that the people who came up with these rules didn't have enough to do and were always looking for some reason to turn their button noses into the air.

"In detail, explain how bread should be buttered and eaten at a meal," the professor demanded.

After reading the entire book in front of her, Paris knew that the night before and at breakfast, she'd buttered and eaten her bread wrongly, according to etiquette. How very atrocious, she joked to herself.

Drawing in a breath, she feigned indecision, giving the woman before her a moment where she thought that she'd stumped her. The bitter professor probably believed that Paris would say, butter the roll with a knife and tear into it, as she had done at the dining table. However, according to the book, that wasn't the correct method. There was a much stuffier one.

"One should never butter the entirety of their bread at once." Paris ensured she didn't repeat the words exactly as she had read them but rather put them in her own words. "Instead, one should tear the bread into bite-sized pieces as it is going to be eaten, butter it individually, and put it into the mouth with one's finger and thumb. Additionally, one should never use their knife for buttering as mixing food on the plate is not considered good taste."

Although she knew the answer was correct, Paris still tensed, waiting to be graded. No one said a word, the entire class all seeming to hold their breath.

"I'm not sure how you knew all the answers to that quiz," Professor Butcher said bitterly. "Your answers were suspiciously accurate as if you used a spell. No offense intended, but for someone with your background, I find it unlikely that you'd have naturally learned the information."

"Would you believe that I had an extra hour this morning to study?" Paris posed, technically not lying.

"I guess that's the only reasonable explanation," the flustered woman said, her face flushing pink and a calculating look on her face. She wasn't buying it, but Paris didn't care. Professor Butcher couldn't prove anything.

"No offense intended," Paris said and stretched to a standing position. "I think it's better that we made this little arrangement because if I had to stick around in this class, it would probably have crushed my normally sunshiny disposition."

"About the arrangement," Professor Butcher said in a high-pitched voice, sounding suddenly flustered. "I'm not sure the head-mistress would allow—"

Paris held up her hand. "A deal is a deal. The class all heard our agreement. Don't worry. I'll go and work out everything with the headmistress right now." She looked at her wrist, although she wasn't wearing a watch. "I mean, I do have an extra hour or so before my next class since I'm done with this one…for good."

Before the angry professor could object, Paris breezed out of the classroom, all eyes on her back. The quiz she'd passed wasn't the most complex test that Paris ever had, but without her crash course speed-spell reading the book, she would have failed without a doubt. However, she didn't think she could get through all her classes the same way.

CHAPTER THIRTY-THREE

"Wilfred," Paris said once she was in the hallway outside the classroom. "Can you help me—"

Before she finished the request, the magitech AI fairy butler materialized beside her. Paris shook her head, still not used to such an invention. It was strange to think that Wilfred was solid and yet also like a hologram.

"Yes, Ms. Westbridge?" He bowed. "At your disposal."

"Am I not interrupting you when I call on you like that?" she asked, so many curious questions occurring to her all of a sudden.

"Is that why you called me?" he questioned, his white-gloved hands behind his back.

"No, but now that you're here, I have to know."

He nodded. "I can understand your confusion about how I operate. There are multiple renditions of me that can be used for assisting those throughout FGE."

"Oh," she said with surprise. "Like an army of posh English butlers?"

Wilfred shook his head. "Not really. I consider myself an assistant to the staff and students of Happily Ever After College."

"We're going to have to work on your sense of humor." Paris laughed. "I didn't think of you like an armed soldier who was guarding the college."

"I'm not programmed to have a sense of humor," he stated matter-of-factly.

Paris scratched her head. "But you have opinions, it seems."

"Why would it seem that way?" he questioned.

"Well, because before in the kitchen you said, and I quote, 'I'm afraid that discipline isn't the strong suit of the college.'" Paris slipped into the butler's English accent for the last part of the sentence. "That statement isn't fact-based. It's an opinion, although I'm sure it's supported by evidence."

He nodded. "It's true that due to my longevity with the college and my experiences, I've evolved to have opinions. It's a result of being both magical and tech as well as having the fairy component. That magical race is considered more sensitive than the others, and I was modeled to emulate them."

Paris shook her head. "I think that trait skipped me then. I don't think I've been called sensitive once in my entire life."

Wilfred gave her a thoughtful expression. "It's my observation that you're not a normal fairy. Maybe this is due to your upbringing or because you don't eat enough sugar or that this is simply an anomaly unique to you."

"You know, describing a trait of mine as an anomaly isn't as complimentary as you might think." Paris winked at him with a faint grin on her lips.

The butler didn't return it. Instead, he rocked forward and back again, his arms still pressed behind his back. "To further explain your questions regarding how I work. Many versions of me can pop up to assist staff and students. However, I'm not able to be in the same room with one of my renditions. It scrambled my programming and was therefore disallowed."

"So we can't have a cheerleading pyramid of Wilfred's, then?" She laughed.

"That was another joke, was it not?" he asked, quite seriously.

Paris deflated. "Apparently not a good one. We'll work on this for you. I suspect if time allows you to form opinions, we can get you laughing."

"With such evolutions, that opens the flood gates to many other possibilities."

"What do you mean?" Paris asked.

"Well, it goes to reason," Wilfred began. "That if I evolve to laugh, that means I'll also have the capabilities for other emotions. Ones that could be destructive to my productivity."

"Oh." She drew out the word. "You mean that if you learn how to laugh, you'll also be able to cry?"

He thrust out his chest. "It was Kahlil Gibran, the great poet who described not experiencing emotions as a seasonless world. To sum up, he said, one could not laugh all their laughter unless they wept all their tears."

Paris had never cared much for poetry. Well, not until that morning had she read a book, and now it had been two books—one that she read in a few seconds using magic. Her life had drastically changed. But this Kahlil Gibran sounded like an interesting writer and his poetry may be worth checking out.

"Well, we do live in a seasonless world here, don't we?" Paris threw her arm out and gestured at some windows down the hallway where perfect sunlight streamed through from the Enchanted Grounds. "But it does seem that working at fairy godmother college, which is all about promoting love, that you as a staff member would have some emotions." She shrugged. "What do I know?"

He considered this. "More than you might think. That's an interesting observation and holds some merit, although I will admit that promoting love is mostly done here using an equation."

Paris blinked at the butler in confusion. "Again, I have a lot to learn because I didn't think that love and math had anything in common. One is all organic and frilly things, and the other linear with clear rules and laws. Am I right?"

"It is more about how fairy godmothers are taught to create a match," he explained. "It's believed that a Cinderella who displays certain traits is in the best possible position to attract a Prince Charming and maintain a healthy relationship due to their mutual refinement."

Paris groaned, showing her annoyance. "Yes, I learned about this ridiculous notion when I tested out of Cotillion. I never thought that love was about etiquette. I thought it was for everyone and not reserved for those who tucked in their blouses and drank their tea with their pinkies in the air. However..." She swept her hand at her attire and shrugged. "What do I know? I'm the picture of being a slob, and I've never once been in love, not even remotely close. So maybe if I starched my pleated skirt, I'd feel my heart flutter...although I'm not sure I have one at all."

Wilfred arched one of his white eyebrows at her. "It's highly unlikely that you don't have a heart."

"Wil...that was a joke."

"Right, madam." He bowed. "Of course it was. You've given me some interesting things to consider, although I don't have any answers to your questions."

"You calling them interesting again proves my point about you having opinions," she sang. "Seems like only a matter of time before you're laughing at my jokes."

"We shall see, Ms. Westbridge. Now, you called me because you needed assistance. Is that right?"

Paris nodded. "I'm looking for Headmistress Starr's office. Will you please point me in the right direction?"

"I'll do one better and lead you there." He started forward down the long corridor.

Paris hurried after the butler, finding that she had more questions now than when she tested out of Cotillion class. Hopefully, Willow could shine some light on things.

If Mae Ling wanted Paris to voice her opinions, she would hopefully be happy with her performance this far.

CHAPTER THIRTY-FOUR

When Wilfred paused in front of a door labeled Headmistress Willow Starr, Paris was about to thank him and knock.

Before she could, the butler rapped on the door, and when Willow said, "Come in," he pushed the door open in a dignified manner. Then he stepped forward and stated, "Ms. Paris West-bridge to see you, Headmistress."

Paris had never been announced before, and it all felt very formal. Then again, what else should she have expected? So far, everything at Happily Ever After College was quite stuffy.

"Oh," Willow said with surprise. "Yes, please send her in. Thank you."

He nodded and held out a presenting arm to Paris.

She nodded in appreciation and stepped past him into an office that very much resembled the sitting room at the front of the manor. It exuded the feel of "grandmother's house" with the crocheted blankets draped over chairs and lace doilies adorning rich wood tables.

The headmistress sat behind a modest and elegant desk,

wearing the blue gown with the pink sash, her grayish hair draped over her shoulders, and a dainty felt-tipped pen in her hands. Beside her was something that looked like a tiny telephone, then something that resembled a phone but one of those older rotary kinds.

Willow's eyes swiveled up to a pendulum clock on the wall and back to Paris. "You're supposed to be in class."

Wilfred had disappeared, pulling the door shut immediately. Paris nodded, feeling suddenly nervous about interrupting the headmistress.

"Yes, I realize that, which is why I'm here," she started, knotting her hands together. "You see…" Paris trailed away, realizing that she hadn't planned out what she was going to say to Willow.

She couldn't very well say, "Mae Ling told me to be myself, which means to rebel against your curriculum and ways of doing things." Without the head professor saying it, Paris knew that she wasn't supposed to tell anyone the advice she'd given her. She had gone silent when Headmistress Starr entered the room upon meeting Paris. No, that conversation and her direction to Paris was between the two of them.

"Something is wrong," Headmistress Starr guessed.

Paris nodded, chewing on her lip.

"Take a seat." Willow held out her hand to the cushy armchair opposite her desk. "You look a little peckish. Have you been eating since you got to the college?"

As if invited to complain, Paris' stomach grumbled on cue. She remembered then that the spell she used to read the book using magic would have depleted her magic reserves. She'd been too excited about the win against Professor Butcher, and she'd forgotten about the huge expense.

"I have been," Paris admitted.

"Well, maybe not enough sweets." Willow pushed a crystal dish of butterscotch candies in her direction.

Paris had never liked the candies. She also didn't like other candies—or sweets. Still, calories were calories. Maybe that was the thing. The fairy godmothers thought they needed to eat sweets to be sweet and refill their reserves, but maybe it was about eating what one likes. Paris would rather have a quesadilla the size of a pizza filled with grilled chicken and peppers or a hamburger and fries. Why did she have to eat cake and cookies if that wasn't for her?

These were the things she needed to voice, but doing so was harder than she would have thought as she looked into the thoughtful eyes of the headmistress.

Unwrapping a candy, she popped it into her mouth and attempted a smile. "The reason that I'm here," Paris began, finding it difficult to speak with the hard candy in her mouth, "is that I didn't agree with the curriculum of Professor Shannon Butcher's class."

Willow glanced down at a notebook, scanning it. "You mean Cotillion?" She looked up, having reviewed the class schedule.

Paris nodded. "I realize these classes are important to you all here," she began, trying to sound as respectful as she could while also trying to say this was complete bullshit. She liked Willow and didn't want to disrespect her at all. "But—"

"You don't think they're relevant," Headmistress Starr guessed, offering a polite smile.

Sighing, Paris nodded again. "Professor Butcher and I didn't get on very well from the beginning. We agreed that if I tested out of the class, I didn't need to take it."

Surprised, Willow tilted her chin to the side. "Did you test out of Cotillion?"

Another nod. "She gave me an impromptu quiz, and I got one hundred percent."

"Well, I can't say I'm not surprised," Willow stated, "but I'm very impressed." She sighed and looked around at her desk as if she'd lost something. "This is very unorthodox, as I'm sure you're aware. We don't usually allow students to do things in such a manner."

"I'm not the typical student," Paris offered.

"That's true," Willow agreed. "Still...I'm not sure how to handle this."

"It's just that, if I may Headmistress Starr..."

The fairy godmother lowered her chin and smiled. "Go on then."

"Well, it's just that as much as I respect what you all do here, promoting love and all, I'm not sure that we need to refine women so they fit into a mold that makes Prince Charmings like them," she explained in a rush. "I didn't agree with all the etiquette of the Cotillion class. And I'm not sure about my schedule. Like, why do I need to learn baking and cooking and gardening?"

"Because your charges need to," Willow explained.

"But that's the thing," Paris argued. "What if they don't? Why don't regular women and men who aren't all proper get to find true love? Why is it only those with Ph.D.'s in refinement who get to be matched?"

Willow considered this for a moment. After a long pause, she glanced up at Paris, her gaze penetrating. "I'm not going to argue that you're altogether wrong, Paris. However, I want you to also keep in mind that I'm not wrong. Maybe we're both correct, but we need to meet somewhere in the middle. You see, I recognize that our ways are dated. It's one reason I allowed you entry to Happily Ever After College. Most don't want to be fairy godmothers anymore, so I can reason that we haven't adapted to the modern world. But I'm not sure how to proceed. You may be a little extreme for us. We've yet to see. Here's what I do know that's relevant, besides the fact that we're losing fairy godmothers and therefore much more."

Willow stood from her desk and walked to a side wall where a red velvet curtain hung. She pulled it back by simply using her finger to draw it to the side magically. Behind it, hanging on the wall was a meter that had a small heart at the bottom. The arrow was set well under halfway along the dial, about at the twenty-five percent mark on a scale of one hundred percent.

"This love meter is the same one they monitor at Matters of the Heart and the Fairy Godmother Agency," Willow explained. "We're all responsible for it. I churn out skilled fairy godmothers. They assign then Saint Valentine monitors and governs. On all fronts, we've decided we're failing. We're not sure if it's the teachings, which are the foundation or if the assignments are wrong, or if Saint Valentine's oversight isn't catching problems. However, what is evident is that worldwide, true love is down. It's at around twenty-five percent, which is a dangerous number for our globe. It's never been so low."

Paris thought for a moment. "And the repercussions of that..."

"There are many," Willow began. "Love affects everything in this world from our planet to the ecosystem to the economy to population. It's the most far-reaching effect of any."

Paris gulped. "So we have to do something."

The headmistress nodded and smirked. "Hence the reason that I allowed an untraditional student into our ranks." She took her seat at her desk once more and folded her hands in front of her casually. "I don't know if I'm doing things right or wrong, or if the Fairy Godmother Agency or Matters of the Heart is. All I know is that we need to do something differently. You have a different, younger mindset, so I'm open to learning from that."

Paris sensed a "but," so she decided to stay quiet.

"But..." Willow drew out the word.

There it is, Paris thought.

"I would be remiss if I didn't ask that you do the same thing," Willow stated. "I'll allow you to test out of Cotillion, but please note that you have to prove yourself. Our curriculum was established for a reason so you can't simply dismiss it. I'll be open to your new ideas as long as you try and master what we offer."

That was a lot. Paris pondered. She could offer her input, but she had to study what they'd already established. It would require more than if she simply went along with the status quo. Still, Paris didn't agree with how things were. Plus, her gut told her that she could offer the college a good change.

So she extended her hand to the headmistress, which apparently wasn't how fairy godmothers agreed on things. Not backing down, Paris offered her a smile. "You've got yourself a deal. Let's shake on it."

As if it was her first handshake, and maybe it was, Willow took her hand in hers and gingerly wrung it. "Okay, we have a deal."

CHAPTER THIRTY-FIVE

Never in her entire life had Paris been in a ballroom. Why would she? It wasn't a place that a kid from Roya Lane found herself. There weren't ballroom dancing lessons or ballet or anything similar.

Still, Paris was enchanted when she stepped into the large, elaborately decorated hall, more than the rest of the mansion, which was saying a lot. The ceilings were high with several large chandeliers dazzling with crystals that hung like snowflakes.

The floors felt different under her boots as if she was walking on air that clapped with each of her steps. She glanced behind herself, wondering if she was leaving prints.

"You made it," Wilfred said in his distinguished voice from the corner, striding over to her.

Paris whipped around to find the butler smiling regally at her.

"Yeah, this is my second class." She looked around at the students putting on special heels in the corner of the ballroom. "Will you please point me in the direction of the instructor? I guess I should introduce myself."

"You already have," Wilfred stated proudly and pressed a hand to his chest. "I'm the instructor for ballroom dancing."

"Oh," Paris hiccupped, not having expected the butler would be an instructor. He was the most refined person she'd met there or anywhere else, so it made sense. "Well, then I hope it comes as no surprise that I don't know the first thing about ballroom dancing or any type of dancing."

He nodded. "I concluded as much. Don't worry. You can observe today and join us as you pick up the moves."

"Great. I'm used to sitting on the bleachers. Where are they?"

He gave her a blank expression, confused.

"It was a joke, Wil…"

"Right, madam." He clapped his hands good-naturedly. "Well, I hope that you don't mind sitting in a seat along the wall. We don't have any of these bleachers that you speak of." He pointed to where padded armchairs were lined up along a wall where two familiar faces already sat—Chef Ash and Hemingway.

Paris nodded. "Okay, so I get to sit and watch? No pop quizzes or making me do the Zumba on my first day?"

He gave her another look of confusion. "We're doing the foxtrot today. I don't think we'll be covering the Zumba."

"I think that's a workout that housewives do at gyms," Paris explained. "But honestly, I wouldn't know since I'm not a housewife and have never been to a gym."

"Then how do you know?" Wilfred asked curiously.

"Because I watch a lot of Netflix," she admitted.

"Well, please try to pay attention," Wilfred instructed and pointed at the class that was filing into orderly rows.

Paris backed up to the row of chairs while looking back and forth between the class and Chef Ash and Hemingway. She slid into one and finally asked her burning question. "What are you two doing here?"

"We're dance partners, obviously." Hemingway pretended to sound offended.

"Excuse me for not knowing that. This is my first ballroom dancing class. I guess I figured the students would partner up."

"They do," Chef Ash agreed with a smile. "But it's nice for them to have someone who knows how to lead."

Paris lowered her chin. "Because a woman couldn't do that, right?"

"It's not traditional," he admitted.

She watched as the butler clapped, gaining the students' attention, and reviewed the moves that they'd learn during that class. It still seemed so strange to Paris that she had to learn ballroom dancing and not only to help others find love, but this was her method for staying out of jail. "To think, I could be learning how to smuggle pixie drugs into a place."

"What's that?" Hemingway leaned over as if he hadn't heard her right, although she suspected that he had.

The news from the class with Professor Butcher would be spreading, and soon everyone would know that Paris was jail material. She looked like it, so it was only a matter of time before everyone treated her like it. Or maybe she'd change things…she hoped so.

"I was remarking how strange it is that I'd have to learn ballroom dancing," she lied, pointing as Wilfred demonstrated a move for the class, and the students all tried to copy it.

"Oh, I don't know," Hemingway began. "It's a lot like fighting, I'd think."

She spun to face him, wondering if news about her jail sentence had already rapidly spread. "Why would you say that?"

He drew back. "Because last night you said you couldn't throw a roundhouse kick with the fairy godmother gown on, so I figured that was your thing."

She nodded, trying to cover her alarmed reaction. "Yeah, I prefer martial arts."

"Which," Chef Ash held up a finger in the air, "I'll point out is an art, hence the name."

Paris nodded while watching the class try to follow Wilfred and not look quite as graceful. That gave her little hope that she'd pick this up if they'd been doing it for a few weeks or months and she was only beginning.

"Yeah, the funny thing is, I can take out a minotaur with one arm restrained, but ask me to waltz, and I'll probably sweep your legs out from under you by accident." Paris laughed.

Hemingway gave her an uncertain yet entertained expression. "Why is it that you would have to fight a minotaur?"

She shrugged. "How else was I going to get back the jewelry he stole?"

Wilfred clapped and turned elegantly in a circle. "Now, I'll have some dance partners join you to practice. The rest partner up with each other until we rotate." The butler waved to Chef Ash and Hemingway.

"That's our cue." Chef Ash tipped his imaginary hat to Paris as he strode for the class.

Hemingway pointed at her and winked. "I want to hear stories about kicking minotaur's butts and more over a glass of sherry."

"I don't drink sherry," she replied.

He turned, walking backward. "Whiskey it is."

"I never said I was victorious," she stated.

"I want the story then," he fired back before spinning.

Paris sat back, laughing and wondering what she'd gotten herself into by agreeing to give all this a chance. It all felt like a silly game, but the love meter wasn't a joke, and she desperately wanted to help the world…if that was within her powers.

CHAPTER THIRTY-SIX

From the doorway, unseen by the class or Paris Westbridge, were Willow Starr and Mae Ling. The pair watched the proceedings of the ballroom dancing class, and listened in using an eavesdropping spell.

The headmistress visibly flinched at hearing Paris' admission about fighting a minotaur. Mae Ling, however, hid her grin after hearing this.

"You think she's what we need?" Willow asked the head professor.

"I do," Mae Ling stated with confidence.

The headmistress shook her head. "I've always trusted you on these things...your process, but I wish you could be more forthcoming with your reasoning."

"I think she has a good instinct," Mae Ling admitted, observing as Paris slumped in her seat, watching the class practice as she threaded her arms across her chest, disinterested. "I think that as fairy godmothers, we've lost that instinct. We're too textbook, and it's outdated. We need something different."

Willow sighed heavily and looked at the rebellious fairy. "She's definitely different. Not only for a fairy godmother either. She's different for…well, a fairy."

Mae Ling shrugged. "I'm a fairy."

"Yes, but you know how to behave," Willow stated.

"I know when to behave and when you're not looking," Mae Ling teased playfully.

"Oh, you always behave, even if you don't conform." She pointed at Paris. "That one doesn't do either."

"I like that about her," Mae Ling stated proudly.

"I do too," Willow admitted. "That doesn't mean she's going to work out. We'll have to keep an eye on her. How she acts today is crucial. Saint Valentine is breathing down my back on several things: Our low enrollment, the fairy godmothers flunking out once in the field, and now this decision to allow an unorthodox student into our college. If at the end of today, Paris doesn't seem like a good fit, I think we need to reassess."

"I think she'll pass our exams tonight," Mae Ling declared. "But…" She held up a finger while drawing out the word. "Consider that she might pass using unconventional means since she is an unorthodox student. We all need to be prepared for that."

Willow lowered her chin and gave the head professor a knowing look. "You mean me. I need to be open to such things."

"Possibly," Mae Ling sang and glanced back at Paris. "For now, we simply observe. See what she does and how she does. Grade her as she progresses through the day."

Willow nodded. "Then tonight, the final exam to see if she's right for Happily Ever After College. If not, we have to figure out something else. If the answer isn't unconventional students for the college, then I have to figure out something else. Everything at Happily Ever After depends on this. Love is at stake."

CHAPTER THIRTY-SEVEN

Paris had never been in an observatory before. She didn't know much about the solar system since she'd never read about it in her online science classes. Unfortunately, she knew too much about astrology because under her flat on Roya Lane there had always been a strange astrology shop that sold crystals and star charts.

The woman who ran it was named Cosmos, and she often gave Paris unsolicited advice when she passed by her store. Even stranger was on the few times that Paris had moved to different places on Roya Lane, the shop had too. Cosmos had various reasons like her lease was up or the old shop's energy was stagnant.

The astrologer would always tell Paris not to make any business transactions or to limit communications because Mars or Venus was in retrograde. "Wait a fortnight or more before signing anything," the old woman would advise Paris on her way to the coffee shop.

"Right," she'd muttered, striding past the shop. "Because I sign so many things each day."

The whole idea of astrology seemed so far-fetched, even in the magical world. The fact that Paris was now required to take a class on it at Happily Ever After College completed the farce that was becoming her life. She couldn't fathom how astrology could be relied upon for matchmaking, but Paris had promised Willow that she'd keep an open mind.

So as she filed into an auditorium inside the observatory, Paris decided not to sit in the back. The space was impressive with stadium seating and a massive screen at the front. Hovering high up in the air were models of the solar system's planets circulating as they did in space.

Once in her seat and surrounded by whispering students, Paris imagined she looked strange surrounded by women in blue gowns while she sat in the middle in her all-black clothing and sporting her blonde hair.

She hadn't been seated for more than a minute when chimes filled the air like soft music. From the side of the stage, a fairy godmother with the pink sash on her blue robes emerged out of seemingly nowhere. The professor had dark skin and one bright blue eye and one brown one. Her long dreadlocks were braided down her back and were the same grayish-blue color as everyone else's hair.

"For those new to my class, my name is Professor Joyce Beacon. Welcome to Astrology," the woman said in an airy tone while looking out over the students.

Paris wanted to laugh since this introduction was aimed at her, although the professor didn't look at her directly but rather around the room as if searching for the newbie. It was evident to all that Paris was the new student, but she didn't raise her hand to draw more attention.

"February is going to be a very unusual month due to the many planets in Aquarius, creating a celestial equinox of energy," Professor Beacon explained, launching straight into the lecture. "This hasn't happened in such a way for over sixty years, which relatively speaking is a very short time for fairies, but still note-worthy for its rarity."

Paris didn't understand half of what this woman was saying, but she worked to keep the confusion off her face, as well as the ever-growing skepticism.

"What does this activity with Aquarius mean?" Professor Beacon asked matter-of-factly.

Not a damn thing, Paris thought.

Before any of the students with their hands eagerly raised could answer, the fairy godmother stated, "February is going to be a flurry of activity. For our charges, that means there are several more factors that you all will have to take into account when evaluating successful matches. Now I understand that all you first-years aren't yet doing real matches. These rehearsal ones will prepare you, and having a unique situation like this with so many planets in Aquarius is also good practice."

Paris had to cover her mouth to hide her laugh. This woman couldn't be serious. They weren't really pairing up potential matches based on their zodiacs? These were seemingly intelligent individuals at Happily Ever After College. How could they put such stock into things? Then Paris realized that she should have expected this was what the class was about. It was astrology, after all.

On the trek to the observatory, Paris had deluded herself into thinking they'd watch interesting shows in the planetarium at the back or study constellations through the powerful telescopes in the observatory. She wanted to convince herself that they'd study astronomy using the ideas of physics and mathematics and science to understand the actual chemistry between two people. Alas, it looked like the fairy godmothers were putting stock into a bogus science founded in zero fact.

"It's important," Professor Beacon continued, "that when assessing matches, you always look at both your Cinderellas' and Prince Charmings' sun signs as well as their rising sign."

Oh dear, this class was going to be a true demonstration in restraint. Paris didn't know how she was going to keep her mouth shut.

"For those new to the class, who wants to explain where the two charts come from?" the professor asked the class.

A round of hands shot into the air.

"Yes, Rainbow?" The fairy godmother pointed toward the back of the auditorium.

The universe was really testing Paris now. There was a student named Rainbow in the class? No doubt a name that was the product of two hippy parents who probably birthed their child in the river and cut her umbilical cord with a stone. A woman named Rainbow was exactly the type of person that Paris thought would follow astrology and not do certain things based on the moon's position.

"The sun sign is based on one's birthday," Rainbow answered. "The rising sign is calculated by the precise time of birth, place of birth, and day, month, and year of birth."

"Correct," Professor Beacon stated proudly and walked along the stage. "You should always read the full forecast for your charge's month. Otherwise, you could miss something. If you disregard one of the signs, you might plan a date for them on a particular day due to their sun sign, but their rising sign might state that leaving the house at that time could prove grave for your charges. So to get the whole picture, you have to consider both."

To Paris' surprise, she found her hand in the air. It was such a shock that she looked up at the extended arm, wondering how it got there.

"Yes, Ms. Paris Westbridge," the professor called on her.

"So are you saying that two people born at the same time, place, and everything else would be the same person?" she challenged. "Or that if two people all have the same place, date, and year of birth, but are one second apart that they'd have entirely different star charts?"

"It's impossible for two people to both be born at the same place, time, and everything else since two people can't occupy the same space," the professor shot back, annoyance flaring on her face.

"So they are born a few feet apart," Paris offered. "Is that what shapes their life differently? Not different genetics or cultures or whatever else would affect them?"

"This is not a topic of nature versus nurture, Ms. Westbridge. Regardless of upbringing, our sun and rising charts define us from birth."

"I simply can't agree with that," Paris argued. "How is it that the day I was born would have more of an impact on who I am rather than social and economic factors or hereditary or a ton of other factors?"

The students in the class all leaned away from Paris as though not wanting to be associated with her by proximity. Maybe Professor Beacon was known for zapping challenging students with lightning spells or something.

"Our sun charts are critically significant for explaining who we are," the fairy godmother explained through clenched teeth. "You can't argue that the sun isn't important, right?"

"Well, without it we'd all die, so no, I'll give you that one," Paris joked dryly.

The professor sighed dramatically and planted her hands on her hips. "The sun is the center of our solar system and therefore the center of everyone's universe."

"I don't know much about science, but I think our solar system is in the universe, meaning that the sun can't be the center of the universe," Paris quipped, realizing she could shut up at any point, but the little nagging voice in her head wouldn't allow it. She'd opened this can of worms and now was letting them wiggle out and do as they pleased.

"My point is," the professor seethed, "that it's the sun that dictates the twelve signs as it is what moves through these constellations. Ignoring its impact on a person's life based on that chart is negligible at best. A compatibility guide that didn't take into account both the sun and rising charts could prove to have negative results when matching two people."

"So are you telling me, if a Prince Charming is a Capricorn, then I have to wait until his sun and rising charts are in alignment or something before introducing him to the Virgo?" Paris asked, earning many gasps from around the room.

The professor grinned in reply. "You have much to learn, Ms. Westbridge. If you had done the proper studying on the subject, you'd know that those signs are rarely compatible. A Virgo's rigid nature would never do well in a romantic relationship with a Capricorn's ignorance of schedules."

"I can't help but think you're missing the point I was trying to make," Paris remarked. "I simply don't think we can dictate people's future based on their zodiac. It's not an exact science. I mean, it's not a science at all…"

"Astrology is an age-old method that has been used for centuries to determine multiple factors about a person's life," Professor Beacon said smugly.

"I'm not discounting that there could be validity to astrology," Paris stated. "I simply think that blindly following something that could never be one hundred percent correct seems illogical. Instead, it should be more of a guide in making matches rather than seen as a guarantee. I mean, the weather forecast often tells us one thing but is off. If we lived and died by that, we might miss out on a not forecasted sunny day or not take an umbrella along even though we felt the rain in the air."

The fairy godmother narrowed her eyes at Paris. "You make some interesting points. I'm not saying that you're right, but maybe we need to take into account other factors as well as compatibility charts. For now, you need to learn the fundamentals and fully understand astrology. Only then will I entertain such radical notions that you're offering."

Paris nodded, feeling victorious. It wasn't a total win, but it wasn't a total loss. She'd voiced her opinion, and unlike with Professor Butcher, Professor Beacon had heard her. Paris hadn't compromised her beliefs, and hopefully the more she learned about astrology, the more she could support or debunk its claims.

For Paris, it was always about using logic, which she thought the strange practice ignored, but the only way to argue against something was to understand it. In truth, she didn't think that astrology was altogether wrong. It simply wasn't fact-based. Such things should be taken with a grain of salt rather than blindly sprinkled onto an entrée and eaten freely.

CHAPTER THIRTY-EIGHT

The headmistress and Mae Ling stood in the auditorium's doorway, watching the proceedings down below involving Paris and Professor Beacon. Willow had tensed when the new student had first spoken up, wondering what trouble Paris would bring on herself.

To her surprise, the fairy had made some relevant points and in a way that wasn't disrespectful. It did appear that the young fairy found it impossible to keep quiet and simply learn. Paris questioned everything, which had never been the way at Happily Ever After College.

The students at the school were never the questioning type. Fairy godmothers and those training for the role were notorious for being accepting individuals who went along with what others told them. They didn't rebel. They didn't argue. They were polite, pleasant, and conforming.

None of those traits fit Paris Westbridge.

"I think that overall, Paris should be assessed positively for that round," Mae Ling whispered.

Willow brought her attention up to regard the head professor.

"She challenged a professor in her first five minutes in the class, not knowing much about the actual subject matter."

"Well, sometimes those with an objective perspective, who know the least about something, are in the best position to pick it apart," Mae Ling offered.

"Maybe." Willow drew out the word.

"We both know that astrology is an archaic part of our curriculum," Mae Ling continued. "Employing it in matchmaking has never been a success factor. Paris brings up an excellent point that it should be used as a guide, rather than a definitive method."

"Why are you so supportive of this new student?" Willow asked, having seen Mae Ling's usual neutral manner shift with Paris' arrival.

"Nothing that we've been doing seems to work," Mae Ling explained. "The love-meter keeps dropping. Enrollment is at an all-time low. Our graduates aren't having great success out in the field. We can't do much to make things get worse, and anything new we do has to be better than what we've been doing. I think that something needs to push us into the modern world."

Willow nodded, these words echoing the same thoughts in her head. Change was scary though. Everything that Paris stood for was the opposite of the fairy godmother principles. They were old, grandmother-type figures who were dainty and pretty and full of sugar and spice and everything nice.

Paris Westbridge was dark and rebellious and probably full of salt and a lot of pent-up angst.

"Look at the Dragon Elite," Mae Ling continued. "That ancient organization of dragonriders was dated a couple of decades ago. Then one woman strides in there and shakes them up, pushing them into the twenty-first century."

Willow nodded proudly. "Sophia Beaufont—the first female dragonrider in history. You're right. If it weren't for her, the Dragon Elite would still be living in the Dark Ages. Maybe it does take new blood to reenergize an old school. We'll have to wait and see. However, I fear there are only two ways that someone like Paris can take us. Either up and to better places or down and farther away from our goal."

Mae Ling agreed with a nod. "She has two more classes and an exam set for today. Then we make our final decision. Let's keep an open mind."

Willow drew a deep breath. She was trying to stay open to these changes although they were challenging her on every single level. Evolving at the college was scary, but failing with her mission as headmistress was terrifying.

CHAPTER THIRTY-NINE

B y the time lunch rolled around, everyone at the college had heard about the Cotillion class incident. These rumors had circulated fast and were now pretty far-fetched.

"I heard you threw the textbook at Professor Butcher while you recited it verbatim," Christine said beside Paris, having joined her again for the meal. It made Paris feel comforted, thinking that the other woman was sitting with her because they were becoming friends and not because she was some sideshow that she wanted firsthand information from.

Paris laughed, cutting open the yeasty roll and slathering butter across it, in the very naughty fashion of buttering and eating bread. "I didn't throw anything at her except insults about how outdated the whole method of these manners was. I mean really, am I supposed to put a book on my head next and stride around the class to show I'm a proper lady?"

"Well, no, that's next week's lesson, I'm pretty certain, and you've already tested out of the class," Christine offered in a hushed voice. "I think that's the first time someone did that."

"I wasn't as lucky to test out of ballroom dancing or astrology," Paris related.

"Oh, you might start to enjoy those," Christine stated. "Wilfred is a nice instructor and astrology can be fun although Professor Beacon takes it way too seriously."

"That's what I told her."

Christine nearly dropped her fork filled with leafy greens. "You told her that? What did she say?"

Paris nodded. "She said, I made some interesting points but that I needed to learn the fundamentals of astrology before I could discount them."

"Wow, you're already shaking things up."

That was the part that scared Paris. She hadn't been at Happily Ever After College long and already felt like a bizarre change agent. "I will say," she began in a whisper. "That most, like Willow and Professor Beacon, are fairly level-headed. They could have told me to suck it up and accept things, but they seemed open to my opinions."

Christine nodded. "Most fairy godmothers are very under-standing. It's a trait that makes us successful in our role." Her gaze traveled down the table to a group of gossiping girls led by Becky Montgomery. "Of course, there're always exceptions to this."

"What's the bully's story?" Paris indicated the brunette.

"Oh, her family has been funding the college since the begin-ning," Christine explained. "They have deep pockets and throw money at their problems. If one of theirs gets in trouble, there's a donation. If Becky doesn't make the grades, they donate. The college has hit hard times, and most are aware of it, so I don't think the Board is in any position not to be swayed."

"That's sad," Paris grumbled, never having liked it when people bought their way into something or out of it without earning it fully.

"What's sad is that no one ever stands up to Becky," Christine whispered. "I've wanted to a ton of times, but it isn't my nature.

Then yesterday you threw a pie at her face, something we've all wanted to do a thousand times."

Paris laughed. "I didn't really throw a pie at her face like some slapstick clown bit. I dropped one on her head and only because the tray of brownies sitting beside the pie would have done physical damage. I wait until someone deserves it before I make them pay painfully."

Christine giggled with her, shaking her head. "You're not like anyone here."

Paris nodded, not sure how she felt about that.

"Totally true," a woman across from Paris stated. "I heard a rumor that you were supposed to go to jail, but your uncle is a detective and cut this deal for you."

Sighing, Paris realized that was the other reason most were whispering up and down the table and pointing at her. "Well, he didn't buy my way in here, but yes. I'm the bad sort that your mom warned you to stay away from."

"So what, you make it here, or you go to jail?" Christine asked.

Paris nodded. "I'm afraid so. The college, as you said, has fallen on hard times, and I'm the result of desperation."

"Did you kill someone?" the woman across the table asked.

"Yes," Paris retorted sarcastically. "I'm a murderer, and you have to sleep down the hall from me."

The woman looked suddenly ill.

Christine laughed, slapped the table, and broke the tension. "She's joking. Obviously, Paris isn't a murderer." Giving her a suddenly serious look, Christine tilted her chin to the side. "But seriously, what did you do?"

"I punched a giant who stole someone's lunch money," Paris stated. "And I was in the wrong place at the wrong time a few dozen times. Trouble has a way of following me around as you've already witnessed. But I've never done anything really bad, not in my opinion anyway. When I see something I don't like, I speak up about it, and usually, that's to someone who doesn't want to hear my protest. They throw a low blow, I counterattack, and then we're both carted off to the Fairy Law Enforcement Agency, also known as FLEA. Then the whole thing repeats itself the next week. It's all very boring."

Christine shook her head, appearing impressed. "I've never so much as given someone a dirty look for doing something awful. That's pretty amazing that you stand up to people like that."

"Yeah, well, if it were amazing, I wouldn't be here," Paris remarked. "It's apparently not my job and gets me in trouble more than it gets me accolades."

"Being here isn't so bad though," Christine urged. "I know we all must seem like a bunch of goody-two-shoes compared to you and the types you're around, but we're fun. On Saturday nights we stay up late and watch romantic comedies and have pillow fights."

"I'll politely bow out of competing in the pillow fights since I suspect that I'll turn it into a gross form of warfare," Paris muttered.

"I think you'd have us all beat," Christine concluded.

Paris wasn't sure that watching romantic comedy and pillow fights were something she'd find herself doing. Maybe she could convince the women to have a casino night instead or a murder mystery night. Sure, they were supposed to be about creating romance, but that didn't mean she had to stomach movies about two airheads blindly falling in love. The fairy godmothers deserved to have a life too, which meant a little adventure.

Convincing the fairy godmothers and professors to change would be a challenge, but one that Paris was up for. She glanced down the table, her eyes connecting with Professor Butcher, who was shooting visual daggers at her.

Still holding her fully buttered roll, Paris crammed half of it into her mouth, disgracefully tearing off a chunk and chewing with her mouth open, eating very much against the rules of etiquette and loving every bit of it.

CHAPTER FORTY

The heathen was mocking her now, Shannon thought, watching as Paris Westbridge tore into her dinner roll like a savage. She'd seen many things at the college in her time, but nothing like the rude fairy who sat farther down the table chewing with her mouth open.

This rebel might have gotten into Happily Ever After College, but there was no way that she would stick around. That morning's debacle was a rarity and had caught Shannon Butcher off guard. It wouldn't happen again. Paris might fool the headmistress and Mae Ling and maybe some of the staff, but her antics wouldn't blind Shannon.

She didn't know how, but the Cotillion professor was certain that strange spell work had been employed for Paris to pass the quiz that morning. Many spells might have worked, but Shannon couldn't figure out how Paris had successfully pulled it off.

Fairies had magic but many times needed an object to harness it, like a wand or a stone or an elemental force. Fairy godmothers often turned birds into vehicles or flowers into dresses, pulling on the object's powers. However, Paris didn't appear to have anything she was drawing on when using what Shannon thought was an osmosis spell to study the textbook's contents.

That was beyond bizarre. It wasn't like fairy magic at all, but rather like the brand of magic that a magician used. That didn't make any sense at all, which was why Shannon Butcher would have to do some investigating on her own. She would find out who this fairy was who was disrespecting their tried and true ways at Happily Ever After College. Once the fairy godmother learned who Paris Westbridge really was, she would expose her and hopefully get her kicked out of the college.

CHAPTER FORTY-ONE

Hemingway was propped up against the wall in the hallway outside the dining hall when Paris exited. He straightened to attention when he saw her.

"Hey there," he greeted her with a wide smile. "I figured I would walk you to the greenhouse for your next class."

"Thanks," Paris said awkwardly, wondering if the Jack-of-All-Trades for the college had heard she was a criminal and was keeping an eye on her. "Yeah, I have Gardening, which makes about as much sense as me learning how to tango."

He laughed, and a dimple surfaced on his cheek. "I don't think Wilfred teaches the tango in ballroom dancing, but you could always request it."

She shook her head. "I don't get what good playing in the dirt will be for helping me to match lovers."

"From my perspective, which isn't remotely close to being a fairy godmother," he began while leading her out onto the sunny Enchanted Grounds. "Much like ballroom dancing, gardening is a skill and a discipline, which doesn't hurt to learn and understand. I believe the skills we learn lend themselves to other things. Yes, the headmistress does expect Cinderellas to know the fundamentals of gardening, and therefore you must learn them."

"Right." Paris grunted. "Before I can help a gal land a catch, I have to teach her how to prune roses. Makes total sense."

He nodded understandingly. "I get how it seems strange. But also, in gardening, you'll learn lessons that hopefully relate to the matters of the heart. Growing things is very much about love. At least it is for me. There's a unique passion that goes into gardening. Well, and also, you aren't only going to learn how to plant regular old seeds and trim back topiaries. In this class, the instructor also likes to dabble in magical gardening, which fairy godmothers can use to create herbs, flowers, and unique plants for potions and all sorts of other uses."

Paris found herself smiling at this. "Hey, this might be the first class I've taken all day that's useful. I like the sound of this. I hope the professor isn't some snobby jerk with a gardening hoe up their butt."

Hemingway threw back his head and chuckled. "I hope you don't think that about them. I hear they're pretty down to Earth."

Paris shook her head and rolled her eyes at him. "Did you just make that terrible pun?"

"I did." He feigned hurt. "I thought it was pretty good. It appears I'll have to step up my comedy routine to get a laugh out of you."

She nodded. "Yeah, I'm not stealing your material to get a laugh out of Wilfred."

Hemingway gave her a look of surprise. "I don't think there's any joke that can get him to laugh. He's not wired for it."

Paris shook her head, undeterred. "I have a mission. I'm going to get that man to laugh if it's the last thing I do at this place—or the only thing."

After opening the door to the greenhouse, Hemingway held out a hand for Paris to enter first. "You might be the first student here ever to have that as a goal. Usually, they want Wilfred to polish their shoes and tell them the latest gossip in the manor. That butler sees and hears everything."

Paris discovered that the greenhouse was humid and pulled off her leather jacket once inside. "No thanks. I polish my boots, and gossip is super boring. I'd prefer the challenge of getting a magitech AI to laugh."

"I like it. As Eleanor Roosevelt said, 'Great minds discuss ideas, average minds discuss events, and small minds discuss people.'"

Chatting students filled the greenhouse, and they all hushed at the sight of the two when they entered. Planters lined the perimeter and baskets with flowers hung from the ceiling. In rows were individual workstations with a flat surface and drawers of supplies and tools underneath. Paris took the first empty one at the back and looked around for the instructor as Hemingway breezed past her to the front.

Once there, he turned and looked out at the class. "Hello, class. Let's go ahead and get started on today's lesson."

Paris froze, never having considered that the professor for this class was none other than the gardener for Happily Ever After—Hemingway Noble.

CHAPTER FORTY-TWO

Hemingway slapped his palms together and rubbed them back and forth with an eager look on his face. "Who's ready to get their hands dirty today?"

The students all nodded, but none of them seemed as excited about this as him. Paris had a hard time picturing any of the pretty and neat women in blue gowns getting their manicured hands dirty.

"All right. First two rows," Hemingway began and motioned to the set of students at the front. "I want you in the Bewilder Forest today extracting the red juice from the Dragon's Blood Tree. For twenty extra points, who can tell me what benefits the juice offers, besides looking like real blood and being great makeup for Halloween?"

A few hands shot up into the air. Hemingway pointed at a woman at the front. "Go ahead and indulge us, Moondrop."

Moondrop, Paris thought. Did most of the students here have hippie names like Rainbow and Moondrop? Thankfully her maybe new friend Christine had a normal name. Paris realized that she couldn't really talk since hers was unique.

"The juice of the Dragon's Blood Tree can be extracted and used to heal various ailments and improve mood if used in elixirs. Taken in too high a dose, it can cause euphoria," Moonbeam answered in a rehearsed manner as if she'd memorized the textbook.

"Correct," Hemingway praised. "Why is euphoria a bad thing?"

The students all looked around at each other as though searching for the answer. When no one said anything, Paris dared to raise her hand.

"In the back there." Hemingway pointed at her with an intrigued smile on his face.

"Well, although euphoria sounds like a nice state of being," Paris began, her voice low at first but rising as the students turned to look at her and leaned in her direction like they couldn't hear her well. "It's an extreme on the emotional scale, and it doesn't seem that rational judgment could be used when in such a state."

She had never heard herself talk that way, as if she was all educated or something, but the words had all flowed effortlessly. *Maybe reading one book had exponentially raised my IQ,* Paris thought and wondered where she came up with the word "exponentially."

The room was silent, all eyes on her. Hemingway blinked at her, also seeming as surprised by her answer as she was.

Finally, he grinned and threw his hand into the air. "Ding, ding, ding! Ten points for you. Since you're new, please note that points are only used for bragging rights. They aren't transferable, have no monetary value, and expire after an hour. So use them right away. That's my advice."

Paris discovered she was smiling again. Maybe the gardening class wouldn't be as dull as the others. So far, so good.

"You were correct as well, Moonbeam." Hemingway looked at the student at the front of the class. "There are tons of healing qualities that the Dragon's Blood Tree is used for. Incidentally, it also can strip paint if used in concentrated form and is a clever cleaning agent for hard to eliminate stains."

He then swept his arm to the side of the greenhouse where there was a row of plants with fuzzy pink blossoms. "My middle row, I want you all to work with the shame plants. Talk to them, tell them jokes, play them music, give them your life story. The point of today's lesson is that you must spend the entirety of the class with them without them folding in their leaves or bowing down. If they do, who wants to tell me what that means?"

Most of the class raised their hands. Hemingway indicated a tall woman toward the back. "Yes, you, Queen."

Paris nearly laughed. There was a student named Queen. She'd heard it all now.

"If a shame plant folds in its leaves or bows," the student began, "it means that you've hurt its feelings, offended it, or made it upset in some way. They're sensitive plants that pick up on the emotions and moods of others who are in proximity to them and respond in kind."

Paris eyed the strange plants on the far side of the greenhouse, suddenly fascinated that such flowers existed.

"Well put," Hemingway commended. "Twenty points. Yes, that's correct. The shame plant is extremely sensitive, and we use its extract to create mood rings that sense real feelings. However, as fairy godmothers, you're going to need to present yourself lovingly in stressful situations. Your charges will be like the shame plant, and your job will often be to keep them from wilting. So grab a plant and pretend it's a brokenhearted Cinderella and make it smile. Or at least keep it from bowing."

Many of the students got up and rushed for the plants as if they were eager to get a specific one.

"My back rows," Hemingway said over the shuffle, "today you're going to be in charge of finding, collecting, and trimming the roots of the living stone plant and tending to it. Who can tell me why trimming the roots of this plant is difficult?"

A set of hands shot up.

Hemingway smiled, the participation making him happy. "Yes, Tilly?"

"The living stone plants grow in rocks and have invisible root systems," a woman explained.

"Correct," Hemingway chirped. "The plants blend into their surroundings, so finding them in the Bewilder Forest will be your first challenge. Then you'll need to collect them by carefully trimming these invisible roots so we can replant them in the greenhouse. Trim too much of the roots, and the plants will die, so you'll need to be careful. The only way I know to uproot one is to feel for the invisible roots and trim using touch. In this way, you're going to have to rely on this sense. Delicacy is the key—also an important characteristic for a fairy godmother."

Hemingway clapped as he buzzed with excitement. "Okay, without further ado, go and garden."

Encouraged by his enthusiasm, the students all animatedly started in various directions. Paris was in the back row, which meant that she had to go foraging through this Bewilder Forest, searching for a plant that she had no idea what it was. Trying to hide her reluctance, Paris kept her head down as many students filed past her for the door.

She was about to follow them out, hoping one of them could explain what she was looking for when Hemingway strode in her direction, carrying a large green book.

He plopped it down in front of her with a sideways smile, showing his perfectly straight top teeth and crooked bottom row. It made for a cute combination. "I have a different task for you, Paris."

CHAPTER FORTY-THREE

Paris eyed the book in front of her. It was entitled: *Magical Gardening*. "Do you want me to read that book?"

"Eventually," he answered. "Since it's your first day, I want you to start with basics. Under your station, you'll find everything that you need: pots, soil, and some starter seeds. Your task today will be to plant six seeds and nurture them to grow."

Paris angled her head, looking under the workstation briefly, pulling out several packets of seeds. "What magical properties do these have?"

"None. They're regular old sunflower seeds," Hemingway explained. "New students always start with planting those and tending to them over their first year. Hopefully, in twelve months, you've transferred them successfully to the outside of the greenhouse, and they are towering over it. That's the idea, and I like that it represents the growth that students make during that period."

Paris deflated. "That doesn't sound as fun as milking a Dragon's Blood Tree."

He offered her a sympathetic look. "I get it. You have to start with the basics. You'll progress to magical gardening, but only once you've mastered the mortal way of doing things. It's important to know the fundamentals, which aren't as glamourous as trimming invisible roots, but critical."

"Okay." Paris tried to keep the disappointment off her face.

Hemingway glanced over to where the students were interacting with the Shame Plants. "Becky, what did you do to yours?"

In front of Becky, her plant had fallen over, looking entirely lifeless.

"I didn't do anything to it." Becky scowled. "I just told it about my day."

Hemingway shook his head, rushing over. "Maybe you should have sung to it instead. I'm not sure we can rescue this one."

Paris kept her laughter locked away as she pulled out the soil and pots. She'd never gardened before. Then again, she didn't recall ever playing in the dirt. Growing up on Roya Lane didn't offer tree climbing or mud cake-making opportunities. The streets were cobbled, and there wasn't much nature around, but there were fun shops and tons of places for Paris to get into trouble.

When she plunged her hand into the bag of moist soil, Paris instantly enjoyed the way it felt against her fingers. She found the task of filling up the pots and patting sunflower seeds into the dirt to be very meditative. It was also super easy, and she had six pots done within a few minutes.

With nothing else to do, Paris opened the textbook that Hemingway had given her, reading about various spells that could be used to enhance and speed up growing. Fueled from lunch, Paris used the studying spell she'd learned that morning to read most of the book in a matter of minutes. *It was a brilliant spell,* she thought but was still confused why all of a sudden reading was so easy for her. Even without using the spell to speed read, she found the task simple whereas it had been painfully difficult before.

Paris was looking around for a watering can for the new seeds when right on cue, a tiny pixie fairy flew over with a small watering can and sprinkled liquid onto the pots.

"Thanks." Paris smiled at the little female fairy, who was about the size of the small pots with gossamer pink wings and long green hair. The creature squeaked and flew off with the watering can in tow.

Paris hadn't been around many different types of fairies. Now and then she'd see a fae on Roya Lane, but she avoided them because Uncle John said they were so dumb a conversation with them killed brain cells. They were beautiful though, and it was often difficult not to stare when she saw one. Pixies were mostly in nature, tending to gardens and buzzing around forests. It made sense to find them at Happily Ever After College.

Paris was known as a general fairy. They weren't as dumb as fae, but not as smart or as powerful as magicians. They tended to be somewhat like the elves with hippie tendencies as evidenced by the students' strange names at Happily Ever After College. Thankfully that characteristic had appeared to skip Paris because she refused to wear hemp pants or make kombucha—a tea made from fermented mushrooms.

The fairies harnessed the element of ice, meaning that controlling it came easily to them. However, Paris often found that she was better at managing the element of wind, making it die down on Roya Lane. Often it whistled down the narrow street, throwing Paris' hair into her face, which she didn't like.

Fairy magic was also unique because truly powerful spells required an object to control the power so it didn't overwhelm the caster. Paris reasoned that she'd never done a spell that powerful because she'd never needed such an object.

Having read most of the textbook and planted her seeds, Paris now had nothing to do. Deciding she'd skip ahead and employ one of the spells from *Magical Gardening*, she tapped her finger on each of the six pots and muttered the incantations she'd learned.

At first, nothing happened. A few seconds later and one at a time, little seedlings pushed up through the dirt, growing fast until a short but sturdy sunflower unfurled from each pot.

Paris smiled proudly at her creations, grateful the spell worked on her first attempt.

Hemingway glanced over from the other side of the room and did a double-take. He hurried over with a look of surprise on his face.

"Where did you learn how to do a fast-growing spell?" He sounded suddenly anxious, a look of worry on his face.

CHAPTER FORTY-FOUR

Tensing, Paris pointed at the open textbook. "The spell was in there. Is it okay that I used it?"

Hemingway's gaze darted between Paris and the book, confusion on his face. "First, it's perplexing that you were able to use it successfully. I'm guessing that was your first time using a gardening spell, right?"

She nodded.

"Although it worked," he indicated the six sunflowers, "that wasn't the point of the exercise."

"You wanted me to grow sunflowers, though."

Hemingway shook his head. "I wanted you to grow sunflowers naturally."

Paris stuck her hands on her hips. "What's the point if I can do it magically and speed up the process?"

"Well, to be honest," he began, "I'm surprised you were able to perform the spell on your first time. It's not an easy one and requires a lot of magic, especially for six sunflowers."

"I had a big lunch," Paris admitted.

He shook his head, still look confused. "But no, you shouldn't have used a spell to cheat the process."

"I wasn't cheating," she argued, crossing her arms over her chest. "I was speeding up the process. I got done fast, so I figured I'd make the most of the time."

He pointed to the textbook. "You got done early, so you skipped to the advanced chapters at the back of *Magical Gardening* and decided to play around with a spell?"

She shook her head. "No, I read most of the chapters before it."

Hemingway pressed his hands to the sides of his head as if he was trying to keep his confusion from overwhelming him. "You read most of that huge book? In the last hour?"

"Well, I learned some studying spells this morning, and they've increased my reading speed," she explained, wondering if she was in trouble for performing spells and reading ahead.

"You learned those studying spells this morning?" Hemingway asked, his tone dripping with disbelief.

"I'm not lying," she fired back, earning attention from some of the other students on the far side of the room, working with their shame plants.

Hemingway brought his hands down, seemingly to try and calm Paris down. "I didn't think you were lying. It's just that…well, this isn't typical behavior from one of our new students."

Paris laughed at this. "I think we've already established that I'm not the typical fairy godmother student."

He nodded. "I realize that, but I didn't know to what extent."

"I think I've had beginner's luck," Paris remarked. "I've never been a good reader, but since getting here, I really enjoy it. I've never had my hands in dirt, so I think having my first experience lent to my success with the fast-growing spell."

"You've never worked with dirt?" He sounded surprised.

"Well, not because I grew up with servants and always had on my pretty coat and lace gloves," she answered. "I grew up on Roya Lane."

The surprise deepened on his face. "I didn't think anyone lived there. I thought it was only shops and official magical offices."

"Well, a few of the shop owners live there," she explained. "But yeah, there's not a lot of residents. And there isn't any dirt, not that I know of."

He nodded in understanding. "Anyway, although it's extremely impressive that you used the fast-growing spell successfully, the idea is to master these mortal skills first before using the shortcuts of magic. If you don't know how to do it, you won't be able to teach your charges."

Paris sighed. "To be honest, I think that teaching my charges how to prune roses and plant gardens won't be my style. Maybe they don't like gardening, and why should that be a skill they have to learn to match with Mr. Right?"

Hemingway nodded, then lowered his chin. "I don't disagree. But that's the curriculum. As I said, there are benefits in you learning how to garden. For instance, one reason I wanted you to grow your sunflowers the old-fashioned way was to teach you about the process. Many can use magic to grow things." He glanced over his shoulder before leaning in closer. "Well, not Becky Montgomery. Everything living seems to hate her, but the point is knowing how to plant a seed and bring it up using love. When you master the art of growth, you master patience, which is important when learning about love—something you'll need to become an expert on."

Paris nodded, thinking the notion made sense. "Okay, I won't use magic until I've mastered the mortal way of gardening."

Hemingway smiled at her before looking proudly at her sunflowers. "Something tells me that it won't take you long. You seem to have a natural green thumb."

She blushed, never expecting gardening to be something she was good at. This was on the ever-growing long list of surprises from her first day attending Happily Ever After College.

CHAPTER FORTY-FIVE

Willow tapped the side of the scrying bowl with a wand and shook her head, clearing the scene with Paris and Hemingway in the greenhouse. "What do you make of these latest developments with our new student?"

Mae Ling glanced casually across the headmistress' desk. "She's a very powerful fairy."

That observation didn't seem to please Willow. She sighed, worry evident on her face. "That's not necessarily a good thing. Too much power in a fairy has been linked to corruptibility. Look at magicians. They've started so many wars because they're so powerful. Fairies tend to be more about making love, which is why we have the job that we do. We don't fight crime like the House of Fourteen or the Dragon Elite or the Rogue Riders."

"Yet, we're not doing the job that we should." Mae Ling pointed at the love meter on the wall—its dial still indicating twenty-five percent.

Willow's mouth tightened. "I realize that, but that doesn't mean that powerful fairies are the answer. Paris is a wild card, and I simply don't know if taking in a new brand of student is what the college needs to turn things around."

Mae Ling tipped her head back and forth, ready to play the devil's advocate, a role she often took with the headmistress. "Or maybe someone like Paris Westbridge is exactly what the college needs. She's already passed Cotillion class on her first day, challenged some of the more archaic practices of astrology, and mastered the fast-growing spell in gardening."

"That's exactly what worries me," Willow muttered while staring at the surface of the scrying bowl, the shimmering water rippling from the last visions of the scene with Paris and Hemingway. "Something isn't right about her."

"I think what you mean is that something is different about her," Mae Ling corrected. "And we both know that we don't do 'different' well here at Happily Ever After College. That's why all the fairy godmothers look the same and the curriculum hardly ever changes. I think we need to remain open-minded. Paris is challenging us and I, for one, think it could be very beneficial."

Willow nodded, still staring off without seeing. "Well, she has one more class and her exam, so we'll see how she does and go from there. Right now, I'd say she's about fifty-fifty. A lot will rest on how she does the remainder of the day."

CHAPTER FORTY-SIX

The demo kitchens were spacious with multiple individual workstations, similar to the greenhouse setup. There were colorful refrigerators along one wall and shelves with all sorts of equipment. The cooking and baking classroom was different than the kitchen that Paris had seen this morning but similar to it. Chef Ash was there, smiling wide when she entered. He was wearing the white uniform she'd seen earlier, the trademark pencil still behind his ear.

"Welcome to your first cooking and baking class," he greeted and handed her a textbook entitled *Magical Cooking and Baking.* "Do you have much experience?"

"Not really," she admitted, having chosen a workstation. "I can make macaroni and cheese and sandwiches."

"That's a good start." He winked and strode to the front of the class, making all the students in their powder blue gowns quiet their conversations. "Welcome back, class. Today, we're going to pick up where we left off. If you haven't mastered your tidy tarts, you'll continue trying to make those today. Many of your tarts didn't clean up a dirty space when consumed but rather had the opposite effect. Wilfred said it took him a long time to clean up this kitchen after some of your endeavors. You might be putting in too much Bavarian sugar if tasting your tart creates a mess, rather than cleans it up. If you've done it right, you shouldn't have any dishes to do and the windows on the 'back wall will be squeaky clean." He laughed, indicating the bank of windows that looked out on the Enchanted Grounds, shimmering light streaming into the demo kitchen.

"If you were successful with your tidy tarts," Chef Ash continued, "you're moving on to making bad temper eraser confections. The recipes for these are quite complicated, so I encourage you to read through them carefully. Any mistakes with these sweet treats won't put someone in a better mood, but as you might have guessed, it will make them even more sour. With magical cooking, if you don't follow a recipe exactly, it will always have the opposite effect as desired, which is why it's such a risky venture."

Paris knew that many relied on magical baking and cooking. There was an interesting place on Roya Lane called Crying Cat Bakery. She'd gone in there a few times, but the owners were strange, sometimes refusing to serve her something, saying that she wasn't ready yet. The two women who ran the bakery also made threats to each other but seemed to do it in a joking way.

Paris never had any experience with magical baking and cooking. Now that she thought about it, Uncle John didn't rely on magic practically at all. He said there was something honest about doing things with his two hands so when he made her breakfast, it was manually. He hadn't taught her many spells or other ways to use her magic, saying that she'd figure out how to use it in time when she was ready. For some reason, people always seemed to say something about "when you're ready" to Paris.

"Now, for our new student," Chef Ash continued, his gaze connecting with Paris. "I know that tidy tarts and bad temper eraser confections sound fun, but I'm going to require that you start with the basics."

"Because I can't progress to magical baking and cooking until I master the basics of doing it the mortal way," she guessed.

"You're quick," Chef Ash cheered, the wrinkles around his eyes surfacing when his grin widened.

Paris shrugged. "I'm catching on."

Chef Ash picked up a spatula on the work surface next to him. "Okay, I'll put all the recipes on your stations. I want you to read through them carefully and don't get started until you know exactly what you're doing from start to finish." He twirled the spatula in the air, and a piece of paper materialized on every individual workstation.

Paris glanced briefly at her recipe for apple pie, reading through it quickly. Realizing that she needed to get started on the pie dough right away, she started for the refrigerators.

"Paris," Chef Ash interrupted her, stepping in front of the refrigerator as she neared. "Although I appreciate your enthusiasm to get started on your apple pie, you need to read through the recipe carefully first."

She nodded. "Yeah, I did. Just like you said."

He gave her a well-meaning smile. "I understand that apple pie isn't as difficult as what the others are working on, but notice that everyone else is still studying their recipes."

Paris glanced over her shoulder where all the other students were still bent over their workstations, reading through their recipes. She turned back to Chef Ash. "I don't know what to tell you. I did as you said and read through my recipe. I know precisely what I need to do and was going to start on the pie crust first so it had time to chill while I was working on the filling."

Chef Ash blinked at her. "You read through the entire recipe? I just gave it to you."

"I did," she answered. "I'm going to get the chilled butter, egg, ice water, and two and a half pounds of apples. Peeling those by hand will take a while, so I was going to start on that straight after the dough."

"You read through the entire recipe," he stated, this time not as a question but still sounding perplexed.

"Did I do something wrong?" She looked around again. Paris had never made an apple pie, but it had to be easier than making a tidy tart or a bad temper eraser confection.

"No, it doesn't seem as though." He stood back and held up his hands. "Well, I'll get out of your way then and let you get to work. Let me know if you have any questions."

Paris had a ton of questions, but they were more about the "why" regarding learning how to bake and cook. However, she reasoned that, similar to gardening, it was about learning a discipline. Again, she didn't think she'd want to teach her charges how to bake so they could land a guy. Maybe they didn't cook or bake, and Prince Charming was the one who kept her fed. This was the twenty-first century after all.

CHAPTER FORTY-SEVEN

E ven without using magic, Paris found that she enjoyed baking. Something was humbling about rolling out the pie dough and getting her muscles into the activity. She also appreciated the chemistry of the process. Chef Ash, watching from nearby, had stated that baking was all about the precision of measurements, whereas cooking relied more on instinct.

She enjoyed the sentiment and found a strange pride when she pulled the completed pie from the oven. It had a perfectly flaky golden crust and smelled deliciously of apples and cinnamon.

"I think you have a natural knack for this." Chef Ash gave her pie a look of appreciation as she put it on the top shelf of the cooling rack. "Of course, the final test is tasting, which happens after dinner tonight. It will be up to your peers to judge whether you got everything right."

Paris gulped, thinking how awkward it would be on her first day to have the other students judging her work. "Well, hopefully, the pie will be cool by then. The recipe says that it takes two hours on a windowsill."

Chef Ash nodded. "Usually, it would. However, that cooling

rack is magic-enhanced, so I suspect your pie is already cool, but we'll still have to wait to cut into it until after dinner."

"Wow, that's handy." She watched as the other students worked on their desserts.

"I'm sure you'll pass today and be able to progress to other, harder recipes," Chef Ash offered, watching as she observed the other students, recognizing the longing in her gaze. Although Paris hadn't understood why she needed to learn baking and cooking, she had enjoyed the class and looked forward to learning magical recipes.

Lost in thought about future lessons and how incredibly magical cooking could be, Paris hardly registered as something small scurried between her and Chef Ash, disappearing behind a bunch of large sacks of flour and sugar in the corner. Paris noticed that whatever it was had wings and large eyes, but that was about it before it disappeared, hiding away.

She and Chef Ash exchanged looks of surprise. She would have investigated, but before she could, running footsteps outside the classroom's open door interrupted them.

Penny, looking nervous and stressed, jerked her head back and forth, searching the classroom. She looked straight at Chef Ash, urgency in her voice. "Have you seen it? If I lose another zonk, I'll be—"

Professor Butcher raced into the students' kitchen and halted, her hands out as she looked back and forth. "Is it in here?" she asked Chef Ash.

"Is what in here?" Chef Ash appeared nonchalant, although Paris sensed he was lying. They'd both seen something fly past them.

"A zonk!" Professor Butcher stated, her frizzy hair whipping in the air as she jerked her head back and forth. She pointed straight at Penny, who was slowly moving along the room, carefully looking around but hiding the act. "This one says she didn't lose her fixer fairy again, but it's not in its cage, which means she's lying. If that's the case and she's lost another zonk, she's out of here. No more Happily Ever After College for you, Penelope Pullman. The guidelines of your scholarship are clear."

Paris' heart sank when a sad look covered the mousey woman's face.

All the other students had looked up to watch the commotion. However, Chef Ash clapped sternly. "Get back to work. Nothing to see here."

Paris was careful not to look toward the flour and sugar bags where she suspected the zonk was hiding.

"Did you see a zonk fly in here?" Professor Butcher demanded.

Chef Ash scratched his head, appearing confused. "Nope. If it did, it snuck by me. Paris and I were focused on her apple pie."

Professor Butcher narrowed her eyes at Paris. "Oh, so you didn't elect to test out of this class because you were too good for it, then?"

Paris shook her head. "No, I think I'll like magical cooking and baking. Chef Ash is a great instructor. Really supportive and not at all condescending."

Anger flared on the professor's face, but Paris didn't care. Shannon Butcher was proving to be a bully. She'd outed Paris in her first class for being a criminal that her uncle got her into the college and now she was bullying Penny, threatening to kick her out of the college for losing a fixer fairy. Paris had never seen a fairy known as a zonk but had heard they were helpful to have around since they found problems and took it upon themselves to repair them using creative solutions. They were really ugly too, which was not something that most races of fairies had a problem with—being the prettier magical race usually.

Prowling around the perimeter of the room, Professor Butcher gave Penny a murderous expression. "When I find that missing zonk, you're going to have to pack your bags, Ms. Pullman."

Penny's glasses fogged up as tears streamed down her cheeks.

Professor Butcher was nearing the area where the zonk was hiding behind the bag of flour and sugar.

"Really," Chef Ash began in an even tone. "I can't allow such distractions in my classroom. I'll keep an eye out for the zonk, but I think you two should return to your class."

"Oh, be quiet, Cook!" Professor Butcher spat, her face red. "Leave real teaching matters to the real instructors."

Paris nearly went off on the fairy godmother right then, but Chef Ash glanced at her, his expression seeming to say, "Don't."

Professor Butcher was poking her head into the shelves full of mixers, looking into large bowls and behind big canisters of spices. She was close to where the zonk had disappeared.

Paris glanced at Penny when the fairy godmother pushed aside some pots and pans on the shelf, still searching. Discreetly, Paris indicated where she suspected the zonk was hiding. Penny's eyes widened with obvious worry. It was only a matter of time before Professor Butcher arrived at that spot.

Probably sensing the angry woman was about to find its hiding spot, the zonk stuck its head out from behind the back, looking back and forth with a jerking motion. The fairy was ugly with large dark eyes and sharp teeth. It didn't look like the helpful fairy that it was supposed to be, but it also appeared terrified of the stomping professor who was about to pluck it from its hiding spot.

Maybe catching the movement out of her peripheral vision, Professor Butcher straightened, her gaze flying in the direction of where the zonk was hiding. She was right in front of the cooling shelf, only a few paces from the bag of flour where the zonk had disappeared once more.

Paris knew they were out of options. Desperate situations called for drastic actions. Making an impromptu decision, Paris subtly flicked her finger and made her cooled apple pie slide off the shelf, tumble through the air, and land directly on Professor Butcher's head.

CHAPTER FORTY-EIGHT

The apple pie filling oozed down Professor Shannon Butcher's head and face as she screamed, earning everyone's attention. The commotion did as Paris had intended and gave Penny the chance to race over and scoop up the hiding zonk, sliding it into the inside pocket of her blue gown. She was smart too and disguised her actions by pretending to run over to the professor who was still screaming and now wiping apple pie off her face.

"Are you okay, Professor?" Penny asked, vibrating from nerves and all the excitement.

The students all seemed to be hiding their laughter as they stared in disbelief at the dramatic situation that kept getting more entertaining. Chef Ash also appeared to be hiding his reaction, which was shock mixed with amusement.

Paris couldn't believe that in two days, she'd dumped a whole pic onto two different people's heads. Only she would get herself into such trouble so quickly.

"You!" Professor Butcher roared, pointing her finger to Paris.

"You did this, didn't you! You knocked that pie off the shelf and onto my head, didn't you?"

Paris kept her face neutral and shook her head. "I think you knocked into the shelf, professor. In your haste to find the zonk, which I don't think is in here."

"Chef, what did you see?" the fairy godmother demanded.

He crossed his arms over his chest, pursing his lips while he thought. "I don't know. So much was happening at once."

"Oh, this is ridiculous!" Professor Butcher yelled. She snapped her fingers, conjuring a dry towel to wipe the dripping apple pie filling off her face. She still wore a crown of pie crust on her frizzy hair. "I know this was you, Paris."

"Why would I do that?" Paris countered.

"I don't know," the fairy godmother seethed. "But this reeks of something you'd do. You've been in trouble since you got here. Why am I not surprised? You belong in jail or Tooth Fairy College. Not here."

Paris shivered. She'd rather go to jail than tooth fairy college.

"Professor," Penny began in a small voice. "Can I help you get cleaned up?"

"No!" the woman screamed, her face blossoming red. "Penny, if and when I find that missing zonk, you're leaving this college too." She rounded back on Paris. "First of all, I'm going to take care of you. The headmistress will hear about this as soon as I get this… this…" She picked out the crust in her strands, eyeing it. "Whatever this is out of my hair."

"Apple pie," Chef Ash supplied. "I thought it was going to be quite good, but now we won't know and can't grade you on it, Paris."

"Well, you could take a forkful off Professor Butcher's face," Paris offered, hiding her laugh.

The fairy godmother fisted her hands by her side. "You won't do any such thing. No one is eating pie off my face! Ever!" With that, the angry woman stomped out of the classroom, leaving a trail of apple pie in her wake.

Penny looked up at Paris, then to her gown as the zonk tried to get loose again. Before Paris could ask if she was okay, Penny fled for the door, her face full of embarrassment.

Paris shook her head and looked at Chef Ash with an apologetic smile. "I'm sorry for that. Thanks for covering for me."

"Covering for you?" he asked. "I didn't see a thing. She might have knocked into the shelf. I had my eye on that darn zonk." The chef winked at Paris with a knowing look in his eyes. "I'm glad Professor Butcher didn't find it. Otherwise, Penny would be gone. She's been gunning to get her kicked out of Happily Ever After College forever, and the girl is down to her last strike."

Paris let out a breath of relief. "Well, then I'm glad too, but I've obviously failed the grading for your class today."

He nodded, remorse on his face. "I'm sorry, it's true. I can't sign off on your full performance without having graded the taste of the pie. Don't worry, you have the final exam tonight, and if you do well on that, it will make up for this."

Paris sighed. "Let's hope because surprisingly, I don't really want to leave here. This place is strange and backward, but I want time to understand it better."

He smiled at her. "I like that you're open-minded like that, although I get that you're different than most of our students, and fitting in here doesn't come naturally to you."

She nodded, twisting her mouth to the side. "Yeah, I'd guess none of the other students have thrown pies on two people's heads in such a short period."

"I don't think anyone ever has, to be honest." He chuckled. "You're going to get quite the reputation. If you stick around after tonight, I'll always be sure to make extra pies."

CHAPTER FORTY-NINE

Willow Starr had half of her face covered with her hands, cringing as she replayed what she and Mae Ling had seen while spying on the magical cooking and baking class from out on the patio. The pair had disguised themselves to look like statues next to the Serenity Gardens so they could watch Paris Westbridge without being noticed.

Coming to life once more and taking on her usual appearance, Willow shook her head. "I can't believe she threw another pie on someone's head."

Mae Ling's brown eyes sparkled with amusement. "We both know that Shannon deserved what she got. She's so mean to Penny and unfair to many students who she thinks don't belong here."

"It's true that she thinks only the crème de la crème of students should be allowed entry to Happily Ever After College," Willow admitted. "But I think she tries to offer some unique expertise."

"I think that it's in your nature to see the best in everyone," Mae Ling countered.

"Regardless." Willow let out a deep sigh. "Paris hasn't made this easy on us. She's under the grade after that performance. Everything will rely on her exam tonight, and she needs to have an exemplary score. Otherwise, my hands are tied, and I'll have to send her back."

"She did make the pie and didn't rely on magic," Mae Ling stated.

"Without tasting it, there's no passable grade." Willow shook her head. "It's regrettable because it was nice watching her today. She doesn't have a healthy respect for rules, but she also has her brand of magic and could do great things here."

"She seems to like it," Mae Ling offered.

"I thought so too." Willow smiled. "We'll have to see how she does tonight. I hope she makes a true love match. One can't rely on magic to be a fairy godmother. At the end of the day, someone who will promote love has to have a lot of heart, and that's what the test will prove."

CHAPTER FIFTY

P aris should have expected all the whispers and looks when she entered the dining hall for dinner, but it would take some getting used to. The sad reality, she thought, was that she wouldn't have a chance to get used to it because it didn't seem likely that she'd pass as Headmistress Starr said was necessary for her to stay at Happily Ever After College.

Not at all hungry but knowing that she needed to eat before her final exam, Paris filled her plate with crispy chicken tenders, green beans, and French fries. She got more than a few looks for taking a second heaping pile of green beans, one of her favorite vegetables. She reminded herself that fairy godmothers in training were encouraged not to fill up on green vegetables so they didn't spoil their appetite for dessert.

"You've now made two pie heads." Hemingway slid into the chair next to Paris. She was about to reply when Christine took the seat on the other side of her.

"I heard that Chef Ash refuses to make pie anymore after the incidents," she said in a conspiratorial whisper.

"That's exactly why you shouldn't listen to the gossip mill

around this place." Chef Ash took the seat directly across from them and winked at Paris. "I'm thinking of doubling the pie quota now."

"Why pies?" Christine asked. "Do you come from a family of clowns?"

"Not that I know of." Paris laughed and sipped her water, her ears hot from all the attention. "They were what was available at the moment."

"I like it." Hemingway tore his bread into pieces and took a bite. "Pies are soft and sweet and don't cause much damage."

"You could have chosen something much more dangerous," Chef Ash offered.

"Yeah, like a candlestick or a wrench," Christine whispered while looking around the table. Most attention was on the four-some, mainly because of Paris in their midst.

"What is this? A game of Clue?" Paris laughed. "I'm not Madam Peacock killing people in the library."

"No, but you're getting the retribution that we've all longed for," Christine said longingly.

"Well, we will see," Paris said in a low voice. "My impulsive behavior might have gotten me kicked out. We'll wait and see. Any clues you all can give me about the exam?"

"You're a special case," Chef Ash answered. "This isn't a typical orientation day for a student, so no, I'm not aware of how they're testing you."

"Follow your instinct, and I'm sure you'll be fine," Hemingway offered.

Christine snickered, "If all else fails, throw a pie at your problems."

Paris sighed. "I can't wait to go to sleep tonight. This has been the longest day in the history of days."

Hemingway nodded. "I love sleep. My life tends to fall apart when I'm awake, you know?"

She tilted her head at him. "It does? I didn't take you as the train wreck type."

He laughed. "It's a quote from Ernest Hemingway—the real Hemingway. I like to throw them into conversations now and again."

"You're as real a Hemingway as he was," Paris corrected. "Have you read all of his books since you're his namesake?"

"What type of man would it make me if I hadn't read a book written by the man I'm named after?" He popped a piece of bread into his mouth.

"Yeah, I don't know."

"No, seriously." He laughed. "That's the type of man I am. I'm the guy named after Hemingway who has never read one of his books. I've tried, but they aren't for me. I can never get into them."

"But you quoted him," Paris argued.

"Yeah, that's right," he affirmed. "I've researched him and like his one-liners. He has some insightful quotes I like to throw into conversations when they fit, but I've never been able to get through one of his books. I'll keep trying."

Paris nodded. "I can understand. Not until today could I read a book. Now I've read three almost."

"In one day?" He gave her that look of surprise like before in the greenhouse.

Again Paris felt like he didn't believe her. Deciding deflecting was better, she said, "If it makes you feel better, I'm named Paris, and I've never been there."

He scratched his head. "Why not portal there?"

She shrugged. "I didn't get a chance to leave Roya Lane much before this. My uncle is pretty protective. Plus I was always afraid of the trouble I'd find if I went off on my own."

Hemingway laughed at this. "It does seem to follow you around. I understand. I've never traveled. Haven't been outside of Happily Ever After College."

"Really?" she asked. "You were born here?"

He nodded. "Yeah, and what better place to grow up and live than in this bubble? Besides, traveling is more fun when you have someone to do it with."

Suddenly Paris sensed a loneliness in Hemingway and knew there was a complicated story behind his upbringing at Happily Ever After College. It didn't seem right to pry right then, not knowing him that well. However, she hoped that today wasn't her last at the college and she'd get a chance to learn more about him. Paris hoped she could learn more about many at the college and several of the subjects. Everything rested on the final exam.

CHAPTER FIFTY-ONE

"Good thing that packing won't take much time." Paris looked out the open window at the Enchanted Grounds from her bedroom. The sun was setting, and the stars were twinkling in the clear, cloudless sky.

"That sounds like a defeatist mentality." Faraday nibbled on the cheese and cracker plate that Paris had gotten for him from the kitchen.

She glanced over her shoulder at the squirrel, grimacing at the many crumbs he was getting into the sock drawer. "I'm just mentally trying to prepare."

"I find," he began while eating the crackers like a beaver sawing down logs for their dam, "that what we prepare ourselves for becomes our reality. If you want something to happen, then you set yourself up for that to inevitably happen."

Paris shook her head. "Sorry, but my life has never been that fairytale thing. I'm realistic, and it's doubtful that I'll pass the exam with a high enough grade to make up for my performances today in classes."

"Because you challenged your first instructor, testing out of her class and insulting the curriculum, or is it because you argued with the astrology instructor?" He cocked his head, his large eyes full of curiosity.

"How do you know about that?" Paris blinked at him.

"Well, I have good ears, and the incident in Cotillion class was all over the school by mid-morning," he explained. "Then I was using the telescope in the observatory during the astrology class in the auditorium, and I overheard the whole exchange."

"Why were you, a squirrel, using a telescope?" Paris questioned.

Faraday crammed a whole cracker into his mouth. "There wasz somein' shiny inside it got my attention," he said while chewing, as crumbs flew from his lips.

Paris shook his head. "You're such a strange squirrel. What did you do today?"

"Nothing," he chirped.

"Yeah, playing with huge telescopes and listening to gossip around the college sounds like nothing," she muttered.

"Do you think that because you cheated in the gardening class or tossed your pie at Professor Butcher is why you'll flunk out of Happily Ever After College?" he asked,

She looked back out the window at the pristine grounds. "How do you know about either one of those incidents? The one in the greenhouse shouldn't be the topic of gossip since no one but Hemingway and I were aware of it."

"Would you believe me if I told you I spied on the events when I was foraging in the back of the greenhouse?"

"I thought we already established that you don't forage," she countered. "Yes, I think that my various mistakes throughout the day are why I'm going to get booted."

"I'm not sure I see the choices you made as mistakes," he offered. "That seems like a harsh view. It seems to me that you made some interesting strides today, testing out of a class in a single day, reading three books, making a pie, and possibly a few friends for the first time."

She turned and put her back to the window. "How do you know that I read three books? And that I made friends? Or that I didn't have any to begin with?"

"You'll remember that you were alone on Roya Lane when we met, saying goodbye to imaginary friends," he answered.

Paris wrapped her arms across her chest in a challenging fashion. "And the rest of my questions?"

He shrugged. "I'm an observer. It's what I do. There's not much more interesting at this college right now than Paris Westbridge."

"I thought you came here to study this college that exists in a bubble," she challenged.

"I did," he admitted. "I've been all over today, learning all about the ins and outs of this place. It just so happens that wherever I go, I hear things about you. If you didn't know, you have people talking."

"I did know," she stated dryly.

"If it helps, if you have to leave here, I'll leave with you," he said consolingly.

"What?" Paris questioned, shocked to hear the squirrel offer that. "You wanted to come here to do research or whatever secret mission you have up your sleeve."

"I don't have any sleeves," he corrected, holding up his tiny arm. "Squirrel, remember?"

"My point is that you wanted to come here when I didn't," she stated. "You don't have to leave because I get kicked out."

"Well, you haven't gotten kicked out yet," he argued. "Our deal was that I come with you because you didn't want to go or go alone. So if you have to leave, I'll go with you."

"Okay." She drew out the word. "But I don't have a lot of socks at my place on Roya Lane and can't afford to have them all ruined."

"Oh, which reminds me," he squeaked. "I got you some new socks. With no holes."

"How fancy," she joked with a laugh as a knock sounded on the door, making both of them tense.

CHAPTER FIFTY-TWO

Paris cautiously pulled open the door, wondering if she was late for her exam. Talk about a way to put a nail in her coffin. She thought she had another half hour, but she might have got the schedule wrong.

To her surprise, she found Penny Pullman on the other side, her chin down and a shy expression on her face. "I'm sorry if I'm bothering you. I just..." She looked around Paris as if she saw something in the room behind her. "Did I hear you talking to someone a moment ago?"

Paris' hand tensed on the doorknob. "Yep," she admitted. "Myself. I was talking to myself, giving myself a pep talk."

"Oh, I thought I heard you laughing," Penny admitted.

Paris gritted her teeth together. If she and Faraday stayed, they had to be more careful. "Yeah, I was laughing. The problem with talking to myself is that I'm mouthy and tease myself. It's all very strange."

Penny smiled at that. The small young woman with mousey features was quite beautiful when she smiled, the gesture transforming her face. "I wish I was that entertaining by myself. I don't think I could talk to myself, let alone make myself laugh."

"Well, my jokes are pretty bad," Paris teased.

"Anyway, if you have a moment, I wanted to come by to apologize." Penny's voice was low and full of shame. "You're in all this trouble because of me, and I never meant for you to get punished for it."

Paris sighed, leaning against the door. "No, don't. This isn't your fault at all. I accept full responsibility. I'm the one who dropped the banana cream pie on Becky's head and the apple pie on Professor Meanie Face's head."

Penny laughed, covering her mouth. "I didn't think there would be any better a sight than Becky getting covered in banana cream, and then you launched that apple pie at Professor Butcher. It was the best twenty-four hours of my life."

Paris beamed, grateful that even if she was leaving, she'd made a difference for this girl who obviously didn't know how to stand up for herself. Maybe that would change. If Paris stayed at Happily Ever After College, she'd teach Penny to fight her own battles and not be Becky's and Professor Butcher's punching bag. Maybe she'd teach her to throw an actual punch. A fairy godmother might need that skill at some point, she reasoned, although she didn't know when or how.

"Well, I'm glad I was able to help," Paris finally said when an uncomfortable silence rose between the two, brought on by Penny's always nervous demeanor.

"That's my real question," Penny dared to ask, flushing pink for being so bold. "Why did you help me? Today, it ruined your project and messed up your assessment. Why did you risk your place here at Happily Ever After College for me?"

Paris had to think about this for a moment. She tilted her head, laying it against the open door. "I'll admit that it was an impromptu decision and I knew otherwise you'd get in trouble and lose your scholarship. I guess, in the back of my mind, I figured I was probably going home either way. I'm not sure I'm right for this place, or maybe it's not right for me. But you're here and deserve the chance to stay, so I figured I could help you."

Penny's smile again made her look girlish and carefree, not a tame woman with tons of worries. "You're the type of people I thought fairy godmothers were before coming here. Someone who fights for others, giving them a chance they couldn't create for themselves."

For some reason, these words that were supposed to make Paris feel better made her feel a lot worse. She didn't think she was at all fairy godmother material. Paris feared that she'd given Penny the wrong impression. Maybe a false hope. Paris wasn't someone who fought and gave others chances. Usually, she got herself into a world of trouble, created some damage to public property fighting with a giant, and gave her Uncle John a headache.

"Look, I appreciate that, but I'm a rebellious girl who was looking for a second chance," Paris admitted. "I'm not all that you're making me out to be. Besides, I'm probably not good enough to keep my place here at Happily Ever After College. So although it was nice meeting you, I'll probably be gone soon."

The sadness that etched itself on Penny's face was immediate. "I hope you don't leave. You make this place better, and not just because you put Becky in her place and saved me with Professor Butcher."

"But that's part of it, isn't it?" Paris grinned.

"Well, yeah," Penny admitted. "But since you've been here, those who used to smile less, smile more. Those who used to scowl most of the time, well, they scowl more. I like what you do to Happily Ever After College and would like to see you stick around. I'd like to see how you fix things."

Paris shook her head. "I'm no zonk," she joked. "I don't think anyone would call me a fixer, but thanks."

"Well, I won't keep you," Penny said sheepishly. "I know you have an exam. I hope it goes well and just wanted to say thank you for helping me. If I could repay you, well, I would. Maybe there will be an opportunity."

"Don't let others push you around," Paris stated. "That's payment enough. But thanks."

Penny offered her one last tame smile and turned, striding back down the hallway.

Paris closed the door and pushed her back against it, grateful she had made a difference at the college, if only for one person. That was enough.

CHAPTER FIFTY-THREE

The Enchanted Grounds were lit with tiki torches when Paris exited the conservatory, finding the same temperature as when she was outside during the daylight hours. It was weird to think she'd been at Happily Ever After less than two days when it already felt like so long, and still, there was so much she wanted to explore.

Shaking off the distractions of her thoughts, Paris started toward the open grassy area where she saw Headmistress Starr, Mae Ling, and many of the other professors congregated. Paris was grateful she didn't have to perform this exam in front of too many people.

She turned to look back at the manor and spied dozens of faces pressed to various windows, all of their eager eyes on Paris.

"So much for thinking I'll have any privacy," she muttered as she spun back and strode for the congregation of fairy godmothers. Wilfred, Chef Ash, and Hemingway were all present, which again didn't make her feel any better.

"Thank you for joining us," Headmistress Starr began. "This is your exam at the end of your first day. Since your entry into

Happily Ever After College isn't a typical one, we felt it necessary to ascertain that you are in fact right to become a fairy godmother. Is this college still a place that you want to be?"

Paris hadn't expected the question, although it was very straightforward. However, it made her feel vulnerable. If she said yes and failed the exam, would she feel dumb afterward? If she said no, would that be what disqualified her? She didn't know.

Finally, she said, "I'd like the opportunity to see if I'm a good fit. After one day, it doesn't feel like enough time."

The headmistress nodded. "That's fair. Throughout your first day, you were excellent at things that have taken students years to master and not so good at things that only required a little effort from you. So now our job is to see if you have the heart for this place. I believe there are many different methods a fairy godmother can employ to be successful, as you've demonstrated today and argued against. However, a fairy godmother must be able to make two people find love. There's no way around that."

A nervous tickle ran up Paris' throat. She didn't know where this was going, but with each passing moment, she was getting more nervous—an emotion she wasn't prone to. For that reason, Paris worked hard not to look at anyone else behind the head-mistress. She couldn't bear to see Professor Shannon Butcher scowling at her or Hemingway offering her a sideways smile or Chef Ash giving her an encouraging look or Mae Ling's studious expression. Paris didn't want to let any of them down. Also, she didn't want to give Professor Butcher the satisfaction of knowing that she flustered her.

"Your challenge for this exam is simple and complex." Head-mistress Starr pulled a wand from her blue gown. She pointed at one side of the grassy lawn beside Paris and from the ground sprang up the figure of a woman. She then pointed at the opposite side, roughly fifteen feet away, and a man shot up out of nowhere. "To complete this exam successfully, all you must do is help these two matches find love. They're holograms and therefore not real, but they're programmed to act in a prescribed manner. For your purposes, you should know that they're compatible, already have calculated chemistry, and on paper should form a very happy couple. However, a fairy godmother's biggest challenge is always trying to get two people who should be together on the same page. It isn't as easy as putting two well-suited people together so they fall in love. Many complicated factors inevitably get in the way. Your job is to help them to overcome that so true love can blossom. With that, we'll allow you to play matchmaker. Best of luck, Paris."

The headmistress took a step backward, leaving Paris standing between an illusion of a Cinderella and a Prince Charming, making her feel more pressure than she'd ever felt before.

CHAPTER FIFTY-FOUR

"Heeeeyyy," Paris sang while nervously looking between the woman and the man, who both stood somewhat stoically. However, there was no doubt that affection for each other radiated in their eyes. Paris didn't know what chemistry looked like, but it felt like they were drawn to one another. The question for her was how did she push two people together who were meant to be with one another?

Shouldn't they be with each other if they were meant to be? she reasoned. But then, where was the job of fairy godmothers? No, there had to be more to it than that. That meant sometimes people were supposed to be together, but something prevented them. And that's hopefully the job the fairy godmothers served.

So how do I get these two who have the hots for each other to get over their nervousness and match up? Paris thought while looking between the two lovers, realizing that all the professors' eyes were on her, which did little to help her nervousness.

She waved the illusion of the guy over. "Hey, come over here. I have someone I want you to meet."

He glanced over his shoulder and back, pointed at his chest, and mouthed the word, "Me?"

"Yes, you," Paris answered with a grunt.

The guy's gaze darted to the woman on the other side of Paris, then to her. He slid his hands into his pockets and casually but cautiously strode forward. The girl pushed her hair behind her ear, a cute little flirty gesture as she regarded the ground.

"There we go." Paris looked between the pair when the guy had closed the distance. "This is…" Paris held her hand out to the girl.

She coughed nervously. "Cheryl."

"Great," Paris stated. "And this is…" She looked at the guy.

"Phillip," he supplied.

"Perfect." Paris suddenly felt like this might be easy. "Cheryl, this is Phillip."

They nodded at each other, averting their gazes as if they were afraid of one another.

Realizing that these two had a spark that she could feel radiating between them but were going to make this difficult, Paris chewed on her lip. This was the question. How did she get two people together who had a connection? The answer seemed obvious, and yet, she didn't know what to do.

"So Phillip, you're into…" Paris let the sentence trail off, hoping he'd answer it.

"Boxing," he answered diligently.

"Great," Paris said. "And Cheryl, you're into?"

"Classic poetry," the woman supplied.

Paris deflated. *Oh, perfect,* she thought sarcastically. *What better way to connect and fall in love than discussing one's interests in boxing and classic poetry?*

Phillip regarded Cheryl with keen interest, his eyes lustful for her. The way that Cheryl swayed reminded Paris of how girls acted when pining for a guy's affections. There was something between them, but how did she get them to explore that? To fall and cross the gap toward each other.

Maybe she was trying too hard, Paris reasoned.

"Anyway," she said with a jovial laugh. "I got two tickets to the boxing match tonight, followed by dinner at a place called Shakespeare. I can't go, and was hoping that you two would take my tickets and reservations? Seems like the perfect type of date for you two."

Cheryl twisted her lips in hesitation. "I have to get up early tomorrow morning."

Phillip jerked his head to the side, looking away. "Yeah, and I better not go out. I have a lot of work to do."

Paris deflated, wondering if she should shove one of the love birds into the other. Maybe that would seal the deal. "Okay, well, how about this? We make it an early night. Just a drink? My treat. At a sports bar? Wine bar? Wherever you all want."

Cheryl nervously pushed her hair behind both ears at once. "I shouldn't…Tomorrow…"

"You have to get up early," Paris muttered dryly.

"Yeah, and I shouldn't either," Phillip stated regretfully, that longing still bouncing around in his eyes.

"You have work," Paris added, disappointed.

"Sorry, maybe another time." Cheryl took a step backward.

"Yeah, I wish it had worked out," Phillip offered, also stepping backward.

The two were moving away from each other to Paris' horror. She jerked her head back and forth, looking between the two figures that were now farther apart than when they started.

"Wait," she said, suddenly desperate, wondering what she could do to make them fall in love. Her head jerked back and forth, but her mind didn't come up with a solution. Within seconds, both the man and woman had disappeared, leaving Paris alone and with a very heavy weight on her heart—she'd failed her exam.

CHAPTER FIFTY-FIVE

"Paris," Headmistress Starr said in a sensitive voice, stepping up next to her. "I'm sorry to inform you that you've failed your exam."

Paris couldn't help it. Her head automatically fell, hanging low in defeat.

"Unfortunately, after your performance today in the classes, combined with your exam results," Willow stated, "that means that you can't attend Happily Ever After College. It doesn't seem that you'd be a good fit for our curriculum or in the role of a fairy godmother. This is very regrettable, but I hope you've enjoyed your time here."

Paris couldn't bear to look at the headmistress or the professors behind her. It was strange that in such a short period, many people had already felt like they could be friends. Paris had hope for her future there. She had wanted one at Happily Ever After College, but now that felt like a dream that she shouldn't have gotten attached to, especially so quickly.

Unwilling to look at anyone or the manor where all the students were probably looking out the windows at Paris failing, she turned to face the conservatory. She was grateful that she didn't have any possessions she needed to retrieve. That would make leaving that much easier.

"I understand." Paris held her chin high and looked at the glassed-in room. "Thanks for the opportunity. I'll show myself out."

Behind her, she heard Willow draw in a breath. "But…"

Before Headmistress Starr could fully object, Paris set off, striding forward through the conservatory, down the long hallway, and for the front door to FGE. Faraday would meet her on the front lawn. Then they'd portal back to Roya Lane, where unfortunately, Paris would have to tell her Uncle John that she'd failed and had to go to jail. That was the worst part for her. Not going to jail. She could deal with that. Disappointing him, that hurt the most.

Paris' hand was on the handle for the front door, and she was almost free of FGE when a voice sounded behind her.

"Before you leave, I have something I need to say," Mae Ling said, her voice urgent.

CHAPTER FIFTY-SIX

Paris froze with the door half-opened. She turned slowly, deciding that if she was going to look at anyone—talk to anyone at the college, it would be Mae Ling. She'd seemed to have Paris' best interests at heart. *Or maybe she was the reason she was leaving now,* she thought. If Paris had behaved and not been herself, maybe she wouldn't be in this predicament.

"I don't think this is over," Mae Ling stated.

"I think it's better not to hold onto unrealistic expectations," Paris countered. "You told me to be myself and speak out if I didn't like something. I did that, and as you can see, it didn't work out. Now I move on."

"I also said that I would protect you," Mae Ling argued. "I said if you did as I asked, that you wouldn't be expelled from the college."

"And yet I am." Paris uttered a rude laugh and threw her arms wide. "I appreciate your help, but I think this is hopeless. I obviously don't fit in here."

Mae Ling shook her head. "I think we all need a little time to figure out how we fit together. How about you go back to Roya

Lane and unwind and rethink things? Don't tell your uncle anything. Reevaluate. See if anything occurs to you. Then, once you've had a little time to cool down, maybe you'll return and reconsider the situation."

"I don't see what the point is," Paris argued.

"Well, that's why getting some perspective might help."

"So let me get this straight," Paris began. "You want me to go get a drink because that's how I'll magically get to see things better? Are you encouraging confused and frustrated people to drink away their problems?"

A slight smile curved up the edges of Mae Ling's mouth. "It's not as much about the drink as it is about a change in scenery. I think that if you get a chance to think, you might come back with a different perspective."

"Come back?" Paris asked. "I can't get back here."

"You can though," Mae Ling corrected. "As a student at Happily Ever College, you can portal here now."

"But I'm not a student anymore," Paris stated.

"You are," Mae Ling countered. "Until midnight, you are. As long as you return by then, you'll be able to portal back here."

"I don't understand why," Paris stated. "What's the point? I failed. I tried, and it didn't work out."

"It hasn't worked out yet," Mae Ling offered. "Sometimes, what we need to overcome where we've failed is simply to unlock something inside us."

Paris didn't know what that meant, but a drink did sound like a great idea. If nothing brilliant occurred to her, she'd sneak into the apartment and fall asleep and explain her worsened predicament to Uncle John the next morning. That was the last thing she wanted to do, which meant she hoped that she unlocked this thing Mae Ling referred to.

CHAPTER FIFTY-SEVEN

Paris was gone for less than a minute when Mae Ling pulled the cell phone from her pocket. The head professor of Happily Ever After College had locked herself in the sitting room after throwing Casanova, the orange, snooping cat, out of there before closing the door.

She pulled back the curtains on the front window, watching as Paris strode for the center of the lawn where she'd open a portal. Beside her, a small woodland creature scurried to keep up with her.

Mae Ling pressed the cell phone to her ear, hoping the person on the other end didn't keep her waiting. Now wasn't the time for him to be ditzy. Thankfully he answered after three rings.

"She's ready for you," Mae Ling said into the phone. "Be at the bar within the hour. You remember what you're supposed to do?"

The person on the other side of the line replied, offering way more information than was necessary.

Mae Ling nodded. "Okay, do as I instructed you. Right now, this all rests on your shoulders. You can't fail her. Otherwise, we all stand to lose so much. Tell her what she needs to know, but no more."

He replied, and Mae Ling shut off the cell phone.

There was nothing else for her to do at this point. Everything that had led up to this had all been conjecture. Planning and instigating this had been complicated, but it had worked out because maybe, it was supposed to go this way. There was no fate, but some things were destined—like that a very special fairy if given all the right chances, could save love in the world.

Mae Ling hoped desperately that this was destined to come true.

CHAPTER FIFTY-EIGHT

I t was more than evident to Paris that Mae Ling knew something she wasn't letting on. From the beginning, the small, unassuming fairy godmother had instigated something with her advice to Paris. Oddly, Paris trusted her. It didn't at all seem like she was trying to sabotage her if she was telling her to rethink things and return.

Paris had three hours until midnight. She didn't know what brilliant decision could magically occur to her in that time that would change her performance at the college or the headmistress' ruling. Of course, Paris had woken up that morning feeling taller, enjoyed reading for the first time, and discovered she was good at a bunch of things she didn't know about. So she reasoned that anything was possible.

"What are you going to do now?" Paris asked Faraday as they both stood on the Enchanted Grounds of Happily Ever After, looking at the spinning portal that led to Roya Lane. She was hesitating, and they both knew it.

"I'm going to go get a drink as we were told," he stated as if it was obvious.

"First of all, how did you hear about that?" She narrowed her eyes at the talking squirrel.

He sighed. "The door to FGE was open, and I have good ears. You talk loudly, and I'm a master of observation."

Paris grunted and watched the shimmering colors of her portal. "I don't talk loudly."

"When you're excited, you do," he corrected.

"You've never seen me excited since I haven't been since we met…two days ago," she stated dryly.

"It was more of a generalization," he explained. "In the average person, when they get excited, levels of adrenaline spike, which increases oxygen and glucose flow. It also dilates pupils and suppresses non-urgent systems. Excitement extends through to the sympathetic nervous system, increasing heart rate, breathing and causing all reactions to be heightened, i.e., louder volume when talking, sensitivity to stimulus and other factors."

"Serious question," Paris retorted on the heels of his monologue.

The squirrel simply blinked at her.

"Are you a figment of my imagination?"

Faraday considered this. "That's a rational conclusion based on the fact that you met me during a traumatic time in your life when you were searching for a coping mechanism. Also, to further support your point, no one but you has seen or talked to me when in your presence, so it would go to reason that I'm not real and am a product of your imagination."

"Then there's the whole, you talk like a scientist and not like a rodent," she quipped.

"Scientist?" he questioned at once. "You think I talk like a scientist?" The squirrel put his paws to his mouth, made a chirping sound, and flicked his tail. "It's probably because I once lined my bed with a magazine called *Popular Science*. I had trouble sleeping that year and read way too many articles on dark matter and the unconscious mind and other boring stuff."

"You don't sound bored by it," she observed, picking up on Faraday's excitement as he spoke.

"Well, you start reading about string theory, and it's a slippery slope," he admitted. "Before too long, you've graduated to other quantum physics theories and stayed up the entire night."

"Most squirrels probably would have torn up the magazine to make confetti strips for their bed," Paris pointed out.

"Similar to you not being like most fairies, I'm not like most squirrels."

"Obviously." Paris still stared at the portal. "Back to my prior question about what you're going to do after returning to Roya Lane."

"I told you," he insisted. "Mae Ling told us to get a drink. I could use one. It was a fantastic idea."

"Okay, I should probably point out that I was the one told to get a drink, not you," Paris stated. "You're not supposed to be at Happily Ever After College. And I'm not sure that it's a good idea for a squirrel to drink. Your liver probably can't take it."

He shot her a look of offense. "I can too drink. I often enjoy a nice tumbler of brandy."

Paris rolled her eyes. "Why am I not surprised?"

"You keep thinking that I should conform to the preconceived notion you have in your head of how squirrels are supposed to act, and I defy that. I refuse to apologize for it."

"We still haven't determined that you aren't a figment of my imagination," Paris argued. "Of course, my imaginary friend would be a squirrel who acts differently than all other squirrels, has a nut allergy, and enjoys the finer things. Maybe instead of going to a bar, I should turn myself into a mental hospital."

"That's inadvisable because those records register in the Fairy Law Enforcement system," he explained matter-of-factly. "If your name comes up on a roster at the Magical Creatures Mental Health Asylum, the authorities will come and get you and put you in jail. The agreement was fairy godmother college or jail."

Paris lowered her chin and regarded the squirrel with hooded eyes. "How do you know so much about how the magical government systems work?"

"I had a friend that went nutters," he explained.

She shook her head. "Was that intended to be an awful pun?"

"It wasn't intended to be a pun, so definitely not a bad one."

"So you had a squirrel friend who went crazy?" The melodic sound of the portal grew louder. She couldn't hold it open much longer, and she was stalling. Funny that two days ago she didn't want to step through the portal to Happily Ever After College, and now she didn't want to take the one back to Roya Lane.

"I want to point out that squirrels don't only have to have squirrel friends," Faraday stated. "You and I are friends. If you're worried that I'm a figment of your imagination, simply ask someone at the bar if they can see me. That will clear things up. I can say something to affirm that my speaking isn't a product of your traumatic situation."

"Will you stop referring to what's happened to me as traumatic?" she argued bitterly.

"I apologize," he squeaked. "I simply thought that for a normal person, having to give up the only home they've ever known, leave behind their family, and enter a brand-new academy that teaches very foreign concepts to your current interests would be defined as traumatic."

"Is this when you define the word for me, you fluffy dictionary?"

"If you'd like," he stated. "Traumatic means shocking, disturbing or distressing. Does that sound relevant to your current situation?"

Paris ignored the question. "Yes, that's a fantastic idea about confirming your existence by asking some stranger in a bar. 'Hey, Mister, I know we don't know each other, but will you tell me if my squirrel friend is real and actually speaking? Why no, I'm not drunk. Why do you ask?'"

"Is this a good time to point out that you're stalling and your portal is about to close?" Faraday asked.

Paris sighed. "I was trying to figure out what to do with you," she lied.

"I'm going to the bar with you," he stated plainly. "Don't worry. I'll stay out of sight until you get us a booth. Preferably a corner one, away from the pool tables and bathrooms. Those are always the rowdiest areas in the bars on Roya Lane."

"Sounds like you're quite the club rat." Paris chuckled.

"Is that a form of a pun?" Faraday asked, quite seriously.

"It is because people who go to clubs that are like bars all the time are called...oh never mind. If I have to explain the joke, it's not funny."

"I don't think that's why it wasn't humorous," he quipped.

"Do you have any other requirements for our outing?" Paris' eyes watered from staring at the bright portal for so long.

"Pick a classy one," he suggested. "Not one on the wrong end of Roya Lane. Something that has a nice brandy selection and doesn't serve nuts on the table."

"Right," Paris intoned. "Fine, I guess you can go with me to the bar. But yes, stay out of sight. It's already highly likely that I'll get kicked out at some point for getting into a fistfight for whatever reason. I don't want to get thrown out prematurely for bringing a rodent into a food establishment with me."

He huffed, offended. "I'm cleaner than most elves."

"Everyone is cleaner than those dirty hippies." Paris realized that the time had come. She needed to leave Happily Ever After College and return to Roya Lane.

She glanced over her shoulder at the large mansion and felt a twinge of remorse. She hoped against all hope that she'd return before midnight—before it was too late.

CHAPTER FIFTY-NINE

It felt like months since Paris had been on Roya Lane, not days. The smells were so different from the floral and fresh ones at Happily Ever After College. The colors of the street compared to the vibrant ones on the Enchanted Grounds seemed dull and boring.

Paris never thought the place she'd grown up would look and feel so foreign to her. She found a shabby chic bar on the "right" side of Roya Lane that she thought met Faraday's requirements. It was called the Tipsy Goat and not the clientele that Paris was used to. She usually found herself in Chimerick's Bar on the bad side of Roya Lane where the beer wasn't cold, but the regulars didn't look at her as though she didn't belong there.

At the Tipsy Goat, it appeared that most of the hipsters had rolled up their pants and buttoned up their shirts for that night's outing.

Paris kept her head down as she breezed to the corner, unaware of where Faraday had disappeared to.

Finding what she thought was a passable booth, Paris pulled the heart-shaped locket Uncle John had given her from her pocket.

She wished it would open for some reason, as if the answers to all her problems hid inside. She turned it over and read the familiar words engraved on the front: "You have to keep breaking your heart until it opens."

Paris sighed, not knowing what Mae Ling thought she was supposed to figure out in a bar on Roya Lane. This all felt ridiculous and a waste of time.

"Just you?" a waitress with too much eyeshadow asked Paris after she took up residence in the oversized corner booth.

She nodded. "Just me is more than enough company for myself," Paris replied, never liking it when hostesses at restaurants said things like, "Only you?" or if Uncle John was joining her, "Just the two of you?" Almost as if a small number in their party was unacceptable or sad.

As she'd expected, the waitress gave Paris a rude look for her comment. "Well, what will *you* be having?"

"I'm having your finest brandy and a rum and coke."

The waitress arched an eyebrow, either because the two drinks were polar opposites or because she'd ordered two drinks, period. "For the brandy, do you want Hennessy or Louis XIII?"

Paris didn't know, but thankfully from under the table she heard, "Louis XIII."

"Yeah, I'll take the King of France," she joked, not earning a laugh from the uptight waitress who took too many YouTube makeup tutorials.

"And for your rum?" the waitress asked, unamused. "You want Bacardi or top shelf?"

"Let's go with well." Paris realized she didn't have that much money. "But make it a double."

"Well rum and Louis XIII brandy." The waitress shook her head. "That makes perfect sense."

"The brandy is for my stuffy squirrel friend," Paris called after the waitress, realizing that once she was back on Roya Lane she didn't care about perception, not that she was overly concerned about it at Happily Ever After College.

"Smooth," Faraday stated dryly from under the table.

"How is this booth? Is it to your liking?" Paris watched as the squirrel climbed onto the seat next to her, still unnoticed by the crowd in the busy bar.

"There's gum on the floor," he stated.

"What flavor?" she asked immediately, pretending to be curious.

"Haha," he said dryly. "I don't think the waitress believed you about having a squirrel friend."

Paris nodded. "I'm going to start telling people the truth. Since it sounds like a lie, they'll think I'm making it up."

"You really are trying to get admitted to the Magical Creatures Mental Health Asylum, aren't you?"

She rolled her eyes at him. "I hope you have some money because otherwise, we're going to have to drink and dash."

"Classy," he muttered. "I'm sure we'll be okay."

"What's that supposed to mean?" She picked up on a strange tone in his voice.

"Nothing." He dove down as the waitress strode over with two drinks.

"Keep a tab open or close it?" the waitress asked.

"Put it on mine," a smooth, refined voice said as a very handsome fae materialized, a drink in one hand and his arm draping around the waitress' shoulder. Paris knew he was a fae because he was so attractive it almost hurt to look at him. He had shiny blond hair, bright blue eyes, perfectly balanced features, and wore a pink shirt that she was pretty sure he stole off a life size Barbie doll. Like her, he'd glamoured his wings not to appear and probably also to keep them out of the way in the crowded bar.

The guy winked at the uptight woman. "And bring my new friend a new rum and Coke, but with top shelf, please, Brenda."

The waitress shrugged the fae's arm off her. "I told you my name isn't Brenda."

"You look like a Brenda," he argued. "Grow out your hair if you want to look like Bridgette. Get lip enhancements if you want to be a Brittany."

The waitress shook her head furiously and strode back to the bar.

Paris shook her head at the stranger who had offered to buy her drinks and boldly ordered her a better one. She didn't want to rely on the kindness of a stranger, and yet, she didn't want her Uncle John called because some bum couldn't pay their bar tab. That wasn't the way she wanted him to find out that she'd been kicked out of Happily Ever After College.

Holding up the glass of rum and Coke at the fae, she smiled. "Thanks for the drink." She threw back her head and slammed most of it in one gulp, the bubbles tickling her throat and the rum burning in her stomach.

"Noooo," the fae yelled, diving forward, grabbing Paris' wrist to stop her. Right then, he nearly got his nose broken. Instead, she drew back, the almost empty drink an inch from her mouth.

"What's your deal, Weirdo?" she asked the guy, who had large eyes.

He shook his head, daring to take the drink that he'd bought her from her hands. "I got you something that you can drink. There's no reason to put that poison in your body."

"It's rum," she argued. "It's not like I was confusing it with beet juice or something else that's healthy. I know what I'm getting myself into."

He put the drink on the table and sighed. "We always have a choice. Put high-end alcohol into our bodies or low-grade stuff."

"Some of us don't have that choice, Richie Rich." She grabbed the glass before he could stop her, Paris' reflexes faster. She threw the rest of the drink back, draining the glass.

He pursed his lips and shook his finger at her. "You're a defiant one, aren't you? I should have guessed as much."

Paris gave him a confused look as the waitress brought the new drink, depositing it in front of her. "I don't know what that means, Intruder, but thanks for the drink. I hope you're not expecting me to be nice to you in return."

He nodded and slid into the other side of the booth. "Nope. I have to admit that I'm enjoying the name-calling. It's been a long time...too long."

Paris sighed and drank from her new glass. "You're sitting now..."

"Yeah, standing is tough." He sipped his drink. "Anyway, no need to be nice to me. I'm only the king of the fae."

Paris nearly spat out her drink but thankfully didn't waste the rum on the table. "You're what? How drunk are you?"

"Since when?" He lowered his drink, showing her a serious expression. "Since the beginning of the twenty-first century, or since the seventh? Because I really hit my stride in the last few decades."

Paris leaned forward. "Wait, you're serious? You're the king of the fae? What are you doing here? In a bar...on Roya Lane? Don't you have a kingdom?"

He nodded. "I have a huge kingdom with champagne-filled lazy rivers and chocolate fountains and a bunch of fae who tell me how wonderful I am. It's all very boring."

"Sounds rough," Paris said dryly.

"Anyway, let's back up, shall we?" He offered a hand across the table. "King Rudolf Sweetwater at your service."

Paris simply flashed a polite smile at the offered hand. "Pleased to meet you, King. I'm Paris Westbridge. I'd shake your hand, but I haven't washed mine in a while."

He nodded. "It's been a few years for me too."

She grimaced. "I meant an hour."

"Anyhow," the king sang casually, "I'm here to hang out with my people in the real world. Sadly it's been a long time. I wasn't allowed on Roya Lane because meanie Daddy Time said so. He totally banished me from Roya Lane, but today that all changed."

Paris took a drink. "Am I supposed to know what you're talking about?"

King Rudolf shrugged. "Probably not. Most don't."

"Pssst," Faraday said from beside Paris on the booth seat, still out of sight.

She glanced down, seeing the squirrel pointing at his drink on the table.

"Oh," she chirped, remembering his brandy. She grabbed it and slid it under the table.

King Rudolf, spying this, gave her a curious look.

"I'm giving this to my squirrel," she explained.

He nodded as if this made perfect sense. "Whatever floats your boat. I sometimes hoard drinks but say they're for the baby. No one is going to argue with you on that one. We all know how difficult it is to take alcohol from a baby, as the popular saying goes."

Paris wondered for a moment if English was the king's second language…or maybe third or fourth. "I think it's candy. It's as easy as taking candy from a baby."

He laughed. "That's wrong. Everyone knows babies aren't allowed to have candy."

Paris looked down at the squirrel sipping the brandy, wondering if Faraday found this exchange as strange as she did.

"Well, thanks for the drink." Paris held up her glass to King Rudolf. "I don't want to keep you from your party or your kingdom or anything at all."

The fae waved her off. "No worries on that. My party ordered me away from the table. Apparently, I offended them." King Rudolf indicated a nearby table where three gorgeous girls sat, all shooting daggers at him with their eyes. One had brown hair, another blonde, and the third was strawberry blonde.

"Are they mad because you took them all out at once?" Paris

had heard about the promiscuous ways of the fae and never fully understood it.

He shook his head. "Oh, no. They prefer that I take them all out together. That's not why they're mad."

King Rudolf patted his lap and smiled at the table of angry women. "Come on. Don't be mad at me. Why don't you come and sit on Daddy's lap?"

Paris pushed back in the booth, totally shocked. "Wow, well, maybe that's why they're angry at you if you talk to them like that."

"Oh, you think?" King Rudolf asked. "I could try something different." He looked at the table again. "Hey, Boo Boo. Who's your Daddy?"

Paris took a drink to keep herself from punching the king of the fae, which would no doubt put her in jail, no passing "Go," no collecting a toothbrush, or anything else. "You realize that it's super offensive to call yourself their daddy?"

He spun to face her. "I tried to get them to call me King Rudolf, but ever since they were babies, it's been 'Daddy this' and 'Daddy that.' Children do whatever they want regardless."

Paris nearly slammed down her glass with disbelief. "Wait. Those ladies...those are your children?"

CHAPTER SIXTY

"Yeah, but they're mad at me," King Rudolf admitted, finishing his drink and holding the glass in the air to get the waitress' attention. "Another round, Brenda!"

The waitress looked over from the bar and shook her head, but Paris assumed she'd be over with the drinks shortly. Who would defy the king of the fae? Well, besides his daughters.

"You're so young, and they're so young...I didn't think..." Paris found herself nearly at a loss.

"Oh, well, I'm full blooded fae so I'll be hot until the day I die," he explained. "They will pretty much too, but they're halflings, which is why they're mad at me. Apparently, I'm in trouble for them being born. Sue me!"

Paris glanced down at Faraday, wondering if he was making sense of any of this. The squirrel was doing an impressive job finishing his brandy and seeming to enjoy it. "I'm sure I'll regret asking this, but can you back up and explain what happened and why your children are over there scowling at you?"

He nodded as Brenda, or whatever the waitress' name was, brought another round of drinks, including another brandy for

Faraday, although Paris wasn't sure he needed it. "About six hundred years ago, I was born—"

"Maybe we skip to the relevant parts," Paris interrupted.

"Fine." King Rudolf sounded disappointed. "So I sacrificed one hundred years of my life for their mother, to bring her back from the dead. Otherwise, the day was like any old regular one."

"Sounds like it," Paris said dryly.

"We were married in a grand affair," King Rudolf said. "It was really fancy. There were goats."

"Wow…"

"I know," he agreed, nodding. "Anyway, I made their mother my queen. Because she's mortal and I'm the lustrous fae, we aren't supposed to breed, so I brought in a giantess expert and a voodoo doctor, and we were able to do the impossible and have triplet children who are all half-mortal and half-fae. There you have it. Now I'm the scum of the Earth."

Paris tilted her head, her mind cramping. "I'm missing the whole part of why they're mad at you."

"Oh!" he sang and jumped up. "Well, there aren't any others like them. Halflings don't exist since it should be impossible for different races to mix, although there are always exceptions, as we plainly see."

"Plainly," Paris agreed, looking at the table of women.

"So they're mad at me because they're unique and don't fit in anywhere," King Rudolf explained. "They don't fit in with the fae since they're half-mortal and don't fit in with the mortals because they're pretty."

"I guess I do understand that," Paris stated. "But I'm not sure how it's your fault. I mean, you were in love and simply wanted to have a child with this woman…who by the way, you did what for?"

"Went to Taco Bell at midnight most nights to get her food she was craving," King Rudolf answered.

Paris shook her head. "No, I was referring to that part where you brought her back from the dead."

"Oh, that!" He threw his hand in the air dismissively. "Not a big deal. I had to get an illegal stone from Father Time and fight a mermaid and bring my love back and sacrifice a hundred years."

"Yeah, sounds easy," Paris muttered while stirring her drink.

"That's what you do for love," King Rudolf stated. "The Captains were supposed to be our love children, but now they're grown up and mad."

"Captains?" Paris questioned.

"Oh, and not only did I make them unique," King Rudolf stated, "but I named them all Captain."

"Why?"

"So that way they had a title."

Paris sat back in the booth. "You get that's not how it works, right? Please tell me you understand that."

"Of course it is," he argued.

"You have to earn that title or have a boat or something," she countered.

"Captain Morgan has a large vessel." King Rudolf pointed at the brunette. "Captain Kirk has a spaceship…somewhere." He indicated the blonde. "Captain Silver has a fish restaurant." The fae motioned to the last woman.

Paris planted both of her elbows on the table and cradled her chin. "If you were sent here to make me question my sanity, it's working."

"Why does everyone always say that to me?" he asked, quite seriously.

"Anyway, I guess I could understand your daughters feeling different," Paris stated. "But that bit about what you did for your wife is sweet. That sounds like true love."

He smiled broadly, showing sparkly white teeth. "It is. I'd give up more of my life to ensure Serena was always with me. She's the love of my life."

Paris sighed and sipped her drink. "I wished I understood how love like that worked."

"Oh, it's not rocket math," King Rudolf stated.

Paris was going to correct him, but after knowing the fae for only a short time knew it wasn't worth the effort.

"Our story is one for the storybooks, for sure," King Rudolf continued. "Oh, and I once had a friend. Her love story was one to rival ours."

Paris was surprised to find that she was intrigued. Maybe it was the alcohol or because despite being dumb, King Rudolf was charming and entertaining. "Tell me this story."

"Well," Rudolf drew out the word, "I once had a friend, who I don't think you've heard about. Her name was Liv Beaufont…"

Paris thought for a moment, a funny sensation suddenly needling in her mind for some strange reason. However, the name didn't ring a bell. "No, I haven't heard of her. Please go on."

CHAPTER SIXTY-ONE

"Well," King Rudolf began, his eyes dazzling as he sat back in the booth. "Liv and her husband, Stefan Ludwig, had a beautiful love story. You see, they were both Warriors for the House of Fourteen."

Paris didn't know much about the organization that governed magic outside Roya Lane, all law enforcement on that street falling under Uncle John's jurisdiction.

"Back then," the king of the fae continued, "Warriors from different families weren't allowed to be together. The Council who assigned them their missions thought they'd dilute their royal blood. However, Liv, who always fought for what she believed, protested until she got them to change the rules. She risked everything—her family's position, her reputation, and a comfortable life. Warriors notoriously have dangerous jobs and two together, well, they always had trouble barking up their door, never a dull moment."

Paris nodded, having a glimpse of that with Uncle John. He hardly slept, and his jurisdiction was much, much smaller. "What happened to them? Are they still together?"

He shrugged. "Wish I knew. They had a child, but due to the nature of their jobs, they were never seen. It wasn't safe. Liv and Stefan kept a low profile for a few years and one day disappeared. Well, at least Liv doesn't return my calls anymore, but she's been trying to ditch me since I made her fight a mermaid and nearly had her murdered by the queen of the fae."

"Imagine that," Paris chimed dryly.

"I know, some people are so sensitive. Anyway, my point in telling you this story is that when two people are in love, you have to take away what divides them. You can push them together with a mega force, but if there's a wall between them, your efforts are worthless. Instead, remove the wall, and you don't have to push them together—they'll naturally magnetize to one another." He smiled, a twinkle in his eyes. "Because I think that two people who have chemistry want to be in love, they simply need the obstacles removed. Bring someone back from the dead or take away the laws that divide them. Once two lovers don't have barriers, there is no job for a matchmaker. You can stand back and let them love each other."

Paris blinked, wondering why this strange fae was giving her exactly the advice she needed to hear. She wanted to question it, but also, everything in her mind suddenly felt so clear despite the rum and Coke. She knew how to get the two lovers together at Happily Ever After College. How to pass the exam. It all made perfect sense...

"Why did you share this with me?" Paris had to ask.

King Rudolf indicated the locket lying next to Paris on the table. "Because you appear to have had your heart broken, so I thought I'd offer my experience."

Paris grabbed the locket protectively. "Actually, I've never had my heart broken."

He nodded. "Then maybe that's your problem. You have to put your heart out there to have it broken."

She glanced down at the engraving: "You've got to keep breaking your heart until it opens."

"Yeah, maybe," she muttered absentmindedly.

"Anyway, I'm not sure exactly why I shared so much," King Rudolf admitted. "Sometimes you just feel like sharing, and for some reason, it feels like I know you."

Paris nodded, not able to argue with this. The king did seem oddly familiar. For some reason, his stories seemed to unlock something in her, like that morning when she woke up and felt different. All the information he'd shared bounced around in her mind, giving her so many confusing feelings.

"Well, thanks," She finished her drink. "Your stories were oddly helpful." She glanced at the clock on the wall. It was ten to midnight. How had the time gone by so fast? Darting to a standing position, Paris felt her head swim from the drinks. "I have to get out of here." She glanced down at Faraday, who was finishing his drink too, and looked ready to cuddle up for a nap. "Are you coming?"

The squirrel sprang up suddenly on his back paws with alarm on his face.

"Oh, hey there, little guy," King Rudolf chirped.

Paris pointed at the squirrel. "You can see him?"

The fae nodded. "Can you?"

She laughed. "Yes. The question is, can you hear him?"

"Well, no," King Rudolf stated.

Paris deflated, realizing that she was going crazy.

"Maybe that's because he hasn't said anything yet," King Rudolf added.

"What do you want me to say?" Faraday swayed.

King Rudolf leaned forward as though a talking squirrel wasn't weird at all. "That's a good question. Have you heard any good jokes lately?"

Paris laughed again, this time with relief. "Maybe later. We have somewhere to be. See you later. And thanks."

She grabbed the squirrel and ran for the exit, hoping that she had enough time to get back to Happily Ever After College before it was too late.

CHAPTER SIXTY-TWO

F araday sprang out of Paris' arms when they stepped through the portal onto the Enchanted Grounds of Happily Ever After College. She took off at a sprint, hurdling over the stairs and bursting through the front door to FGE, thankfully finding it open. The hallway was deserted but that made sense based on the late hour. Paris hoped that it wasn't too late and she could retake the exam.

She didn't stop running until she rounded the corner to the headmistress' office and found the door open. "I want to retake the exam!"

Headmistress Willow Starr looked up suddenly, worry on her face. Sitting in front of her desk were Shannon Butcher and Mae Ling.

"Paris, what are you doing here?" Willow asked.

"I know what to do now," Paris said between breaths. "Can I please have a second chance?"

"You've already failed," Professor Butcher stated, sounding pleased. "It's too late."

Mae Ling shook her head. "I think this warrants an exception. Paris showed remarkable progress in one day."

"I would agree." Willow rose from behind her desk. "If you think that you know what to do after such a short time, I'd be interested in seeing this."

"Really—"

"Our jobs need to be supporting students, not failing them," Mae Ling reminded her, secretly satisfied that Paris was there. "Wouldn't you all agree?"

"Absolutely." Willow smiled.

Reluctantly, Professor Butcher nodded.

"Well, then I don't see why we should make more of a production of this than we need to." The headmistress snapped her fingers, and the illusions of the two people appeared. Even in the large office, it was still a little tight with all the extra people. Paris tried not to think about this as she stared between the two lovers.

Their chemistry was palpable. She remembered King Rudolf's words about removing obstacles, and two people who were in love would magnetize to each other. Paris had to figure out what the wall was between the two.

She turned to Cheryl. "You said before that you have to get up early tomorrow. Why is that?"

"Oh, well, I have to catch a plane home to Cincinnati," Cheryl answered shyly, her eyes flicking to Phillip several times. "I was here on business, but I have to return to my family."

Paris' heart ached for the girl, who she could see wanted to jump into the man's arms in front of her. She focused her attention on Phillip. "You mentioned that you had a lot of work to do. Why is that?"

"Well," he began, regret in his tone. "I just got promoted to my dream job here in the city."

Paris understood at once. This couple's obstacle was distance. They were afraid to take the plunge, knowing that hundreds, maybe thousands of miles separated them. It would be her job as a fairy godmother to remove the wall between them—giving them the chance to fall in love.

Closing her eyes, she tried to picture the perfect solution. Cheryl's family was pulling her away. Phillip's dream job was keeping him anchored in place.

Paris' eyes sprang open as an idea popped into her mind. "Phillip, I'm the CEO of Random Industries in Cincinnati, and we want to offer you twice as much as what you're making now, doing the same thing. What do you say?"

His mouth fell open, then snapped closed. He looked at Cheryl, then Paris. "Are you serious? I didn't even interview."

"We're looking for the best talent," Paris lied, making it up as she went along. "Your name kept coming up. We'll relocate you and offer you full benefits, but we'll need you to start right away."

Paris expected him to nod. To exclaim that he'd take the job. Instead, as if Paris wasn't there, he strode right past her, threw his arms around Cheryl, picked her up, and spun her around. When he paused, he looked down at the girl, stars in his eyes.

"Did you hear the news?" he asked her.

She nodded, her own eyes starting to spill with happy tears. "I can't believe it. I guess when two people are truly in love, the universe finds a way to put them together."

Phillip pushed Cheryl's hair back off her cheek and leaned close, about to kiss her. "Nothing in the world would have kept me from you, I realize now. But I'm so grateful that it worked as it did."

She smiled and stared into his eyes. "We must have a fairy godmother because this is my perfect ending."

Before the couple kissed, they faded away.

Headmistress Starr clapped, stealing Paris' attention. Mae Ling appeared very pleased, although reserved. Professor Butcher looked madder than hell with her eyes narrowed in vengeance.

"Well, Paris," Willow began. "That was expertly done. You found out what was keeping the lovers apart and found a solution that fit them both. Cheryl kept her family and Phillip got his dream job, although I'm sure you realize that you'd have to instigate the job promotion and everything in a real-life scenario."

"Of course." The fairy's heart drummed wildly in her chest. "So does that mean…"

"Pass," Willow supplied. "I dare say yes. You performed much more capably on that exam than I've seen most of our students do in the past. That was the perfect happy ending." She turned to Mae Ling. "What do you think about having Paris help us with the upcoming event?"

"No!" Professor Butcher yelled at once, her face flushing red.

"Professor," Willow scolded.

"She's been here for one day," Professor Butcher complained and pointed at Paris.

"I realize that," Willow stated. "But she thinks in a modern way. We have a lot of pressure from Saint Valentine. This is our biggest event." She indicated the low love meter. "We can't afford to lose any more lovers."

"I think it's a great idea," Mae Ling agreed. "Otherwise, I'm afraid we'll do our same old stuffy event, and nothing will change. We need to shake things up. Without our interference, Paris could bring flair to the event. Something that will hopefully be a game-changer."

"I think this is an awful notion," Professor Butcher said angrily.

"I'm sorry, but can someone tell me what you're all talking about?" Paris asked.

"Of course." Willow smiled politely at her. "Every year, Happily Ever After College hosts a Valentine's Day ball for mortals. It's not a huge event, but the idea is to try and spark enough true love connections that we can spur energy for the coming year. You see, love has momentum like a spark creates a fire. When we create a lot of true love matches, it has the potential of starting a domino effect. That's always the idea with the Valentine's Day ball, but in recent years, it hasn't worked."

"By recent years, we mean the last several decades," Mae Ling added.

Willow nodded shamefully. "Unfortunately, it's had the opposite effect. Well, you see where the love meter is. We need this one to create a fire of love."

"That means we need to do something different," Mae Ling confirmed. "Not the same old stuffy affair. Before, it was all fancy attire and formality. No matches were made."

Paris couldn't believe it, but she was very excited about the idea. This was a huge opportunity. One she didn't think she deserved, but she wanted to try. "Well, of course not," Paris agreed. "I bet people were too uptight to be themselves."

Willow laughed. "It's like you were present."

"How can people fall for each other if they can't be themselves?" Paris asked. "And if someone does fall for them, they aren't falling for the actual person, but rather the pretentious form of them. We need to put on an event where Cinderellas and Prince Charmings can be themselves. We need to throw out all the glass slippers and ballgowns and magical carriages and create something where people can fall in love with another person and not an appearance."

Mae Ling's brown eyes lit up when she smiled at the headmistress, who also appeared very satisfied by this suggestion.

"Does that mean you'll help us with this year's Valentine's Day event?" Willow asked. "I realize you're brand-new and this is a lot to ask, but we're desperate, and something tells me it's time that we start doing things differently, especially after today."

Paris nodded, feeling a strange sensation bloom in her chest. It was a rare emotion—pride. "Absolutely. I'd be honored to help with the Valentine's Day event."

CHAPTER SIXTY-THREE

"So not only did you pass your exam," Uncle John said over the phone, excitement strong in his voice, "but they want you to help with a huge event?"

Paris was pacing in her small room, only able to take a few steps before having to turn and stride back the opposite way. Her phone shouldn't work at the college, but Uncle John had done something to it using magitech to get past the wards.

Paris had woken up early that morning despite going to bed late and hoped to see Uncle John before breakfast. However, she didn't have enough time to portal out of Happily Ever After College to Roya Lane and back in time. Plus, magical reserves were a factor and Paris wanted to ensure she was fresh for the day's events. So she'd settled for relying on technology and called her uncle.

"Well, the Valentine's Day event isn't supposed to be huge," she replied. "It's supposed to create a spark. Yes, they know they need to shake things up."

His familiar chuckle warmed Paris's heart. "Oh, shaking things up is your specialty. I knew you'd do well there. Well, I think you'll do well anywhere, you just needed to find something for yourself. I think getting off Roya Lane was necessary. You weren't ever going to find anything good here. It's a bunch of trouble."

Guilt prickled in Paris' throat at the notion that she'd snuck back to her old stomping grounds and not told Uncle John about it. Still, that's what Mae Ling had ordered her to do, and she'd met King Rudolf. Oddly enough, the airhead fae had helped her.

All night, the stories he'd told her had strolled through her head, seeming to open doors that had been locked before, sparking ideas she hadn't ever thought about. Paris hadn't known much about the House of Fourteen, never being outside of Roya Lane for the most part.

Liv's and Stefan's story felt like a fairytale, and she wondered what had happened to them. Maybe they'd gotten tired of the dangerous Warrior lifestyle and escaped to a tropical island to enjoy their life and love without the stresses of saving the world.

The idea sounded good in theory, but now that Paris had the opportunity to create real change, she was addicted to it. If the Valentine's Day event had the chance of sparking fires of love worldwide, how couldn't she want it to be a huge success?

This was her chance to make her mark. They were trusting her. She didn't understand it entirely, but she also wanted this more than she'd wished for anything, ever. Having almost lost the chance to be a fairy godmother had made Paris hungry for something she didn't think she wanted. Life was strange like that.

"Well, I'm proud of you, Pare," Uncle John said over the phone. "I've always been proud of you. You have a lot of heart."

"Thanks, Uncle John. I better get down to breakfast. I need to grab something for a friend." Her gaze slid to Faraday, who was pretending not to eavesdrop from his sock drawer. He'd requested a croissant for breakfast that morning, which she could snag and get to him before the meal started if she hurried.

"Look at that," Uncle John cheered. "You're helping with events and making friends. This is good news."

Paris couldn't help but smile. It was true. After getting tipsy with the squirrel and the king of the fae the night before, she couldn't help but think of Faraday as a friend. He had left with her when she'd gotten kicked out. That was a good friend—someone who stuck by you no matter what.

"Well, remember to take your medicine," Paris said in a rush to Uncle John. "And eat vegetables at least now and then."

"Pare, you know they don't agree with my stomach," he argued, as he always did.

"They don't agree with your taste buds," she countered.

He chuckled. "That too."

"Don't overdo it, okay?"

"I won't," he agreed. "But I do have a business trip coming up. I'll be on a stakeout for a while."

"You what?" She was surprised. "Since when do you have stakeouts?"

"Since you're not around," he answered matter-of-factly. "You think I was ever going to go on those with you around? You might want to go off on your own from time to time, but I always needed to be here if you needed me."

"Oh, and now I'm here," she guessed.

"Well, I usually sent Danny on the stakeouts, but you know, I'm tired of paperwork," he grumbled. "I'm up to my ears in it. So I'm going to let Danny get the hand cramp filling out forms, and I'm going to be a real detective for a while."

"You're always a real detective, Uncle John."

"I know, I know," he chimed. "I want to get out, and now that I know you're okay, well, I can do that without worrying."

"Okay, well, be careful," she ordered.

"I will."

"Don't eat a bunch of junk food while on these stakeouts," she demanded.

"How about a little?" he joked.

"Fine, but remember the vegetables." She smiled.

"Okay, well, I love you, Pare. Always and forever."

"I love you, Uncle John." Paris felt a new level of gratitude. "Always and forever."

CHAPTER SIXTY-FOUR

O ver the next week, Paris made so much progress. She also created a lot of problems for herself, but that was standard for her and to be expected.

Each day, she read at least a book if not two or three, learning all sorts of spells and other useful, more practical information. She'd run out of excuses with Wilfred and had to participate in ballroom dancing classes, but she didn't hate it. To her surprise, ballroom dancing felt like fighting, without the nose bleeds and bruised knuckles. There was nice coordination to the whole thing, and she appreciated the flow and grace of the movements.

Hemingway was impressed with Paris' instincts with gardening but often had to remind her not to take magical shortcuts. She didn't understand why even when she mastered the mortal ways that he still wanted her to dig a hole instead of cheating using magic.

"There's a Zen proverb that says, 'Before enlightenment, chop wood, carry water. After enlightenment, chop wood, carry water,'" he told her one day when she challenged him.

"Oh, so you're not quoting your namesake today?" she teased him, her hands on her hips.

A smile surfaced in his bright blue eyes. "I quote all sorts."

"When do you say your own lines?" she fired back, having fallen into a natural playful dynamic with him.

"Oh, I have more than a few of my own lines," Hemingway argued and shook his head. "But you're derailing the conversation. My point is, there are rewards in doing things the honest way."

"You mean, blisters," she corrected. "There are blisters in doing things the honest way."

"Paris, you shouldn't always rely on magic," he stated, suddenly serious.

"Why?" she asked.

He shook his head. "You have to know that you're more powerful than most fairies, right? You see it."

Paris looked around the greenhouse, checking that no one was close enough to overhear them. "So?"

"So, because you have so much magic, doesn't mean you always have to rely on it for everything. You're also clever and resourceful. I'm just saying, partner all your skills because magic is helpful. But when we use magic to do something, we can't always control the outcome. You can't always stop a magical fast-growing spell. Then a plant grows until it hits its prime and starts to die. Keep in mind there are multiple ways of doing things."

Paris knew that Hemingway had her best interests at heart, as did Chef Ash who had been very helpful in helping her hone her baking skills. She enjoyed the art of making things with her hands and didn't always cheat the process. It was different from gardening where one planted something and had to wait. With cooking and baking, the results were much more immediate.

Professor Shannon Butcher was one of the rare people at Happily Ever After College who didn't seem to have Paris' best interests at heart. The fairy godmother shot Paris rude glares when she saw her and insulted her at every opportunity, although

Paris didn't have any classes with her. The professor was still protesting about Paris having any involvement in the Valentine's Day event, but Willow had remained firm about her decision.

To Paris' surprise, the headmistress had endorsed her idea to have a speed dating event for the Valentine's Day celebration. She'd explained that it would be bare-bones.

"Those invited will be encouraged to come as they are," Paris explained when she proposed the idea at the planning meeting, her palms sweating as she stood in front of many of the fairy godmothers and instructors. "The idea is that no one is falling for someone's appearance. Dressing up is nice to show we care, but for this event, we want people to fall for each other, not fancy clothes and perfect hair."

"That idea holds merit." Professor Joyce Beacon smiled across the table at Paris. "Cinderellas make sure they look perfect for their Prince Charmings, obsessing and forgetting to be themselves."

"Yeah, but I contend the two fall for each other's appearances initially," Professor Butcher stated. "Then once a foundation is created, they can look more like themselves."

"Yeah, and she puts on her fat pants, and he gets a gut," Paris argued. "Because they're exhausted from all the prior efforts. What if we encouraged them not to do that? There are years for them to go to black-tie events and be fancy if they want. I'm not saying those things aren't important or shouldn't be done. But if we aim to get as many true love matches as possible, we should encourage people to come as they are. Otherwise, the matches we make will be about infatuation and lust and won't last."

"That's exactly why this event has failed in the past." The headmistress tapped her pink ballpoint pen on a pad of paper. "Last year we had over half the couples hit it off on Valentine's Day. But after ten to fourteen days, most of them had broken things off."

"So we have people come in jeans and T-shirts or whatever." That earned Paris a rude cough from Professor Butcher, but she ignored it. "Then we give them time to get to know each other in a casual setting. Nothing that makes them nervous, so that way, they're really themselves."

"What if we give them something that ensures they're really themselves?" Chef Ash asked. "Like no pretenses."

"Like whiskey shots?" Paris offered with a laugh.

"Sort of," he affirmed. "Maybe a magical elixir that makes them relaxed and natural."

"I think there are some herbs in the Bewilder Forest that have those properties," Hemingway offered.

"I can make them into a punch," Chef Ash affirmed.

"I like this idea." Willow smiled.

"For decorations," Wilfred began, "I like the idea of keeping it simple, but I think a romantic aspect is still important. It is Valentine's Day, after all."

"I agree," Willow declared. "Some music and dancing are always nice. Lighting is important and shouldn't be discounted. And something else that is simple yet sets a nice mood without forcing it."

"I have some doves down by the lake that are very tame," Hemingway offered. "They could be part of the decorations rather than some grand explosion like they do at weddings when they let them out."

"I like that idea!" Willow exclaimed. "Yes, elegant doves sitting around the ballroom and cooing will be nice." The headmistress looked around the table, a satisfied expression on her face. "Well, we all have our jobs. In one week, we'll come together in Los Angeles for this event. I have every hope that we'll make this the best Valentine's Day celebration we've had in a long time. Let's do everything we can to make that happen. A lot depends on this."

CHAPTER SIXTY-FIVE

*Z*huang Lane's area wasn't a place that fairy godmothers ever found themselves, but Shannon Butcher had had enough. The narrow lane was full of both hidden and exposed dangers. The creatures that lurked in the cold shadows spread disease and feasted on the weak. Criminals ran the shops, selling things the House of Fourteen would no doubt deem illegal.

Shannon had been at Happily Ever College for decades, teaching the students etiquette and other important subjects. Yes, true love was dwindling in the world, but changing the curriculum wasn't the way. Willow Starr was irrational. There wasn't any evidence that Happily Ever After College was to blame for matches not being made. It could very well be blamed on the modern world, Shannon Butcher reasoned.

How were people supposed to fall in love when they couldn't pull their attention off their devices long enough? Or maybe Facebook was the problem, creating insecurities in relationships. But fairy godmothers weren't the problem. They simply taught charges how to be poised and pretty and perfect so they could find love. That's how it worked. That's how it had always worked.

Happily Ever After College wasn't what needed to change. It was the world that needed to. However, no one was listening to Shannon anymore.

Against her reason, Willow had allowed a reject into the school. Now Paris Westbridge was changing things. The horror of it all was that the college was adapting to these gross standards. Already Shannon's class numbers were dwindling, many students arguing that it was irrelevant. More and more, Paris was lobbying that love needed to be about intrinsic factors rather than polished appearances.

If Paris was going to affect the future of love on the planet, Shannon knew they were all in trouble. She realized that Willow was scared. Mae Ling had checked out long ago. No one knew what to do. It was up to Shannon to fix things. That's why she'd risked entering Zhuang Lane, a place filled with dark and illegal magic. The fairy godmother didn't like the idea of employing such things. Still, she was willing to do whatever it took to save Happily Ever After College before the modern world—and Paris West-bridge—sent it to the depths of Hell where it wouldn't be recoverable.

At the seer's shop, Shannon knocked six times, as she'd been instructed to do. The door creaked and opened by itself to reveal a dark sitting room. In the middle of it was an old blind woman who looked up from a round table. Deep wrinkles lined her face, and black bags hung under her white eyes. Worse than the sight of the seer was the rattlesnake on the floor next to her, shaking its tail and flicking its tongue at the fairy godmother.

"You are willing to pay a lot of money for information on this girl," the old woman said without greeting Shannon. Some people had lost sight of all proprieties. This was where the world was going without Happily Ever After College if it didn't maintain its curriculum.

"I simply want to know the truth." Shannon had spoken to the woman on the phone and sent her the huge amount of money she'd asked for as an advance. "You have proof that what you share with me today is both useful and also true?"

"That was the agreement." The seer's rattlesnake slithered up the leg of her chair. "I found something that I think will be very useful, which is why I took your money."

Shannon stepped into the dark room, nearly needing to hold her breath due to the smell. She dared to close the door, knowing they'd need privacy for the next part. "What can you tell me about Paris Westbridge?"

"As you suspected, she isn't who she says she is." The seer swayed back and forth, snapping her fingers beside her as though dancing to music in her head, but the sound of the snake's rattle was all there was.

"Tell me everything," Shannon urged.

"I don't have to. What I've seen about the girl is all there in that envelope."

Greedily, Shannon darted forward but paused before yanking the envelope off the table, her eyes cautiously watching the snake. She jerked open the envelope and pulled out the documents, her mouth popping open as she read the birth records.

"This is all true?" Shannon asked in disbelief.

"It is," the woman croaked. "Once I saw who she was, finding proof wasn't hard. It was all hidden in plain sight for those who knew where to look to find it." The seer cackled loudly, throwing her head back.

Shannon shook her head at the woman, repulsed by her lack of decorum. Still, this was what she needed. There was no way that Paris could stay at Happily Ever After College after this. However, getting rid of the girl wasn't the only part of her plan.

"The creatures that I asked for. Did you find them?" she asked the woman, stepping back as the rattlesnake traversed the distance and arrived on the table's surface.

"Of course," the woman cooed. "They're out back. Will you need help transporting them?"

Shannon shook her head. "No, the fewer people involved, the better."

"Very well then, my dear," the woman hissed. "I trust you can see your way out."

A shiver ran down Shannon's back as she started for the door opposite the entrance. She'd be glad to be out of the shop, although her reason for coming here had already rewarded her. Very soon everyone would know the truth about Paris, and she'd no longer be able to pollute Happily Ever After College with her rebellious ideas.

CHAPTER SIXTY-SIX

"Everything is perfect," Headmistress Willow Starr proudly said while standing at the front of the banquet hall in the JW Marriott in Los Angeles. She wore her usual blue gown with a pink bow and had braided her thick hair down her back—and had a sincere smile on her face.

"Oh, why did you have to do that?" Paris joked. She wore her usual black leather jacket and jeans and boots, although she'd gone fancy for the event and brushed her hair.

"Do what?" the headmistress asked Paris, gaining the attention of the fairy godmothers, other professors, and nearby students.

"You jinxed us," she replied. "Next, are you going to say that nothing can go wrong?"

Willow waved her off. "Oh, everything is all set. We open the doors in one minute. Is everyone ready?"

Chef Ash strode forward, wearing his usual white chef's uniform and a tall hat for the occasion. "The buffet is ready."

"All the tables are set," Wilfred stated, looking distinguished as always.

Paris had to admit the two thousand and eight hundred square foot banquet hall was quite impressive. The walls were all pink with gold designs and lit from various angles. The round eight-person tables were elegantly set with white and gold plates and simple rose centerpieces. The entire space was tasteful yet under-stated. No one should walk in there and think they were under-dressed. That's what the invites sent to the one hundred and twenty guests explicitly said: "Come as you are and be yourself."

Paris hoped the guests waiting to mingle and dine did just that. In case any of them planned to be anything but their authentic selves, all they had to do was sip the punch, and they'd be who they truly were. It wasn't dishonest since the elixir was safe and only ensured no one put up any pretenses. This wasn't going to be a night of showing off and trying to impress someone so they fell for the other one. This was about finding real love because people were their authentic selves.

"And the doves?" Willow asked Hemingway.

He pointed up at a perch along the side of the dance floor. "They're all cooing and being love doves to set the mood. I even trained them not to have any accidents on the guests."

Willow giggled. "Very good. So we open the doors, and all the guests know where to go. They meet with a potential date, and after five minutes, rotate. It's unorthodox, but it gives everyone a chance to mingle. Then we have dinner and dancing, and hope-fully, make a match or two."

"Or ten," Paris chirped.

"Or twenty," Christine added.

"Could be thirty," Penny dared to say, then covered her mouth as if she shouldn't have been so bold.

"I think it's time that we open the doors already," Professor Butcher urged. "The guests are getting restless, and that's not good for matchmaking."

"I contend that it's not about circumstances that dictate whether two people will fall in love," Paris argued. "Maybe it's the very act of waiting in line or being inconvenienced that gives them the opportunity to fall for each other."

"We will see, Ms. Westbridge," Professor Butcher said, a bite to her words. "This was all your idea, so if it's a success, we know who to thank. If it's not, well…"

Paris would have thought that Shannon Butcher was extra vindictive that night if she hadn't gotten accustomed to the professor's sour mood. Deciding that she'd focus on the good of the Valentine's Day event, Paris turned her attention to the double doors as Headmistress Starr pulled them open, welcoming all the eager guests into the event.

CHAPTER SIXTY-SEVEN

Paris thought that things would start slow with awkward exchanges and lots of nervous glances. Instead, for whatever reason, things were natural and easy from the beginning between the invitees.

People sat next to each other, asking various questions and giggling about how fast the time went. The conversation seemed to flow and was uninhibited by the light orchestra music that Wilfred had chosen.

The fairy godmothers and students were circulating, greeting guests and making them feel welcomed. There was no polite small talk or frivolities on that night—only genuine smiles and warm gestures that hopefully created the right environment for the inevitable to happen.

Paris believed that's what it all was. If two people were right for each other, they didn't need shiny suits and sequins. They didn't need horse-drawn carriages and chauffeurs. Those were nice and maybe for later when they were indulging. Initially, two people should have a chance to fall for each other and not for the circumstances around them.

Which begged the question for Paris, would Cinderella have fallen for Prince Charming if they hadn't met at a ball? What if they met at a gas station and she'd been cleaning the bathrooms, and he was a trucker named Larry with mustard stains on his sleeves? Paris believed that Cindy and Larry deserved to fall in love as much as the polished Cinderella and Prince Charming. She hoped that this rare opportunity she'd received to take this risk showed the fairy godmothers that too.

Paris looked around the banquet hall, infected by all the positive energy around her.

"I knew you could do it," Mae Ling said at her shoulder. She'd seemingly materialized out of nowhere.

Paris glanced down at the little woman. "What? I mean, why? Actually, how?" She shook her head. "It's so strange that all of you gave me this type of chance to do something when I've been with the college for such a short time."

Mae Ling shrugged nonchalantly. "A Head Professor can pull strings when she wants to."

"But why?" Paris asked.

"You failing and returning to complete your exam the way you did, well, it did you favors," Mae Ling explained. "Much better than if you had passed the first time through. It showed grit, and Willow saw that. I knew you had it in you."

"That's the thing." Paris watched the various couples interact. All seemed to be having a nice time, even if they didn't hit it off entirely. Maybe they achieved friendship, if not true love. There were hopefully many benefits to the night, although love was the desired goal. "Why are you instigating things? What do you know about me that I sense you're not saying?"

"I've been with Happily Ever After College for a very long time," Mae Ling explained. "We've done many great things. But we've failed to change with the world. I simply knew that we'd need something new to push us ahead."

"I feel like you're avoiding my question though," Paris argued, not wanting the fairy godmother to finagle her way out of this. "Do you know something about me?"

"Yes, Paris. I get glimpses of things in the past, present, and future. Not like a seer, more like potential realities. Things that could happen, people who can make a difference, paths that can be taken. Nothing is guaranteed though. To specifically answer your question, I know you have greatness in you. I know you have much to learn about yourself. And I know that you will get your heart broken many, many times. If I explain to you how I know one of those things, I must explain to you how I know all of them. Is that something you want? Do you want to know how your heart potentially gets broken? Because I warn you, it won't stop it from happening."

Paris gulped, feeling her insides suddenly start to churn. She shook her head. "No, I don't think I want to know. That sounds worse, waiting for the inevitable to happen."

Mae Ling nodded proudly. "I agree. If it helps…" She pointed around the room at various people. "Every single person in this room will have their heart broken at some point. You can't live a full life without it happening. So we must simply embrace it as part of life."

Paris thought about that for a moment, noting how similar it was to Wilfred's words from Kahlil Gibran. He'd said the poet had written something about how one could not laugh all their laughter unless they wept all their tears. There was no joy without pain in this world, Paris reasoned, intrigued by the idea. She'd spent so much of her life protecting herself that this whole notion of opening herself up to be vulnerable so she could experience the full spectrum of emotions was scary and also becoming more digestible.

She recounted what King Rudolf had said to her in the bar: "You have to put your heart out there to have it broken."

"Thanks for—" Paris turned to thank the fairy godmother, only to find that Mae Ling had disappeared suddenly. She shook her head, realizing that she might never understand the woman's enigmatic nature.

"There's something to be said about being casual, wouldn't you say?" Hemingway asked at Paris' shoulder.

She glanced at him, noticing that he was wearing his usual, a button-up fleece plaid and jeans with boots. "I'm the queen of casual."

"Well, it does seem to be having a nice overall effect on our guests. Last year, this was a black-tie event, and all the women had on huge ball gowns. Don't get me wrong. Everyone was beautiful. But people were so stiff and full of etiquette that I don't think anyone laughed or truly enjoyed themselves."

"Well, how can you when you can't breathe because a corset is cutting off your air supply?" Paris questioned.

He nodded and looked around. "And now, look at this. It's exactly the opposite as far as the vibe."

Paris did like to hear the various couples laughing and talking loudly. That reminded her of what Faraday had said what people did when they were excited. They spoke loudly—like many of the couples in the room. And excitement was indicative of other, budding feelings. Hopefully, that meant love was in the air.

"Well, I'm glad things are going well." Paris sighed, and for the first time since starting on this project, allowed herself to feel victorious.

"That's strange." Hemingway was studying the perch where the various doves were stationed, cooing.

"What's strange?" Paris suddenly tensed.

He pointed up at the perch. "Those doves...they aren't mine."

CHAPTER SIXTY-EIGHT

"What does that mean?" Paris raised an eyebrow. "How do you know?"

He scrutinized the birds, still staring up at them. "My doves are all white. Those..."

Paris saw what he meant. The doves perched beside the dance floor had a black tip on their tails and around their necks. "If those aren't your doves, whose are they? Also, where are yours?"

Those were the first two questions Paris had. Others quickly followed, like why would someone replace Hemingway's doves? If these weren't trained, what did that mean?

Paris didn't get a chance to mentally cycle through other questions because Hemingway grabbed her arm with such alarm it made her suck in a breath.

"Those doves aren't right," he said with urgency.

She saw what he meant. As the doves looked down on the guests, all enjoying themselves, their eyes flashed red and not with love.

"We have to get everyone out of here." Paris spun and found the doors to the front foyer shut. She rushed over, and to her horror, they were locked. She tried several different spells but couldn't do anything to open them, which meant that magic kept them secured.

She turned and looked up at the perch filled with dozens of doves as the first descended toward the potential lovers, its beak wide as it called loudly—a high-pitched, deafening sound indicative of its murderous mission.

CHAPTER SIXTY-NINE

"Take cover!" Paris yelled as one by one, the birds dove for the crowd like torpedoes, screaming in a very uncharacteristic dove-like fashion. They aimed for the heads of the group, beaks first.

The guests all looked up at the sound of the commotion, confused at first. Panic broke out as they saw the chaos unfolding.

"You can't get out!" Paris yelled. "Get under the tables."

Birds were now grabbing at women's hair and yanking at men's collars with their claws. People were running into each other to escape the craziness.

Paris was trying to figure out the best way to handle things and wondering if it was okay to use force on deranged doves that definitely weren't loving. She caught sight of Willow and Mae Ling in her peripheral vision, and they appeared panicked by the change. "The doves!"

"Yes, I see that!" Willow shouted.

"They aren't Hemingway's," Paris called while ushering a couple under a table as a dove pecked at the top of her head.

Deciding that the birds had to go, Paris threw a fist at it, sadly sending it to the floor, but it was her or it.

"The doors!" Willow tried one.

"We need to get them open," Mae Ling offered.

"I'll cover you," Hemingway told Paris as he arrived beside her with a serving dish that served as a handy shield.

The room was complete pandemonium. Fairy godmothers unused to fighting all cowered under tables. The mortals also sought shelter, although some batted at the crazed doves that swooped down from the ceiling, trying to take jabs where they could. To Paris' surprise, many couples had teamed up to fight a single dove who was targeting them, throwing objects at the bird, or swooshing a plate through the air.

She glanced sideways at Hemingway. "How do you think we take all these rabid birds down most effectively?"

"What we need to do is corral these monsters." He threw his shield in the air as a murderous dove went for his head.

"I'm listening." Paris yanked a tablecloth off a table and swished it through the air like a whip to keep a set of doves back from her.

"Well, although they can fly when wet, they don't like it," Hemingway explained, pointing up at the ceiling.

Paris saw what he was referring to—the sprinklers on the ceiling. "I can activate those."

He nodded, smiling wide. "Do it one by one starting here where there's the largest concentration. We want to drive them toward that intake vent there." Hemingway pointed. "I'm going to go and open it up and create a cage using magic. We'll drive them in there, and I'll shut it."

"And bam," Paris stated, adrenaline pumping in her blood. "We have caged, deranged birds."

"Ready?" He asked

Paris dropped the tablecloth, and prepared to use her magic to activate the sprinklers. She looked around, grateful to see that most people had taken cover. Some were still fending off the crazy birds. Willow was trying to get the doors open with Mae Ling, Penny, and Christine defending her as she worked.

"Let's do this!" Paris watched as Hemingway took off, sprinting for the large vent.

CHAPTER SEVENTY

As soon as Paris got a signal from Hemingway, she activated the first set of sprinklers, pushing the strange doves away from them. That took some pressure off her and the fairy godmothers since it drove the birds toward the center of the room.

However, now Paris was right under a sprinkler and getting drenched, as were many on the room's far side. She didn't care and simply shook her head to keep the water out of her eyes so she could see. Some of the fairy godmothers screeched as if they were suddenly melting.

Hemingway worked fast, getting the grill off the intake vent. Paris wasn't sure what he was doing, but she thought he was blocking the other side of the vent somewhere to create a cage of sorts. It was smart because she didn't want to kill all these animals. It wasn't that she wouldn't if it was between them and her, but she avoided such things when possible.

She was impressed to see many of the couples hadn't taken cover and helped defend each other from the birds. Some cowered under the tables, but even they cradled each other as the weird doves screamed and streaked past.

Thankfully, Hemingway worked fast and seemed to have fixed most of the vent up as a cage. He gave Paris another signal.

She used her magic to activate more of the sprinklers, drenching three-fourths of the room. The doves immediately reacted by flying in the direction of the large opening. Hemingway turned, holding up the large grill that would be the gate to the murderous birds' cage.

"Now!" he yelled, and Paris activated the last of the sprinklers, drenching the rest of the huge banquet room. That did the trick though, and with nowhere else safe to go and stay dry, the deranged doves all flew into the opening, followed by some *thuds* when some must have hit the other side of the makeshift cage.

Hemingway successfully used magic to get the grill back into place before the doves realized they were trapped and turned on him. He secured it in place, and the room was suddenly safe once more, although soaked.

Paris let out a breath of relief, snapped her fingers, and simultaneously extinguished all the sprinklers at once, making much of the loud noise dissipate. The sounds of relieved gasps and cheers replaced it.

CHAPTER SEVENTY-ONE

Many of the guests emerged from under their makeshift shelters looking disoriented. Most were wet, or their hair and clothes disheveled after being assaulted by the birds.

The students and fairy godmothers all moved into swift action, comforting the confused guests who had the strangest and scariest surprise on an otherwise pleasant Valentine's Day.

To Paris' surprise, many of the guests began laughing, realizing they'd survived the ordeal. She heard them joking with each other about how things played out or recounting their experiences.

Thankfully, the doors were finally unlocked. Wilfred and Chef Ash had been locked out and worked with Willow on the other side to get them opened. Several people rushed out to drier areas, but many stayed to collect themselves.

A woman reached out and brushed a wet piece of hair off a guy's forehead, relief on both of their faces. The whole set of scenes was more than bizarre. It was almost as if the craziness had brought people together in an unexpected way.

"Are you okay?" Hemingway had returned to her side.

Paris nodded. "Yeah, I think everyone is okay."

He surveyed the room. "Paris, I think they're better than okay. These wackos are laughing."

She grinned. "I know. I'm not sure what happened with your doves, but at least we survived whatever that was."

He shook his head. "I don't know either, but I want my doves back and want to figure out what the hell those beasts are."

"I think we know what happened." Penny strode over, urging the headmistress to follow her in Paris' and Hemingway's direction.

"What's going on, Penny?" Paris asked her.

"When we ran out of here, we found Hemingway's doves all still caged in one of the rooms we entered. Usually, I wouldn't have investigated, but well, all this action made me feel braver than usual, so Christine and I started checking rooms. Guess who we found in there with them?"

"Who?" Willow asked.

Penny gave her a guilty look. "Christine is bringing her in here. Please don't be mad at what we did to her. We had to because we think she's behind this."

"Who?" Willow asked again, now starting to sound like an owl.

The group turned as Christine led Professor Shannon Butcher through the double set of doors, tethered in ropes and levitating vertically off the floor—floating in their direction, her eyes bulging with hostility.

Penny pointed at the bound professor. "We think that she was behind the mean doves since she wasn't in here and had the real ones secured away."

Paris shook her head, realizing that although she'd tried not to harm any doves, she might have to murder someone that day after all.

CHAPTER SEVENTY-TWO

"Is this true?" Willow asked when Christine paused Shannon Butcher in front of the group. She and Penny had wound up the professor like a mummy. "Are you the one who set these creatures on our guests and us?"

Shannon narrowed her eyes and looked straight at Paris. There was no mistake where her hostility was centered. "I had to. None of you would listen to reason."

"So you set a bunch of rabid doves loose in a Valentine's celebration?" Hemingway asked, anger flaring on his face for the first time. "Where did you get these monsters?"

"It doesn't matter," Shannon stated. "I needed to prove to you all that we need manners and traditions and pretenses. Without it, we're no better than any commoner."

"What's wrong with that?" Paris challenged. "Do commoners not get to find true love?"

"No!" Shannon yelled, fighting her restraints, but Christine had done a good job. Paris was proud of her friend. "True love is for those who are disciplined and refined and have poise and skills.

That's always been the way it was. If we lose sight of that, we will lose love."

"That's been the fairy godmothers' problem all along," Paris countered. "Losing love under the current system was always meant to happen. The fact that it existed for so long is the real surprise."

Wilfred and Chef Ash materialized, having helped many of the guests get out of the banquet hall. Now, most of the school was gathered, witnessing the strange events.

"You're the problem," Shannon seethed, shaking her head and looking crazed. "You're the corruption that this place needs to get rid of. I was trying to show you all that."

"You nearly got us killed," the headmistress charged.

"The doves weren't supposed to kill," Shannon denied. "Only attack."

"There's a fine line there," Paris joked and shook her head. She'd never thought the professor would go this far.

"I want you all to see that we need to do things the way we've always done them," Shannon explained. "What this one has done will destroy us." She glared at Paris, unable to point since she was bound.

"Really?" Willow shook her head. "You've had it out for Paris from the beginning, and it must stop. The event fueled by her good ideas was very successful despite your efforts. Many couples left here with a budding romance."

"NO!" Shannon yelled. "She isn't even a fairy!"

At this, everyone fell silent. Paris' mouth fell open. Of everyone, she was the most shocked.

CHAPTER SEVENTY-THREE

"What did you say?" Willow asked carefully while looking between Shannon and Paris.

Shannon laughed. "That's right. This one you all hailed and thought was so great, can't be a fairy godmother because she isn't a real fairy."

Paris tipped her head sideways, totally confused. She unglamoured her wings, which were periwinkle blue. "What are you talking about, Psycho?"

"Yes, technically you're a fairy, but you're not really a fairy. You're not a pureblood," Shannon declared.

"Okay, this is stupid." Paris shook her head. "I'm tired of being villainized by you."

"It's true," Shannon said in a rush. "Headmistress, you'll find evidence inside my gown. Paris looks like a fairy, but her DNA is both that of a fairy and a magician."

This produced gasps from everyone in the crowd. Paris remained silent, not sure what was happening here.

"Halflings are almost impossible," Willow stated.

Paris knew from her discussion with King Rudolf that this was true. However, they were possible. His children were proof.

Paris suddenly found it difficult to swallow. "How am I a halfling?" She couldn't believe she asked the question, but it was hovering on the tip of her tongue. This was crazy and the wrong place for it to come out, yet it didn't feel like a lie.

Shannon cackled, enjoying relating this. "You, Paris, aren't a true fairy."

"You've already said that." Hemingway's anger flared in his voice.

"She isn't even Paris Westbridge," Shannon continued. "Her real name is Guinevere Paris Beaufont."

CHAPTER SEVENTY-FOUR

"B-B-Beaufont," Paris said, the name feeling suddenly strange on her tongue. Just like that, she got a flash of memories.

She was young—a toddler. There was a blonde woman in a black cloak, her smile Paris' whole world. A man with jet black hair, his blue eyes so captivating. They never called her Paris. It was always, "Gwen." Every time they hugged her, which was often, they called her "Gwen." Every time they kissed her, it was "Gwennie."

Paris saw her childhood in so many different flashes. She didn't know how or why, but suddenly she knew without a doubt why King Rudolf had told her about Liv and Stefan and their lost child. It was her. She was Guinevere Paris Beaufont.

Looking straight at Mae Ling, who hadn't said a single word, Paris gave the fairy godmother an inquisitive look that asked only one question.

The small woman simply nodded, affirming everything.

She was both a fairy and a magician. She was a Beaufont. But how? More importantly, why didn't she know this before?

CHAPTER SEVENTY-FIVE

Paris' knees felt ready to give out on her.

"There's no way that can be the case." Willow looked between Paris and Shannon. "She's a fairy. The child born to Liv Beaufont disappeared, and she was a magician."

"She was a fairy," Shannon argued. "If you release me and take the paperwork from my gown, you'll see the evidence. It's the child's birth certificate, which has her magical DNA. All you must do is a simple spell to see if it's the same as Paris'."

Paris wanted to run and hide. To call Uncle John, but none of those were options for her. So she stayed still, pretending that all the events unfolding didn't directly pertain to her.

"Hold her, please," Willow instructed Wilfred, Chef Ash, and Christine. "I'm going to retrieve the evidence."

The bonds fell off Shannon all at once, freeing her once more. However, she was pinned by the invisible restraints of the fairies' collective force, working together.

"I knew that she couldn't be a fairy," Shannon said as Willow retrieved an envelope from her gown. "She acted too much like a magician, so self-assured and pompous. Her magic felt wrong. Felt like that of a magician."

"You mean she was more powerful than you," Hemingway spat, seemingly personally insulted by all this. "You didn't like that she's so powerful, like a magician."

"You will thank me for this," Shannon stated. "A magician has no place in our college. We are fairies, and those types don't mix with ours."

Paris was so confused. She'd always thought of herself as a fairy. Not that she'd ever felt like one. She hadn't felt like any particular race, just like herself. But now…this was so confusing for her, and she couldn't think with everyone staring at her.

Willow had unfolded an embossed piece of paper from the envelope and ran her eyes down it carefully. She looked up at Paris. "I won't do this here if you don't want me to. I won't do it at all if you don't want me to. Still, a simple spell will tell you whether your magical DNA matches that of this child, a fairy named Guinevere Paris Beaufont born to Liv Beaufont and Stefan Ludwig, Warriors for the House of Fourteen, who were both magicians. I don't know how that happened, but according to these records, it did. Do you want to know if you're this child?"

Paris didn't remember nodding, yet she did. She had to know. If it was true, her entire life was a lie. If it wasn't, her reputation was cleared. If it *was* true, she didn't know where that left her…at Happily Ever After College or anywhere. She remembered the plight that the Captains had being mortals and fae. Was that what Paris was set up for? She didn't know, but she was about to find out.

CHAPTER SEVENTY-SIX

W illow simply ran a wand down the length of Paris' chest, her hand a few inches away. She felt nothing, but when the headmistress looked at her, she felt suddenly punched in the gut.

"Paris, it's all true," the headmistress stated. "You are Guinevere Paris Beaufont. You're half-fairy and half-magician."

Everyone around Paris let out their reaction of surprise or disbelief. Well, not Mae Ling. She simply drew in a breath and gave Paris a reassuring look. She must have known all along. Or she suspected it as part of reality.

Paris looked around at the people who had been her friends and wondered if they'd shun her now. Where would she go? She wouldn't be able to talk to Uncle John for a long time since he was on a stakeout. There were so many questions. So many things to do.

The sound of laughter interrupted her thoughts. "You're a halfling, and you thought you could come into our college and ruin things. Magicians can't deal with love. They know nothing about it."

Paris didn't know where it came from, but she was suddenly grateful for the story that King Rudolf told her. "I know about Liv and Stefan and what they did for love. My parents were more in love than most. They sacrificed everything to be together—their reputations, their jobs, their family. If that isn't love, I don't know what is. But love isn't confined to one magical race. Love is what's in our soul. And we all have that."

Willow nodded and pressed the envelope with Paris' birth records to her chest. "It's pretty amazing that for the first time, Happily Ever After College has a fairy and a magician training to be a fairy godmother. I think that bodes well for the college's evolution. Maybe this is what we needed all along to get a more holistic perspective and approach matchmaking from unique angles."

"What?" Paris gasped, surprised by the headmistress' words.

"No!" Shannon boomed. "She can't be a fairy godmother. She's not a fairy."

"Technically," Willow rounded on the woman. "She is a fairy. Thanks for the records. She's both a fairy and a magician. I think that might be why she's such a good contribution to this college."

"You can't allow her to stay!" Shannon protested. "She doesn't belong here."

Willow pointed at the exit. "The only one who doesn't belong here anymore is you, Shannon Butcher. We'll take you to the proper authorities and allow them to deal with you. I'm sure you'll find that your new confines will give you a chance to reflect on all this. I hope you find peace in your heart since you've brought so much negativity to the college. But it will be gone when you are."

CHAPTER SEVENTY-SEVEN

"Christine said that you taught her the binding spell she used on Shannon Butcher," Headmistress Willow Starr said, sitting behind her cozy desk.

Paris twisted her mouth to the side. "Technically, I told her about the time I used it to restrain a troll doing damage on Roya Lane. He was having a bad day and taking it out on a street lamp. She asked how I did it, and I explained how the spell worked."

"Because of that, she had the tools to do something that a fairy godmother never would've been able to accomplish before." Willow didn't sound at all upset about the knowledge Paris had passed on, as the younger fairy would have expected. "We don't teach combat spells here at Happily Every After College. We never have."

"Maybe we should," Mae Ling suggested, sitting in the chair next to Paris on the other side of the desk.

"Maybe," Willow mused. "I think we're going to need to evaluate the curriculum and think about what will best serve us. I don't foresee fairy godmothers getting into fistfights in the future. At least, I sincerely hope not. Still, I think the way we approach things will be different, and maybe that means we'll need a new set of skills, although this doesn't mean I plan to erase the current curriculum. I've learned that too much change isn't good. We need to find a balance."

Paris hadn't had a chance to process everything she'd learned that night. She suspected that would take some time and many answers. The questions were already pouring through her mind. She was back at Happily Ever After College though, and that's what mattered to her most. Twice recently she'd thought her time here was finished, first when she failed the exam, then when she learned she was half-magician.

Paris still couldn't fathom it. She wasn't a pure fairy. She was a halfling. Did King Rudolf know? Is that why he told her about her parents and shared the information about his halfling children? There were so many questions. So many people she needed to talk to. But first, she wanted to sleep. That would help her to process.

"So I get to stay here at Happily Ever After College?" Paris had to ask. She needed to hear it one more time. To know the head-mistress hadn't changed her mind.

"Of course," Willow answered at once. "I know that it's untraditional, and fairy godmothers have always been fairies. That's the way Mother Nature designed it. You are a fairy. You're also something more. Plus, we can't ignore the impact you've had on this college in a short time. We knew we needed a change and your uncle called me at the right time. I'm a firm believer in divine fate, and when I was at a crossroads, looking for answers to the college's problem, the universe sent us you."

Paris couldn't help but beam. A tenderness erupted in her throat, making her think she might cry. Paris wasn't one to cry. The last time she did, it was because she broke a finger on a gremlin's head. They had surprisingly hard skulls.

"I also brought problems," Paris had to admit. "I've thrown more pies in the time I've been here than in the college's entire history."

Willow giggled pleasantly. "It's true. You're a feisty one. You'll have to learn to control your impulses, but I think there's a good reason why you are the way you are. I'm sure that you're eager to learn who you are and why. I would caution you not to run out and seek answers to the questions right away though. Give yourself time to adjust, and we will help you to uncover the truth if we can."

"I'm sure Paris' history will be revealed when she's ready to understand it," Mae Ling stated with a knowing edge in her voice.

Willow nodded. "I suspect you're right."

"I don't feel like rushing out and learning anything new just yet," Paris admitted. "I need time to wrap my brain around what I've learned so far. And the only person I know who can answer the questions is away and unreachable. For now, I'm going to be grateful that things worked out and Professor Butcher didn't ruin the Valentine's Day event."

Willow's eyes lit up. "Oh, she didn't at all. Take a look at this." Swiping her hand to the side using magic, the headmistress pulled back the curtain that covered the love meter. The dial hadn't moved a lot, but it had moved! It was now pointing at around thirty percent. "True love is up worldwide five percent. Although that isn't a lot, it's progress that we haven't seen in quite some time."

"You think that's from our event?" Paris asked.

"Well, it is Valentine's Day, but on that holiday, we usually see the dial go down," Willow explained. "You see, people feel obligated to do things that are loving on Valentine's Day, which negates true love. Usually, we see a ten percent drop that steadily recovers as we progress through February."

"But we saw a rise?" Paris questioned. "Why?"

"I think the event was successful and that many guests made true love matches," Willow answered. "When those happen, there's usually a ripple effect. When someone falls in love, they're happier and nicer to all they come in contact with. That's exactly the reason that our college exists, to create true love and spread more of the emotion all over the world."

"Then it seems we should focus on creating more than true love between couples," Paris reasoned. "We could do even more and really get the meter off the charts."

Willow gave her a patient smile. "Maybe in time. I'm open to changes, but again, not too much too fast. We want to focus on our curriculum and helping people to fall in love. Then we can look at expanding."

"Wow," Paris declared. "So although killer doves attacked our event and we flooded the banquet hall, things still worked out. Maybe that means people need to have a bad date first. Miss the train, have bad service, have a bad hair day. You know, be real and see if love is sparked in the worst-case scenario because then it will happen in the best ones too."

Willow nodded. "The idea holds merit. There were no pretenses, and when things got stressful, our charges were their authentic selves. Hopefully the matches we made stick, but we have to wait and see. For now, I'm very happy with the results."

Paris pulled in a breath, feeling grateful that although her world had turned upside down that night, it was still intact.

"Now, I think after all this, you should go and get some rest," Willow advised. "Since I'm sure you'll need extra sleep, you can skip classes tomorrow morning."

Paris shook her head and rose from the chair. "Oh no. I'm more motivated than ever to learn. We're making a difference." She pointed at the love meter. "I can't quit now."

Willow smiled proudly at her. "Paris, I'm very grateful that you're with us and hope you stay for a long time after you've served your sentence for your crimes."

Paris nodded, having forgotten all about the reasons that brought her to Happily Ever After College. She'd come here out of obligation and now she wanted to stay due to an intrinsic, unwavering motivation.

CHAPTER SEVENTY-EIGHT

Paris and Mae Ling walked in silence until they arrived right outside Paris' room on the second floor. She turned to face the fairy godmother, having spent the entire trek wondering what to ask her first.

"Do you know what happened to my parents?" she finally asked.

Mae Ling gave her a regretful expression. "I honestly can say that I don't."

Paris sighed. "I have so many questions."

"I realize that. But I have a warning I must disclose to you now that you know who you truly are."

"So you knew all along that I was a magician too?" Paris had to ask. "That I was Guinevere Paris Beaufont?" It sounded so weird saying her name like that.

"Of course," Mae Ling answered boldly. "There was zero way that I could tell you. I will never lie to you, Paris. I promise you that. But in many instances, I literally can't tell you what you want to know. In some instances, it would do you little good to know

313

what I know. Please understand that nothing that's happened to you was done out of deception. It was to protect you."

"Protect me?" Paris asked. "From what?"

Mae Ling shook her head, and it was clear that this was something she couldn't reveal. "This situation is extremely complicated. I know you want answers. You want to know why you weren't raised with your parents and why your name was changed. In time, you will discover the truth. I promise. But it will take just that—time. There is only one person who can tell you your history."

"Uncle John?" Paris guessed.

Mae Ling's face lined with wrinkles, making the answer clear.

"I guess you can't tell me who can share the truth with me?" Paris asked.

Regret filled the fairy godmother's eyes. "Powerful magic has been used to protect you. That's all that I can say."

"You can't tell me," Paris guessed. "You've been spelled, haven't you?"

Mae Ling sighed.

She couldn't answer that question. This was getting more complicated by the moment.

"What I can tell you is that as you seek the truth, which I know you will undoubtedly do, you must be very careful," Mae Ling explained. "It's only a matter of time before your secret of being a halfling spreads. There is a danger out there that is so great, and once it learns who you are, it will come for you. Be careful outside of Happily Ever After. Here you are safe. Outside our borders, you are not."

A violent chill ran down Paris' back. Of course, this got more complicated. She was safe there, but when she sought to investigate her history, she'd be a target. That only created more questions—ones that Mae Ling wasn't able to answer.

"Okay," Paris finally said, exhaustion making her feel like she might pass out at any moment. "I'll be careful. I have one last question, and maybe you can answer it. Did you know my parents?"

Mae Ling smiled, a rare gesture on her face. "Oh, yes, and it's because of them that this planet still exists."

CHAPTER SEVENTY-NINE

"Did it happen the way you thought it would?" a woman with grayish-blue hair and a southern accent asked. She stood at the edge of the Bewilder Forest, regarding the Fairy Godmother Estate.

The man known as Father Time, currently in elf form, shook his head. "It rarely ever does. But the dice have been rolled, so we have to take the turn regardless of whether we were ready, regardless of whether I thought Guinevere was ready."

"Shannon Butcher wasn't spelled," Mother Nature guessed, although she preferred to go by Mama Jamba, as her counterpart beside her preferred the name Papa Creola.

The elf with long stringy hair, wearing loose pants and a tie-dye shirt shook his head. "The magic it would cost to silence everyone was too costly. I only spelled those who were most likely to share the information with her."

Mama Jamba smiled sweetly. "I'm glad she found out now. I was getting tired of waiting."

"You were never good with waiting," he countered.

"Time is your thing, Papa. Not mine." The old woman in her

pink velour tracksuit surveyed the Enchanted Grounds. "It's overdue that my fairy godmothers get their act together. We've always known they needed Paris to evolve."

"Her name is Guinevere," he corrected.

"Her name is also Paris, and it's what she's used to being called," Mama Jamba argued.

"The college might need her, but she can't create change if he gets to her," Papa Creola stated, his voice suddenly heavy.

"Yet, you need her to stop him," Mama Jamba sang good-naturedly. Nothing ever got her down. Her planet could be hurtling toward the sun, and she'd be smiling. Such was the perk of being the creator of everything. She simply didn't sweat the small stuff…or the big stuff…or sweat at all.

Papa Creola sighed. "Yes, and it's only a matter of time before the Deathly Shadow discovers who the halfling is. Then my job will really begin."

Mother Nature giggled. "Great, because you've been slacking for a good part of this century."

"I've been planning," he argued, sounding offended. "Getting to this point hasn't been easy."

"But we're finally here, and if you're successful, I'll be successful." Mama Jamba hummed for a moment while swaying back and forth. "Oh, won't it be wonderful when love takes over the planet once more?"

He grunted. "I guess. Love has never been my thing."

"Oh, I don't know, Papa. I think you have more of a heart than you think."

"If you start holding me to that standard, I'm going to expect you to be on time for our meetings in the future," he grumbled.

Mama Jamba slapped him playfully on his shoulder. "Please don't hold your breath on that one."

"I don't breathe," he said, always having to be utterly literal.

The old woman threaded her arm through Papa Creola's.

"Come on. Take me for pancakes. There's nothing to be done here tonight. Let the girl sleep. She has a big job to do."

Papa Creola reluctantly allowed himself to be led away into the Bewilder Forest, knowing that Mama Jamba was right. The halfling was the key to everything.

CHAPTER EIGHTY

Faraday didn't say a word until Paris had finished talking. He stared at her for a long moment and finally said, "You are one of a kind."

Paris shook her head, sliding into bed. "I'm not sure. All I know is that halflings are rare."

"I've never heard of a magician and fairy halfling," Faraday stated. "They can't breed together. It's impossible."

"Well, my parents were both magicians. So I'm totally baffled."

"This will take some investigation."

"Will you help me?"

"Of course!" he exclaimed. "If there's a question, I must learn the answer. And you're an anomaly, which I must study."

"You're an anomaly," Paris teased and pulled her sheets up to her chest.

"Why, thank you, Paris…" He hesitated on her name. "Is that what you still want to be called?"

"Yes," she answered without having to think about it. "That's my name. That's who I've always been, as far as I can remember, at least for the most part. Although I don't know about being a West-bridge now. That doesn't sound like who I always was."

"I'm sure this will all make sense in time." Faraday scurried around in the sock drawer, trying to get comfortable.

"Yes, this will all take a lot of time to understand." Paris turned out the light using magic. "What will you do tomorrow?"

The squirrel finally stopped moving around, having found his spot nestled between the fuzzy socks. "I'll continue my investigations. Did you know the Serenity Garden is off-limits on Tuesdays?"

"I did." Paris remembered that from her tour of the college.

"I must discover why." He sounded tired.

"Tomorrow is Monday," she pointed out.

"Yes, and that gives me time to prepare."

"Oh, well, let me know what you discover," she said through a yawn.

"Let me know what you find out."

"About being a magician?" Paris questioned.

"No, about how to make a soufflé," he joked. "Of course about being a magician. Although, I am curious about the chemistry of making a soufflé. It's apparently a very delicate process."

"You're so weird." Paris closed her eyes, feeling sleep ready to crash down on her.

"Why, thank you," he droned, sounding ready to start snoring. When the squirrel slept, he made a gentle purring sound that Paris quite liked.

"Hey, Faraday…"

"Yes, Paris."

Although she was exhausted and confused, Paris was also happy. Like, really happy, maybe for the first time or the first time in a very long time.

She'd made a difference for love that night. The headmistress wanted her to stay at Happily Ever After College. More importantly, she'd made friends…finally. Yes, there were so many things to discover about her history, but she would, and she was most grateful that she didn't have to do it alone.

"I'm glad you're here with me," she finally said, nearly having fallen asleep while thinking of all the good ways her life had changed—and it had changed a lot recently.

"Thank you, Paris. I'm happy to be here with you, and I look forward to more adventures, starting tomorrow."

"Yes, tomorrow..." Paris Beaufont whispered into her pillow, falling into a dreamless sleep that would prepare her for all the adventures to come.

SARAH'S AUTHOR NOTES

FEBRUARY 24, 2021

Thank you! A huge thank you to you the reader for taking a chance on this new series. I hope you enjoyed book 1. If you didn't, please call Mike at 555-555-5555. Do you ever wonder if that number gets a ton of calls since people are always using it as a made up number? Anyway, thank you.

So if this is your first series with us, welcome. If it's not, thank you and welcome back. You regulars know how my author notes go. MA has just opened them to read and probably groaned, thinking, "Great, Noffke has written another novella of author notes for me to respond do." I have, Bird Killer and I expect you to respond line by line.

For those new to us, I call Michael Anderle, Bird Killer because this one time he was a young lad and killed a bird. Then he grew up and told me about it. He now has two regrets, that I'm aware of. I have been nicknamed Tiny Ninja by Mike and the readers, so when I sign off as that, please don't think I really think of myself as a ninja or tiny. I'm small. About the size of an elementary school child, but I curse like a sailor to make up for it. Really confuses adults sometimes. They are like, where are your parents and why haven't they taught you any manners?

See! See how I just derail this part of the book into my own senseless ramblings? You'll get used to it. Mike, you're still following along, right? You haven't skipped to the end so you can just respond to the last part and pretend you read the whole novella, right? There will be a test. The square root of pie is banana. Get that wrong and there will be repercussions.

Speaking of pie, Paris throwing pies at the villains throughout the books was unexpected. I actually asked my alpha reader, Juergen, if that was too slapstick. He said no. He's the boss.

So let's talk book. I loved writing this first installment. Like it was this fun little break away from reality everyday when I got to visit Happily Ever After College. The characters soon became my friends and I found myself longing to skip all the adulting everyday and get back to writing.

It should be noted that I don't go outside much these days and interaction with real humans is limited due to restrictions. Just saying. It's been almost five months at the writing of this since I've seen my boyfriend, who from this point forward, I will only refer to as the Scotsman, because we all get nicknames in the author notes. Anyway, my point is that I write because I have to. I literally feel like I was chosen for this profession whether I like it or not. But in this instance, it was such a nice escape for me.

Most days I love writing. At three o'clock in the morning, when the story won't let me sleep...well, I still love it. But some days, it's exhausting. I also write because you lovely readers have told me of the escape that it gives you. That's kept me writing on the really hard days when I'd rather turn off my brain and watch Netflix. But for this book, well, I wrote it as my escape. I needed it. And as someone who isn't a romantic, I found it so easy to relate to Paris. She would rather clock a giant for being a bully than listen to a sappy ballad. I've never punched a giant, mostly because I couldn't reach their face, but also I don't really do rom coms or romance very much. So it was easy to write Paris, who didn't understand romance but would stomach creating true love for others if it made the world a better place.

At the start of a new series, the world building and characters takes a while. So how did I come up with the characters? Well, I watch a lot of British television. Lately I've been obsessed with The Great British Baking Show. It's relaxing and unlike American television, the Brits aren't overly competitive. They are supportive of each other and there's less sensational drama. Anyway, Chef Ash and Wilfred were inspired by real world contestants on the show. You can't beat real.

Now Hemingway, well, he's probably inspired by my Scotsman. How did I come up with his name? You ask so many good questions. Names in this series are supposed to have symbolic meaning. So we have Paris who has never been to Paris. Hemingway who has never read one of the famous author's books. Faraday who is scientific minded. Penny who is poor. Professor Butcher who is evil. Willow who is adaptable. You get the idea. Things with the names will come full circle but I won't give you spoilers.

Christine is inspired by my hair stylist who is one of the coolest and funniest people I know. She told me once that people always mess up her name calling her Christina or Christy or Christa. She regretted telling me that because what I never called her since? If you guessed Christine then you get one-hundred worthless bonus points. Why my friends tell me anything, ever, I'll never understand. But I get it. I get Diana and Diane messed up all the time.

Mae Ling, who came over from the Sophia series, is what I call my sister, who isn't an old Asian lady. But a few years ago, my sister, whose actual name is Beatrix, after the author, but I call her Bea when I'm not calling her Mae Ling, pranked called a boyfriend of mine. He's obviously not my boyfriend now, which is why I was like, yeah, that's fine, let's pretend we're fifteen and prank call people. My sister was probably about fifteen at the time because she's twenty years youngers than me. Anyway, she calls the boyfriend, blocking her number and says, "This Mae Ling and you have nail appoooointment with me."

He was like, "What?"

And in her really bad accent she says, "Your nail loooong. You come in for appooooooointment."

He hung up.

I broke up with him. And that's why my sister is named Mae Ling and inspired the crafty and mysterious fairy godmother.

Anyway, I hope you all enjoyed the book. I know I loved writing it.

Without further ado, I turn you over to MA. So Bird Killer, please tell all the loyal readers, what's the square root of pie?

Much peace and love,
Tiny Ninja

MICHAEL'S AUTHOR NOTES
MARCH 9, 2021

Thank you for both reading this story and trudging through the mindless ramblings of a ninja who never grew up.

Or very tall.

Oh, and the answer to the question is the song from a famous pop star who spelled the word out.

You are VERY welcome to those who now have the song stuck in your head. I'm writing these damned notes while dancing around and typing out the beat right now.

And Sarah wonders why I would skip her author notes? Even a teensy little bit?

For those who know who I am, please just drop below to **#ABitMoreStuff.** For those who don't, I add this part to the author notes for book 01s I'm a part of so there is a bit about who I am.

A Bit About Me

I wrote my first book *Death Becomes Her* (*The Kurtherian Gambit*) in September/October of 2015 and released it November 2, 2015. I wrote and released the next two books that same month and had three released by the end of November 2015.

So, just at five years ago.

Since then, I've written, collaborated, concepted, and/or created hundreds more in all sorts of genres.

My most successful genre is still my first, Paranormal Sci-Fi, followed quickly by Urban Fantasy. I have multiple pen names I produce under.

Some because I can be a bit crude in my humor at times or raw in my cynicism (Michael Todd). I have one I share with Martha Carr (Judith Berens, and another (not disclosed) that we use as a marketing test pen name.

In general, I just love to tell stories, and with success comes the opportunity to mix two things I love in my life.

Business and stories.

I've wanted to be an entrepreneur since I was a teenager. I was a very *unsuccessful* entrepreneur (I tried many times) until my publishing company LMBPN signed one author in 2015.

Me.

I was the president of the company, and I was the first author published. Funny how it worked out that way.

It was late 2016 before we had additional authors join me for publishing. Now we have a few dozen authors, a few hundred audiobooks published by LMBPN, a few hundred more licensed by six audio companies, and about a thousand titles in our company.

It's been a busy five years.

#ABitMoreStuff

So, I tried to use my outdoor pizza oven (it's made of sheet metal and sits on a rolling cart out back) for the second time yesterday. Maybe the third?

I can't remember. I'd like to suggest it was the second time because it went less than stellar.

My idea to use wood charcoal (not Kingsford) to keep the heat going did work well—up to a point. A point that the temperature gauge said was 950 degrees.

A portion of my pizza was burnt.

This little pizza oven is pretty small and barely holds a 12" pizza. I'm responsible as the Pizza Chef Guy to turn the pie a bit every little while. The major problems are: the pizza oven loses too much heat, and when I do this, the pizza glues itself to the pizza stone, making turning it a challenge.

One step forward, three steps back.

I figure I will try purchasing some cheap pizza pans to slide into the oven so I can turn the pizza more easily. At least until I learn how to pre-heat the pizza oven correctly. There HAS to be a way to cook on the stone.

I have learned a valuable lesson: cook pizza outside on beautiful days. That way, if you burn a third of the pie, have a soggy crust, and leave a mess, at least you enjoyed mother nature.

Enjoy the supernatural shenanigans of Paris Beaufont while I go use my Google-fu on how to cook a pizza without...problems.

Ad Aeternitatem,

Michael

ACKNOWLEDGMENTS
SARAH NOFFKE

I have so many people to thank who make this all possible. Firstly, thanks to Mike, who really pushes me to be a better writer, coming up with the best ideas, not just the really good ones. We work together pretty well, I'd say. I wonder what he'd say... Anyway, MA gave me the opportunity to write with LBMPN a few years ago and it's been life changing. He's very supportive and really cares. Thanks Bird Killer.

A huge thank you to the LBMPN team who work tirelessly so that I have less stress. Thanks to Steve and Kelly for making my life easier and being on top of everything. Thanks to Tracey and Lynne for fixing all my editing mistakes. A big thank you to the JIT team whose feedback at the 11th hour before publishing is invaluable. Thank you to my alpha readers Juergen and Martin. Thank you to everyone who makes getting the books to the reader possible. I really can't do this without you. And you make it so much more fun.

Thank you to my daughter, Lydia, who inspires my stories over and over again. She's my muse and we are always discussing story. She's an avid reader and listens to the Liv Beaufont series at night and reads the Sophia Beaufont books with me before bed. She also reads other authors, which I guess is okay. But my point is that she's supportive of me in so many ways. I need to stay immersed in this universe and remember all the details. There are 12 book in each series so there's a lot to remember. And Lydia loves my stories and then also supports me by listening and reading them so I can keep crafting. But also, she puts up with me when I go all psycho pants during a big crunch of a deadline. I will be the first to admit that I'm pretty intense a day or two before a book is due. And she always just smiles and says, "Mommy, you can do it."

Thank you to my family, the Scotsman and all my friends. You all are always so supportive of me and for that, I'm infinitely grateful. I really couldn't do this without the encouragement of those I love. On the really tough writing days, the Scotsman points out all the things that I don't see, like my dedication to the craft or how much readers are enjoying the books. I don't know what I did to have the most loving and thoughtful people in the world in my corner, but I'm going to do everything to keep them and hopefully keep making them proud.

And finally, thank you to you the reader. Without you I wouldn't be able to do what I love. Your support means so much to me and my family. Thank you from the bottom of my heart.

Love,
Tiny Ninja

BOOKS BY SARAH NOFFKE

Sarah Noffke writes YA and NA science fiction, fantasy, paranormal and urban fantasy. In addition to being an author, she is a mother, podcaster and professor. Noffke holds a Masters of Management and teaches college business/writing courses. Most of her students have no idea that she toils away her hours crafting fictional characters. www.sarahnoffke.com

Check out other work by Sarah author here.

Ghost Squadron:

Formation #1:
   Kill the bad guys. Save the Galaxy. All in a hard day's work.
   After ten years of wandering the outer rim of the galaxy, Eddie Teach is a man without a purpose. He was one of the toughest pilots in the Federation, but now he's just a regular guy, getting into bar fights and making a difference wherever he can. It's not the same as flying a ship and saving colonies, but it'll have to do.

That is, until General Lance Reynolds tracks Eddie down and offers him a job. There are bad people out there, plotting terrible things, killing innocent people, and destroying entire colonies. **Someone has to stop them.**

Eddie, along with the genetically-enhanced combat pilot Julianna Fregin and her trusty E.I. named Pip, must recruit a diverse team of specialists, both human and alien. They'll need to master their new Q-Ship, one of the most powerful strike ships ever constructed. And finally, they'll have to stop a faceless enemy so powerful, it threatens to destroy the entire Federation.

All in a day's work, right?

Experience this exciting military sci-fi saga and the latest addition to the expanded Kurtherian Gambit Universe. If you're a fan of Mass Effect, Firefly, or Star Wars, you'll love this riveting new space opera.

NOTE: If cursing is a problem, then this might not be for you.
Check out the entire series <u>here</u>.

The Precious Galaxy Series:

Corruption #1
A new evil lurks in the darkness.

After an explosion, the crew of a battlecruiser mysteriously disappears.

Bailey and Lewis, complete strangers, find themselves suddenly onboard the damaged ship. Lewis hasn't worked a case in years, not since the final one broke his spirit and his bank account. The last thing Bailey remembers is preparing to take down a fugitive on Onyx Station.

Mysteries are harder to solve when there's no evidence left behind.

Bailey and Lewis don't know how they got onboard *Ricky Bobby* or why. However, they quickly learn that whatever was responsible for the explosion and disappearance of the crew is still on the ship.

Monsters are real and what this one can do changes everything.

The new team bands together to discover what happened and how to fight the monster lurking in the bottom of the battlecruiser.

Will they find the missing crew? Or will the monster end them all?

The Soul Stone Mage Series:

House of Enchanted #1:

The Kingdom of Virgo has lived in peace for thousands of years...until now.

The humans from Terran have always been real assholes to the witches of Virgo. Now a silent war is brewing, and the timing couldn't be worse. Princess Azure will soon be crowned queen of the Kingdom of Virgo.

In the Dark Forest a powerful potion-maker has been murdered.

Charmsgood was the only wizard who could stop a deadly virus plaguing Virgo. He also knew about the devastation the people from Terran had done to the forest.

Azure must protect her people. Mend the Dark Forest. Create alliances with savage beasts. No biggie, right?

But on coronation day everything changes. Princess Azure isn't who she thought she was and that's a big freaking problem.

Welcome to The Revelations of Oriceran. Check out the entire series here.

The Lucidites Series:

Awoken, #1:

Around the world humans are hallucinating after sleepless nights.

In a sterile, underground institute the forecasters keep reporting the same events.

And in the backwoods of Texas, a sixteen-year-old girl is about to be caught up in a fierce, ethereal battle.

Meet Roya Stark. She drowns every night in her dreams, spends her hours reading classic literature to avoid her family's ridicule, and is prone to premonitions—which are becoming more frequent. And now her dreams are filled with strangers offering to reveal what she has always wanted to know: Who is she? That's the question that haunts her, and she's about to find out. But will Roya live to regret learning the truth?

Stunned, #2

Revived, #3

The Reverians Series:

Defects, #1:

In the happy, clean community of Austin Valley, everything appears to be perfect. Seventeen-year-old Em Fuller, however, fears something is askew. Em is one of the new generation of Dream Travelers. For some reason, the gods have not seen fit to gift all of them with their expected special abilities. Em is a Defect —one of the unfortunate Dream Travelers not gifted with a psychic power. Desperate to do whatever it takes to earn her gift, she endures painful daily injections along with commands from her overbearing, loveless father. One of the few bright spots in her life is the return of a friend she had thought dead—but with his return comes the knowledge of a shocking, unforgivable truth. The society Em thought was protecting her has actually been betraying her, but she has no idea how to break away from its authority without hurting everyone she loves.

Rebels, #2

Warriors, #3

Vagabond Circus Series:

Suspended, #1:

When a stranger joins the cast of Vagabond Circus—a circus that is run by Dream Travelers and features real magic—mysterious events start happening. The once orderly grounds of the circus become riddled with hidden threats. And the ringmaster realizes not only are his circus and its magic at risk, but also his very life.

Vagabond Circus caters to the skeptics. Without skeptics, it would close its doors. This is because Vagabond Circus runs for two reasons and only two reasons: first and foremost to provide the lost and lonely Dream Travelers a place to be illustrious. And secondly, to show the nonbelievers that there's still magic in the world. If they believe, then they care, and if they care, then they don't destroy. They stop the small abuse that day-by-day breaks down humanity's spirit. If Vagabond Circus makes one skeptic believe in magic, then they halt the cycle, just a little bit. They allow a little more love into this world. That's Dr. Dave Raydon's mission. And that's why this ringmaster recruits. That's why he directs. That's why he puts on a show that makes people question their beliefs. He wants the world to believe in magic once again.

Paralyzed, #2
Released, #3

Ren Series:

Ren: The Man Behind the Monster, #1:

Born with the power to control minds, hypnotize others, and read thoughts, Ren Lewis, is certain of one thing: God made a mistake. No one should be born with so much power. A monster awoke in him the same year he received his gifts. At ten years old.

A prepubescent boy with the ability to control others might merely abuse his powers, but Ren allowed it to corrupt him. And since he can have and do anything he wants, Ren should be happy. However, his journey teaches him that harboring so much power doesn't bring happiness, it steals it. Once this realization sets in, Ren makes up his mind to do the one thing that can bring his tortured soul some peace. He must kill the monster.

Note This book is NA and has strong language, violence and sexual references.

Ren: God's Little Monster, #2
Ren: The Monster Inside the Monster, #3
Ren: The Monster's Adventure, #3.5
Ren: The Monster's Death

Olento Research Series:

Alpha Wolf, #1:

Twelve men went missing.

Six months later they awake from drug-induced stupors to find themselves locked in a lab.

And on the night of a new moon, eleven of those men, possessed by new—and inhuman—powers, break out of their prison and race through the streets of Los Angeles until they disappear one by one into the night.

Olento Research wants its experiments back. Its CEO, Mika Lenna, will tear every city apart until he has his werewolves imprisoned once again. He didn't undertake a huge risk just to lose his would-be assassins.

However, the Lucidite Institute's main mission is to save the world from injustices. Now, it's Adelaide's job to find these mutated men and protect them and society, and fast. Already around the nation, wolflike men are being spotted. Attacks on innocent women are happening. And then, Adelaide realizes what her next step must be: She has to find the alpha wolf first. Only

BOOKS BY SARAH NOFFKE

once she's located him can she stop whoever is behind this experiment to create wild beasts out of human beings.

Rabid Wolf, #3

Bad Wolf, #4

CONNECT WITH THE AUTHORS

Connect with Sarah and sign up for her email list here:

http://www.sarahnoffke.com/connect/

You can catch her podcast, LA Chicks, here:

http://lachicks.libsyn.com/

Michael Anderle Social

Website: http://lmbpn.com

Email List: http://lmbpn.com/email/

Social Media:

https://www.facebook.com/LMBPNPublishing

https://twitter.com/MichaelAnderle

https://www.instagram.com/lmbpn_publishing/

https://www.bookbub.com/authors/michael-anderle

Made in United States
Troutdale, OR
03/10/2024

18356255R00199